Summary
Rhythm, Smoke, Inc. 3

As far as Smoke, Inc., CEO, Marty Jones is concerned, although he's only thirty-eight, the meaningful part of his life is over. He has only one pastime that brings him joy—dancing. That usually often requires a partner, a willing body; some woman he doesn't want to know.

To participate in a charity dance-a-thon, Marty meets the contest requirements by hiring a dance partner from Baby Doll's Escort Service.

Underneath all her quirks, serial job-hopper, Holly Smith is a tough, no nonsense, kind of woman. She doesn't date, has two friends, and concentrates most of her time and energy on restoring the old house she bought at auction. She has one form of fun—dancing. When her best friend asks her for help, she agrees to play partner to a local CEO at a charity dance-a-thon.

What could go wrong?

Rhythm

Smoke, Inc.

Gem Sivad

Rhythm
Copyright © 2017 by Gem Sivad
Print Edition
ISBN: 978-1-626229-09-9

Published by Gem Sivad, LLC

Cover Design: Kristian Norris
Editor: V. N. Johnson

Sivad, Gem (11-30-2017). (Smoke, Inc.)
Gem Sivad LLC.

Dedication

This book is dedicated to firefighters, smoke jumpers, and hotshot crews from all over the world. To all the men and women battling the deadly wildfires currently raging up the US Pacific Coast Line, thank you all for your courage and strength. God Bless!

Find the beat...

Chapter One
Marty Jones

WHEN I BOARDED on the twentieth floor, a steady beat of pain danced above my right eyebrow, a thumping ache filling my head. At least today I had the elevator to myself.

After I'd begun getting weird looks over my obsessive rides, I'd announced I was evaluating the building's security system. Not that its anyone's fucking business. So, okay, sometimes I need a little self-therapy. Make that, often. I don't know shit about running a big company. But, dammit, I'm running a big company.

So, lots of times I board the elevator for a little sanity time. Smoke, Inc. is twenty floors up and if I push multiple buttons to slow the ride, I usually have a grip on my senses by the time the doors open on ground level. As for the elevator itself, there aren't any real problems other than, in my opinion, the doors are open too long when the car stops on each floor, and the piped-in music must go.

I had a pile of paperwork waiting on my desk, Elaine, my office assistant, threatening to stay after clock-out-time to *help me with it,* and Noah March, a friend in hell, on his way to my office to make my life more miserable.

Shit. I had to get my paperwork done because I live in my office and no way do I want to entertain Elaine in my after-work hours. But my administrative assistant, secretary, or old harridan, whatever name fits her, knows I don't want her hanging around and uses it to get work out of me.

Jesus, I'm such a fucking pussy. Resentment rose inside of me. *I did not ask for any of this.*

Unpleasant realities and my own short-comings had me grinding my teeth when I arrived on ground level. I braced myself for the inevitable company, and when the doors opened, I automatically stepped back, making room for incoming. Instead of entering the car and moving aside, the passenger stood between me and the buttons on the wall. I liked to look at the buttons. It helped me calm down.

Without shoving the body sideways, I couldn't see squat. That, plus the insipid piano music droning from the hidden speakers, made the vein in my forehead pulse even harder.

"Twenty," I growled and got nothing more than a nod. So much for reminding my fellow passenger he wasn't riding alone. Denied the control panel, my interest switched to the person standing in front of it.

Maybe not a he. The knit cap pulled low left no clue about whether the wearer was man or woman. He/she fidgeted in front of me, as if feeling my stare. *Tough shit, you should have moved.* I leaned on the back wall and crossed my arms over my chest, analyzing the intruder.

There was a time when men wore the jeans and women wore... womanly stuff. I pondered that. A lot of things had changed and most of the time I felt like a whale beached in the middle of a four-lane highway.

I could feel my blood pressure rising and stared harder at the passenger. Denim jacket and jeans offered the same gender anonymity. Thick wool socks pulled high under laced-up work-boots completed the unisex outfit.

Male or female? And why do I care? Nevertheless, my gaze trailed upward, stopping when I reached hip high. Long legs ended where a nicely rounded ass began. Woman.

Who the hell is she? I hadn't seen her during my recent elevator escapes. She was either a new hire in one of the offices or a visitor/client just here for the day. I leaned against the back wall speculating about the newbie. *Probably heading up to one of the insurance offices.*

Since she didn't move, I continued my inspection.

Nice coat. Though it had spots worn shiny with age, it still looked good, fitting her shoulders and tapering in enough to hint at a narrow waist beneath, before it eased out again. I approved the sheepskin lining as I pondered her identity. When the doors opened on the fourth floor, she stepped from the elevator.

Huh. Didn't see that coming. Surprised, I gazed at her as her long strides carried her toward Baby Dolls Escort Service. While I watched, her feet did a little skip as her shoulders swayed to a private beat. For once I didn't mind the extended length the doors stayed open.

Guess she's one of Maxine's girls. Renting office space to an escort service in the company's old building had been a financial decision. Smoke, Inc. had needed the money coming in and Baby Dolls Escort Service had needed a business headquarters.

After the old building burned, it had seemed only fair to offer the former tenants space in the company's new digs.

That, like the elevator music, might have been a poor decision. I pondered yet another one of my possible mistakes on the way up. Elaine stood outside the elevator, ready to grab me as soon as the doors opened.

"You have two courier messages on your desk. Since Noah March delivered one of them and refused to wait outside, he's in your office, too."

I would have preferred a root canal. *Playtime over.*

"Cancel the elevator music contract as soon as it comes up for renewal, tell security to make the doors shut faster, and call Maxine to get me a dance partner for the dance-a-thon we signed up for this month."

Elaine put-on her cranky face. "You could just invite someone you actually know. Like a woman. On a date."

When I ignored her suggestion, she added, "I'll ask Gable Matthews to take care of it."

"That'll work." I plastered on a genial smile and said, "Specify tall," as I headed for my office.

Holly Smith

BIG. MAN. ALERT. I'd pretended to pay no attention to him, but being neither oblivious nor blind, I hadn't missed the behemoth wearing a frown and lurking in the corner of the elevator. After I'd turned my back, I'd wished I hadn't since I could *feel* his gaze, marking a spot between my shoulder blades.

I hurried from the elevator as soon as the doors opened, resisting the urge to shake my booty at tall, dark and grumpy. I was in a good mood and he wasn't changing it for me. As soon as we met in her Aunt Maxine's office, I asked Megan, "Who's the tall guy who rides the elevator up?"

"Which tall guy?"

"The one taller than me by a half a foot." Given my own height, that should have limited the possibilities.

"Probably works for Smoke, Inc. They're all big men and when they're not out on a job, they're up and down all day."

"What's Smoke, Inc.?"

"Fools on parade," Megan grimaced. "If it's dangerous they'll do it."

I didn't wonder until later how she knew and why she cared.

Chapter Two

Holly

Three weeks later

T RIPLE-DIGIT DAMN. I'D been sitting on the edge of the cab's seat, leaning forward so I wouldn't crumple my dress, feverishly gripping a twenty in one hand and my dance ticket in the other when we arrived at my destination. I paid the driver and hopped out. Unfortunately, I didn't realize I'd left my purse inside the cab until the taillights disappeared.

Way to go, Holly. Can't wait to see what's next. At least I had the dance-a-thon ticket in my hand. Otherwise I'd be stranded outside in the cold.

I frowned. I'd need a ride at the end of the night, or money to pay a cab…and I had no phone since it had been inside the purse. As soon as I entered the building, I turned away from the beckoning lights and music to walk down a dark hall instead.

At least the office is open. A youngish man with big ears and a small smile sat behind a desk. He didn't invite me in or look encouraging. Nevertheless, beggars can't be choosers.

"I left my purse in the cab dropping me off. May I borrow your phone to call the company?" It wasn't a trick question, but the way he studied me I wondered if I'd lapsed into Klingon.

"The office phone is unavailable. Business only."

Right. Of course. I looked around. Not a lot happening tonight. Maybe not most nights. "Would you have a personal phone I could use?"

He waited again, then produced a cell phone from his pocket.

"Thanks." I called the cab company. The dispatcher said he'd let his driver know to look for a purse and phone. Okay. I gave him Megan's number to call in case he found it. I also called Megan. She didn't answer. The entire harebrained scheme having been her idea, it would have been nice if she'd hung around to make sure all was well.

"It's easy money. Just show up and forget about everything else. There's never been a song you can't dance to. You'll be fine." Megan's assurances didn't resonate now.

Girlfriend, you owe me big time. I felt totally stupid being Marilyn Monroe. The platinum wig itched. So did the spot where Marilyn's black beauty mark decorated my lower left cheek. And, under their heavy gloss of red, my lips felt stiff. *Zombie woman dressed in glamour.*

An older guy in a suit walked in. The kid gave me the snake-eye, indicating it was time for me to get out. I handed back his phone.

"Thanks." *Okay, showtime.* I left the office and retraced my steps back down the hall to the arched door leading into the ball room. On my right as I entered, a stage had been erected where a DJ tested his equipment.

I headed that way. The music man had set up an el-shaped table arrangement with speakers, mixers, and stuff I couldn't identify. The microphone though, I recognized. I climbed the three steps to the stage and crossed to where the

DJ sat looking bored.

"Could you announce Marilyn's here?" At my request, the DJ spoke into the mike. "Marilyn Monroe's looking for her hook-up…every sexy inch of her."

It wasn't quite how I'd phrased it. When he flipped a switch and a spotlight surrounded me on the stage, I twitched my jacket closer over my chest and squinted out over the floor.

It wasn't much more than a moment before a cowboy came to the edge of the elevated platform, and held my arm as I climbed down, which was nice. The steps were shallow and my heels high. I appreciated the help.

As soon as I hit the floor, he dropped my arm, walked away, and motioned me to follow. Okay. If this was my partner, we were going to have a problem. Also, our outfits didn't match. I winced when I looked at his boots, already anticipating painful toes if those leathers miss-stepped. My eyes traveled upward to settle on his butt. Uh huh. That part of him looked fine.

We arrived at our table and it became clear the cowboy wasn't my dance partner. His very own cowgirl waited for him and frowned at me. I guess she'd seen me ogling *her* partner's ass. I gave her a sheepish look and mentally clocked on.

"Hi. I'm Marilyn. Nice to meet you." I smiled at the cowboy couple and batted my fake eyelashes. The woman part of the couple waited expectantly for me to fill in the usual social blanks. When I didn't, she assumed the role of hostess and introduced herself.

"I'm Dale Evans, tonight, and this is Roy Rogers, a.k.a. Gable Matthews. My real name is Harley-Jane Arthur."

"Soon to be Matthews," the cowboy added and possessively slid his arm around her shoulders. He wore a Stetson, plaid shirt, jeans, boots, a huge belt buckle, and a wide smile. She wore a western style vest and skirt, both fringed, and a long-sleeved plaid blouse matching her significant other's.

"My friends call me Janie." She hugged the guy at her side and laughed. "I told you we'd look dumb." She poked Gable in the chest and gave me a wry grin. "He won't dress up like anything but a cowboy, and I'm willing to compromise since I like fringe."

"Roy and Dale," Matthews growled. "Here to dance."

It seemed clear Gable didn't care for the contest rules. Participants had to dress in fifties-era costumes. Megan had filled me in on the requirements before the event. I nodded understanding at him. My costume made me into something I wasn't, which was okay with me, but not everyone's idea of fun.

"You should dance. I'm sure my partner will be along sometime soon." I smiled without volunteering more personal information.

I didn't introduce the real me because these were not people I'd ever see again, and hopefully if we met, they wouldn't recognize Holly Smith as the fifties-era blonde bombshell who'd shared their table.

The *Couples Only* sign made it clear I couldn't dance alone, so, leaving, seemed like the only reasonable option. As if he'd read my mind, or my face, Janie's cowboy offered an update.

"Your dance partner's running late. He'll be here soon."

How late was late? It was already 7:15 p.m. on a Friday night. My expression, no doubt, reflected impatience.

"You're on the company payroll, tonight."

"Company?" The sign on our reserved table read: Smoke, Inc. Oh yeah, the elevator ride and Megan's *fools on parade'* comment came back to me. *Adrenaline junkies who get paid for danger.*

"Private fire fighters. I'm a mechanic." Gable downplayed the danger but if Janie's frown was indicative, she didn't care for his job.

"You work for Maxine, long?" he asked, changing the topic to me.

"First dance gig," I answered glibly, then settled back ready to become invisible.

After an initial, awkward beginning, I shifted on the chair, bored and wishing I had my phone. I could have read a book or ranted in text at Megan.

After I made it clear I didn't intend to get friendly, my table partners, for the most part, talked to each other. They were sweet together. He straightened her collar. She patted his arm. They sat hip-to-hip on chairs pushed close.

I read somewhere a couple's *compulsive* touching indicated lots of sex. If the suggested predictor was accurate, Gable and Harley-Jane went at it like rabbits.

Not wanting to be a voyeur, I quit watching the table's occupants to study the room. There weren't many people on the dance floor. If I could, I'd join them, but of course, the big bad sign written in bold letters, declared that to be an absolute no-no.

Couples Only. What a crock... I dance by myself all the time. When I work at home, I always have the music on for background, and more often than not, I end up dancing through most of my projects.

"You two should go on and have some fun," I urged them again. I wished they would, so I could be alone and not worry about being polite.

See that's the flaw in Megan's escort advice. At some point, you're expected to be nice on cue. I had nothing in common with these people, and my date, still to be met, might be a complete troll. The later it got, the more I wanted to leave.

"Nope." The cowboy didn't offer explanation, but his girlfriend rolled her eyes.

"Okay, how's this for the truth. If I can't dance, *I* want to leave." I scowled in frustration at my tablemates and clamped my mouth shut on more words fighting to get loose. Because I'd agreed to help a friend, I found myself sharing a table with Roy and Dale. Delightful as they were, with no dance partner in sight, it was time to say good night.

On the other hand, if I could just keep my mouth shut and my seat planted on the chair, I'd get paid. Except for the fact I enjoyed the contracted work—dancing—it didn't matter whether my escort appeared or not. I'd still earn enough to replace the hardware on my sink without suffering trampled feet in the process.

We sat at one of the tables ringing the wooden dance floor. The dance-a-thon had been organized to raise money for a local firefighter who'd sustained third degree burns in a recent fire.

It seemed like a good cause. I hoped they collected a lot, but from the half-hearted participation on the floor, it didn't look promising. Let's just say there wasn't any fancy stepping going on. Regardless of the background music, most of the participants, some old enough to probably need the support, leaned on each other.

"…Gable just finished replacing my kitchen floor."

While I'd been drifting mindlessly, Gable had apparently left Harley-Jane on her own to talk to me. The mention of kitchens and floors caught my attention.

"What kind of material did you use?"

"Oak," she answered and smiled big. "I love it. I'd planned to replace the old linoleum with laminate someday, but Gable nudged me toward the real wood. It's gorgeous."

"Did he install it himself?" *I have a house I'm working on.* I swear, I strangled on the words, forcing myself to keep my lips shut. I yearned to swap remodeling horror stories.

"No, while the guys were living there, they helped Gable reroof my barn and put in the kitchen floor."

"You own a barn?" My covet gene went into overdrive, and I couldn't keep quiet a minute longer.

"My husband and I bought our farm and dreamed." She paused for a moment, and I could see the sheen of tears in her eyes. "That's all we had time to do before he got sick and died."

Nooooo… Janie had just jumped into personal history land, a place I did not intend to go. On the other hand, the barn and house…

"So, you're finishing it by yourself?"

Her sad expression changed to a grin. "Not any more. Gable's sister is my neighbor, and my brother is a firefighter who knows Gable because he works for Smoke, Inc."

While I attempted to sort it out, she explained. "We've known each other a while, but we only got together as a couple at the first of the year. I saw a murder, got stranded during the big snow with Gable in the old Smoke, Inc. building. The murderer, a cop I might add, tried to kill me and burned the building to the ground during his attempt."

Huh. I'd thought my life exciting. Go figure. I really wanted to know her. Impulsively, I leaned forward.

"My name's Holly," I told her. "Holly Smith." Her eyebrows went up on the Smith. "For real, my name is Holly Smith, but I'd just as soon keep it between you and me." At her puzzled expression, I kept talking. "Since I'm already disguised as Marilyn Monroe, I'd rather remain anonymous to the world. I don't work for the escort agency. The owner didn't have anyone who knows how to dance. Her niece, my best friend, asked me to stand in for a real escort because I *can* dance."

Janie grinned and nodded as Gable returned to the table. He kissed Harley-Jane's forehead before he took his seat, again. She resumed her story as if I hadn't interrupted.

"The crew had been living *there*, at the old building. Gable had to keep the furnace going, and even then, the building stayed cold."

He slid his arm around her and looked smug. "Got you where I wanted you, just the same."

"Yes, you did. And it worked out well for everyone when the Inferno burned down, and your crew moved to my farm."

"Crew sounds like a lot of men. How many?"

"Eight men, two months. They were gone a lot of the time, but when they were there, they made repairs." She beamed happily and added, "And they paid rent."

It's wrong to be jealous, but damn. "Wow." I had no intentions of being drawn into a discussion of Smoke, Inc. I knew nothing about the company and suddenly wanted to know everything. Nope. I reined in my curiosity and went back to safe topics like remodeling projects.

"I live in the worst house on the best block I could afford and dream about the day it will be the best house in the area and I can sell the money pit." I gave her my disgruntled look, which she mirrored and nodded her head.

Honestly though, I'd never sell my house. But being careful of who knew my business, and a lot superstitious, I never openly loved it. Instead, I poured my heart, soul, and cash into it and called it a money pit.

"I don't have a crew of eight men making repairs. I'm learning as I go. Kind of a do-it-yourself girl." That was an understatement. "Parts are cheap, but labor costs the earth. I've been reading up on electrical wiring, building construction, plumbing, and carpentry." So far, my projects had been defined by what I could do now, not what I wanted to do.

"Electric isn't something you should play around with," he drawled. He looked ready to lecture me on safety issues, and I forestalled his advice by agreeing. Electric I left alone.

"Janie says you installed an oak floor. What did you use to cut the planks?" I didn't have a saw and knew I'd have to buy one eventually.

"Miter." He warmed to the subject and took out a pencil. I gave him some dimensions and he diagrammed the floor showing me how to calculate how many cartons of material I'd need for my kitchen. We'd found common ground and spent the next forty-five minutes discussing upgrades.

As the time approached 8:00, I decided to give my absent dance partner until the exact top of the hour. Then I'd leave and go to the sports bar where I'd spend the rest of my Friday night waiting tables for steady tips.

I tapped my foot to the beat as the rhythm danced in my veins. A talented DJ provided a steady background of rock and roll music from the forties, fifties, and sixties. On the dance floor, two enthusiastic couples bumped and gyrated to the sounds of The Mystics.

The rules seemed simple. Couples clocked on and danced until they couldn't dance any longer. For every hour completed, the participants earned money from pledgees they'd solicited.

I'd decided I didn't want to be stood-up. If I could keep him dancing long enough, I could earn a sink and the hardware to hook it up. I'm no plumber, of course, but Googling directions had served most of my projects, so far.

I grinned inside at the compelling reason I was here. Kitchen upgrade. My date's reason seemed sad. Evidently, he had enough influence to earn high dollar pledges, but he didn't have enough charm to find a dance partner.

I didn't waste too much time feeling sorry for him. He *could* afford Maxine's exorbitant fees, and his need for a dance partner would underwrite the cost of my bronze, oil-rubbed, Kohler faucet.

I didn't doubt I could fulfill his expectations if he ever arrived. I could dance to two pennies bouncing on the floor. My hips shifted impatiently. I'd given up holding my shoulders still. Every musical note sent a pulse of excitement rushing through my bones.

I looked at the clock and automatically reached for Roger's tiny evening purse containing cab fare and my cell phone.

Darn it. I groused to myself. I'd borrowed the evening bag from my other best friend, Dr. Roger Valentine, City

College Professor by day and Regina, The Comedy Zone's opening act every Friday night. The phone I could replace, the vintage clutch, probably not. I sighed.

My dance partner had evidently decided to be a no-show. Too bad for the lost revenue. Disapproval warred with relief. I wouldn't need Megan's final instructions.

"God knows I want you to have sex, Holly, but if you do, make sure you clock off first. You never know, he could be vice. It's best to skip naughty behavior when you're escorting for Aunt Maxine."

"Vice?" She'd laid her advice on me on the way out the door, absolutely insuring there would be no sex on the job.

Unfortunately, my best friend's advice hadn't included instructions about being stood-up. I didn't know if Megan's Aunt Maxine would suffer repercussions if I left, but I feared we were about to find out. Patience wasn't my strong suit. If I couldn't dance, I wanted to get away from the sounds driving me into jitter-bugging on the seat of my chair.

Roger had examined his Regina outfits and produced Marilyn Monroe without me having to rent a thing. Maxine via Megan had confirmed he'd be reimbursed for the costume. I smoothed the material of my dress. It was a far cry from my usual khakis and turtleneck.

It was the bomb and I loved it. It had a floaty bell skirt with a bodice covering my breasts and tying behind my neck. The white halter framed my chest and my abundant bust rested on a shelf-bra. It showed too much of everything, so over his protests, I'd searched Roger's closet, supplementing the outfit with a white satin, capped-sleeved bolero jacket to cover my problem area.

Other than that, the dress clung to my frame, flowing

smoothly from shoulder to waist before flaring out in a bouncy skirt. I suffered inside the iconic outfit shown in most of the pictures of the Hollywood sex bomb. Neither the dress nor the shoes were comfortable. Especially not the shoes.

But aside from the halter barely covering my breasts, the cut of the dress accented my waist, making it appear narrow. From there it flared out, defining my hips in a totally sexy way. Under the skirt, I was sexy too. I'd have pulled on a pair of pantyhose, but Roger wouldn't allow it.

Instead, I wore a thong, a garter belt, and my long legs were encased in silk stockings. Dark seams marched up the back of my legs, and according to Roger, tempted even his gaze to climb higher.

My meandering thoughts were abandoned to ogle a new arrival. Few men were tall enough to impress me. I salivated along with every other woman in the room as this specimen mopped snow from his brow.

He was both tall and big. Even though he wore a heavy, finger-tip length outer coat, I could see he had the physique of a linebacker—wide shoulders and muscular thighs. Recognizing a prime male when I saw one, drool pooled in my mouth and my stomach muscles clenched.

He shrugged out of his coat, stepped further into the light, and scanned the room. I felt a tingle of shock when Gable stood and waved his cowboy hat in the air. I looked closer.

Whoa. I know him. Why I remembered him, I couldn't say, but I had no doubt. The man who'd kept me waiting for over an hour was none other than the grump from the elevator in Megan's building.

Chapter Three
Marty

AFTER THE INTENSE heat of the California fire I'd left behind, the fierce Pittsburgh cold revived my flagging energy. Three days earlier I parachuted with the rest of the crew into an inferno on the other side of the country. Between then and now, we'd managed to cut, burn, and beat a firebreak into existence before being relieved by local hotshot crews.

Half way home, Elaine had called on the SAT-phone reminding me of the damned dance-a-thon commitment I'd made. As soon as we'd landed earlier, I'd cleaned up, driven across town, parked, and made it to the door by the DJ's stage without falling down. But, shit, I was tired. *Maybe Maxine's girl will be a no-show and I can go home.*

I scanned the tables lining the dance floor and spotted Gable immediately. And Marilyn.

Well I'll be damned. Cowboy did good. My evening took a turn for the better when I saw my dance partner. As ordered, the escort wore a Marilyn Monroe costume and looked like the actress in the flesh.

Surprised, I locked gazes with the blonde at the table. When I saw her deer-in-the-headlight expression, I started moving fast since it appeared Miss Marilyn was considering flight. I figured my ugly mug scared her, but tough shit.

Instead of walking the parameter of the room, I cut through the dancing couples, intent on getting to the table before she decided to run. More than one man thumped me on the back during my journey. Good. It was the point of the evening. I said my hellos and pumped hands on the way through, doing my bit for the company.

Good for business. Kit, my late wife, had always claimed public relations as our reason for going to events. The truth was, she'd loved mixing it up with people. And I loved watching her. Since she'd been gone, usually I sent a check and stayed home. If I did show up it was a business process without personal pleasure.

Tonight, would be no different. The people who controlled budgets would see me here and remember Smoke, Inc. had attended and helped the community. I'd dance a couple of songs with the glamour star and then leave.

I arrived at the table and wasted no time, ditching my overcoat, and then my suit jacket. I enjoyed her startled look. Okay maybe the pinstriped pink shirt was over the top, but I kind of liked the color. I draped the suit coat over the back of a chair, then flexed my back and shoulder muscles, testing the fit of the shirt. I didn't want it constricting my movement.

I didn't eye her directly, but I gave her a good once over just the same. Marilyn looked to be an armful. No chance I'd get her confused with Kit who'd been as light and airy as a hummingbird in my hand. When we'd danced, it had been a sight to behold.

"Elaine did you up proud," Cowboy drawled, calling my attention back to the now.

"Yep," I agreed and snapped the white suspenders clipped to the front-pleated gray flannel pants. On my feet, no joke, I wore gray suede shoes. At least, they weren't blue. I'd drawn the line there when she called me in California before she ordered the clothes.

"You'll be that mob boss, Sam something or other and your dance partner will be Marilyn Monroe." Elaine got excited about shit like that. She probably didn't get to dress up dolls enough when she was a kid. Anyway, she got a kick out of ordering my costume and I'd promised to get a couple of pictures before the end of the night.

So much for thinking my escort might take flight. My dance partner didn't wait for introductions. She stood up, shoved her hand at me, and said, "Marilyn Monroe, nice to meet you. Let's dance."

Holly

BEING TALL MYSELF, I had the unusual experience of tilting my head to see my dance partner's face.

Sun lines marked his wide forehead, a shaggy lock of hair dangled above unruly brows, and dark eyes met my gaze as he frowned down at me. Apparently, his expression never changed. I resisted the urge to tidy him, as he removed his suit jacket and flexed his arm, showing off bulging pecs. Oh yeah, macho man in pink.

Did I mention his height? At five feet eleven barefoot, I didn't often gaze *up* at anyone. At six feet three in the strappy four-inch silver heels Roger had insisted I wear, it should have been even less likely. And yet, there he was, looming *above* me, my own personal dancing bear.

Without a word of greeting, he led me to the official starter table and registered.

"Good to see you Marty." The guy at the table beamed at him and barely looked at me, which was good.

Okay, I can do this. I gritted my teeth and scrunched my toes inside barely-there sandals, wincing as I surveyed my partner's humongous gray suede shoes.

"At least fourteens," I muttered, staring at the intimidating foot gear.

"Fifteens," he grunted without looking at me. "Wide."

I was saved from further embarrassing conversation when the DJ announced us.

"Jones and partner, Team One for Smoke, Inc." Though the audience was meager, a smattering of applause and a few cheers from the balcony greeted us. It surprised me. He had fans.

Gable and Harley-Jane-soon-to-be-Matthews followed behind us, registered, and were announced as *Smoke, Inc. Team Two.*

"Let's get this show on the road." My dance partner frowned down at me as if I'd kept *him* waiting. His scowl deepened as he reached for me. "I'm Marty Jones."

Couples surrounded us on the dance floor. Whether I was ready or not, Marty snagged my hand and deftly swung me into the Beatles singing *Twist and Shout.*

"I've been ready," I answered, tartly, taking control. My partners until now had been shorter than me so I always navigated. I didn't expect to steer him around, but I needed time to ease into the subordinate dancing position since it wasn't my usual. Marty didn't agree.

"I lead. I'm boss. Understand?"

Really? His grunted declaration made me defiant. "I said I'd dance. I didn't say I'd take orders."

Before he could answer, I danced away, emphasizing my hip movement as I gazed at him over my shoulder.

"Get back here," he demanded, and crossed his arms in front of his chest, glaring at me like a petulant child.

I grinned at him over my shoulder, shrugged, and gave the audience an exaggerated Marilyn wink. Laughter greeted my antics, and I glanced back at him. I don't know if he was playing along or remembered me from the elevator, but his expression changed to a frown as he stared at my butt.

I strongly doubted he'd recognize me from the elevator. It had been a four-floor ride and he'd never seen my face, only my backside which wasn't memorable. On the other hand, I'd seen his frown and never forgotten it.

While I mulled it over, I waved my index finger at him, *Naughty, naughty,* scolding him as I danced backwards, away. Frankly, I considered giving him a middle finger salute. Someone in the balcony hooted at my antics which of course encouraged my insanity. I hoped my Marilyn lashes wouldn't stick together as I batted them at him.

Who knew a costume would be so liberating? Little Richard screamed as Jerry Lee Lewis hammered out *Good Golly Miss Molly,* and I totally owned Marilyn.

Honestly, prior to this moment, I'd always maintained a low-key, lips-zipped profile. But the laughter and applause from the audience was intoxicating. I hammed it up. And, if you discounted all the frowns, Marty Jones was hot.

"Did you decide to quit pouting?" I taunted when someone blew a whistle and Marty went into dance mode again.

His expression was grim as he approached, but I was pretty sure I detected a smirk trying to break loose from his outrage.

I faced him, dancing backward, guarding my flank, and resisting the urge to sprint toward the nearest exit. At the same time, I couldn't stop giggling as Marty demonstrated his alpha qualities, not following, so much as giving chase.

Before I grinned too big, he caught up with me and turned me around, pulling me into a hug that seated his groin against my rear.

"Are you going to dance or put on a show," he growled into my ear.

"Put on a show," I sniped back and exaggerated my hip sway, grinding my ass against his very impressive package.

"Be careful what you ask for," he warned, holding me in place with a left hand on my hip when I tried to spin away. Securing me even more, he caught my right hand and locked fingers, raising my arm with his to cradle my breasts.

His cheek pressed against mine as his long legs framed my long legs, his big thighs plastered to the back of mine, and his hand moved from where he'd placed it on my hip to my stomach. He surrounded me with his body, demonstrating his authority as he pressed me backward against his massive frame.

"See if you can follow this." His breath brushed my ear as he whispered his order.

He rocked left, my body followed. He rocked right... Yeah, I got the picture. He was stronger than me and had me locked in place.

"Okay, tutorial over," I muttered.

"Ready?" he murmured in my ear right before he

snapped me out, unfurling me like a ribbon at the end of his arm. When he pulled me back, I was not prepared for the lift and toss, and before he caught me, I'd shrieked loud enough to rival Little Richard.

"Not so sassy now," boss man grunted and slid me through his legs.

I'd previously had a partner where I'd been the *thrower*, not the *throwee*, so I sort of knew the move. When he stood me on my feet again I prepared to dance away but he retained control. "Try to keep up."

I clutched his rock-hard bicep and vowed to use him to polish the floor.

Time fell into an in-between world of forever as we moved to *The Crows*, *The Penguins*, *The El Dorados* and *The Turbans*. The big guy could dance. If his attitude indicated his personality, in real time Marty was a hulking, rude clunk. But set to music he became fluid motion, and somewhere during the evening, his frown changed to a happy grin.

Although few words passed between us, we hit our rhythm and fell into a weird kind of sync with me anticipating every move before he could give a gruff order. As he guided with a light touch, magic happened on the dance floor and I forgot this was a performance and we had an audience.

During the first set, I rode his thigh, wrapped my legs around his waist, and hugged his neck when he slid me between his legs again. When he duck-walked behind me across the room, I was distracted by the size of his package. I mean the guy was obviously big all over, but it didn't slow either of us down.

It didn't matter what music played, we danced as if we'd

known each other forever. Sometimes, I'd pout, close my eyes, cross my arms over Marilyn's abundant chest, and pretend to forget him altogether.

I don't know if the DJ fit his music to us or if we were just that good. But, I heard applause more than once, and I knew it was for Smoke, Inc. Team One.

Hours later, when the music finally slowed to *The Great Pretender* by The Platters, I rested against my partner's big frame and pressed my face into his chest, breathing his spicy scent.

He smelled good. I on the other hand, acutely aware of the perspiration trickling down my spine, doubted the caliber of my own aroma.

I glanced up at the clock. *Shit.* I should be at Balls & Bones serving drinks.

"I need to go to the john."

"You've got fifteen minutes," he growled.

Excuse me? I wanted to tell him to go fuck himself. Before the inclination became reality, Harley-Jane crossed the room and I met her at the edge of the floor.

I had more important things to do than insulting the dance partner from hell. But really, fifteen minutes? I called off work with Harley-Jane's phone, and decided I'd better pee while I was free, since Simon Legree didn't believe in taking breaks.

"You two are hot," Harley-Jane exclaimed as soon as we were in line at the restroom. "Do you, uh, dance professionally?" No doubt Janie thought my dancing included a pole and tit-tassels.

"No, I'm kind of an entrepreneur." I smiled at her, not giving up more personal information as advised by Megan.

Besides, I had too many jobs and none of them particularly interesting.

She took the hint and as we stood in the line waiting for our turn to pee, she pointed at our dance partners.

"He's something, isn't he?" she asked.

"Marty?" He was something, all right. He-Man on steroids. He'd thrown me into the air and caught me as if I weighed no more than a sack of flour.

"Gable," she answered. Then added, "I hope this line hurries along, or it could get messy soon."

I looked at the men's sign outside the male facility beside our line where men entered and exited rapidly.

"Come on. I'm on the clock and time lost, is dance time lost, which translates into money lost."

When Janie looked doubtful, I took her hand and pulled her toward the other sign. Once inside the men's potty-room, Janie claimed the one stall, and I took the time to study my Marilyn costume. No men came in while we commandeered their john. For that, I was thankful.

My bolero jacket had become a crumpled mess. I wrinkled my nose and removed it, then frowned at the cleavage on display.

"Think they'll fall out?" I asked Janie when she emerged from the stall.

"Ah, but it's for a good cause. Think of the pledges." Janie wagged her finger at me and then motioned me to turn around as she studied the dress.

"It really does look great. And with this heat, I'd leave off the jacket."

I accepted her judgment and deposited Roger's bolero at the table before we returned to our partners.

Chapter Four
Marty

"SO HOW DID the job, go? I saw a hotshot team deploying on the news." Gable's question jarred me for a moment. I'd completely forgotten the fire, the crew, and everything else in my head but keeping up with the imp leading me in circles on the dance floor.

"We lost a slew of equipment, but it could have been worse." I clenched my teeth, memory constricting earlier, oxygen-starved, lungs. I leaned on the wall behind me, replaying in my mind my most recent disaster. Not the moment my oxygen had cut off, but the fact I'd thought about letting the inevitable happen.

For a moment, I'd considered cashing out, and it hadn't seemed like a bad idea. Insurance would pay out and pay off. Worries done, day end. Game over. Not until the wind shifted, clearing smoke from the air and providing oxygen for me to breathe, did I remember Jack, my father-in-law.

The old fucker wouldn't know what to do without me to keep him straight. And that wasn't my ego talking. We'd been through too much together for me to bale early on him.

"Equipment check before we go out again," I told Gable. *Maybe a head check, too.* "My breathing equipment shut down. Had the wind not shifted, it would have been my ashes coating Clyde's vineyard."

We were Smoke, Inc.—in this case—smokejumpers for hire. We'd been employed from half way around the world by a friend of my late wife, Kitty Jones. Her buddies ranged from royalty to thugs and all of them had loved her. They didn't all share the same affection for me. But sometimes, knowing Marty Jones still proved handy for them.

This was one of those times. Clyde Ramsey had called when he required a clean-up for one of his problems. Clyde considered me a janitor for the rich which was fine. Dirty jobs didn't bother me a bit. And they usually paid well. He'd had a fire needing doused and I knew his check was good.

"Marty, my people identified a wildfire. Two spotters already pinned it. Hell, it might be out of hand, already. The government's broke. I'm not. I want you to put it out before it gets worse."

Smoke mobilized a crew and had boots and equipment on the ground eight hours after first contact. Once there, it had been easy to see Clyde's *spotters* had started the fire when they'd tried to clear brush with a drip torch.

"We'll collect for our lost equipment. Clyde will pay out a hell of a lot more in fines if the feds realize his people were responsible for the disaster. The locals probably already suspect, but that's the client's problem."

I really didn't want to talk business. I scanned the room until my gaze settled on my dance partner.

"Where'd you find her?" I continued leaning against the wall next to the snack machine and sipping water. In case he didn't understand my meaning, I nodded toward Marilyn now standing in the bathroom line.

"Baby Dolls," Gable answered, not misunderstanding the

question.

"She's one of Maxine's escorts?" Didn't seem possible. Even vamped out in red lipstick, Marilyn mole, and a blonde wig, it was still a laughing kid, wearing four inch *go-to-hell* heels on her already six-foot frame.

"She okay?" Gable asked.

I finished the water and eyed my dance partner. My query, considering my general disinterest in women since Kit died, no doubt flagged Gable's attention.

"Once we settled on who was in charge, she got okay." *Okay, like hell.* I hid my smile. She'd matched me beat for beat, and I'd actually had fun, something that hadn't happened in years.

"You see her dancing by herself, giving me the cold shoulder?" I'd been dancing alone for six years and never wanted a partner. But I wanted this one. "She's a fucking wild woman."

"She's hot stuff," Gable agreed but I was sure he was talking about Harley-Jane since that's who he stared at.

"Didn't plan on staying the night." The audience had gotten considerably bigger and they were eating our shit up. My couple of hours had expanded, and instead of wearing me out, my partner had me rocking.

Kit would have loved her.

Gable pulled me away from that fleeting thought, when he nudged me and pointed at the two women entering the men's toilet.

"I think your wild child's teachin' my sweet girl to misbehave."

I snorted, hard-put to keep a grin from showing. Wild Child sounded about right. Especially when she came sauntering back to the dance floor.

Jesus. My cock tried to punch a hole in my pants and I wasted no time escorting her back onto the dance floor where I concentrated on the music and tried to forget about her tits now on display.

She'd ditched the jacket, and even though the luscious breasts framed by the halter straps on Marilyn's dress were no doubt fake, I and every other bozo in the room enjoyed the show. I had to resist the urge to cop a feel. I settled for pulling her against my chest and hugging her tight. Squashed between us, the tits felt real.

I'd been awake for over thirty-six hours, fighting a fire on the other side of the country during most of the time. But the Marilyn impersonator's sassy strut and perfect timing had me on high alert with adrenaline pumping through my veins.

I rolled her into my embrace, bent her over my arm, and held her for a beat too long while my nose brushed a spot on her neck, and I scented green apples. *Jesus.* I wanted to eat her up.

The brat spun loose and danced another circle around me. I could hear laughter and applause, and I knew it was for her. I figured I'd better rope her in and remind her who was boss.

I linked our hands, whirled her into my arms, and duck-walked her across the floor, pressing my hard-on against her rump to the beat of The Kingsmen singing *Louie Louie.*

My uncontrolled bodily response surprised me. I hadn't had any spontaneous flare ups of lust since well before Kit died. Now I had a full-blown erection for a kid working the skin trade. Shit.

Holly

IF HE NOTICED the change in my costume, my partner didn't mention it. Nevertheless, when Marty's hand rested on the bare skin of my back, I wished I'd left the jacket in place.

And then the DJ abandoned the fifties and changed things up with Elle King and modern swing.

"One, two…" I started counting. As I swayed to Elle's sound, my hips followed the teasing beat. A grin spread over Marty's face and he started snapping his fingers and shadowing my moves. What a dance partner. He wasn't good. He was splendiferous.

The crowd went nuts, clapping and cat-calling their encouragement. And true to my disguise, Marilyn put on a show, teasing, taunting, and flirting to music. Marty laughed out loud, reeled me in, and bent me back over his arm.

His laughter changed to a surprised grunt when his nose brushed my shoulder. He stayed low so long, I was afraid he'd gotten tangled in the wig, somehow. Me being me, I didn't want him snuffling my shoulder.

I had a sinking feeling my deodorant had stopped working three or four hundred spins before. So, I improvised, dancing away from him to give his nose a break from *eau du sweaty Holly*.

Should have known it wouldn't suffice. He captured my hand, turned me so my back plastered to his front, and danced us forward. Aside from his junk grinding against my butt, I was in heaven. Ginger and Fred couldn't have done it better.

Time blurred, and gradually the music slowed until we stopped doing fancy and just leaned on each other. The four-inch heels brought my mouth level with his chin. If I tipped my head the slightest bit, and he did the same, our lips would meet.

The night ended as we danced to Elvis singing *Fools Rush In,* and I tilted my chin, gazing up at my dance partner. His mouth lowered to mine, our lips touched, his lingered for a moment, then withdrew.

I sighed. Applause sounded in the background, and cameras flashed, bringing me out of my trance. I'd forgotten where we were.

"Ten hours, forty-five minutes, and ten seconds. But who's counting, right?" The microphone crackled weird electronic noises as the DJ made his announcements.

The floor had filled and emptied again while we danced. I hadn't paid any attention to the time since I'd taken my one fifteen-minute break.

Whoa. What a ride. I started to ease away, readying to leave, but my dance partner caught my arm, stopping me.

"Standing still isn't a good idea," I muttered. Tired hit me in double time.

Marty must have felt the quaking of my legs, because he dropped my wrist and circled my waist. Sweet. I slumped against him and gazed blearily up ready to say goodnight, or morning, good something, and totter away.

His eyes were heavy-lidded, his chin covered in heavy morning stubble, and his pink shirt a wrinkled mess.

I hated to think what I looked like. I figured when I pulled the wig off, a puddle of sweat might gush out as well. Nor did I want to investigate the black dot on Marty's shirt. It looked suspiciously like the beauty mark representing Marilyn's mole.

Rather than retrieve it, I'd factor the cost of its replacement into the dry cleaning before I returned Roger's dress. My thought tangled with another. *I need to borrow cab fare.*

"Sponsors of Smoke, Inc. Team One, prepare to write those checks," the DJ announced.

I expected a smattering of applause, not the huge roar, greeting his words. Evidently, local news channels had been light on death and murder the night before, so they'd fallen back on the "phenomenal dance for cash" going on.

Anyway, we'd made *News at Eleven*, and because of that, call-in pledges poured in and the station sent a crew over to film the rest of the dance. Wow. Marilyn and Boss were celebrities.

Cameras flashed as Marty raised our linked hands in a victory salute. On the stage, the DJ started putting away his equipment. After we finished posing, I untangled our fingers.

Barbara Carlson, a tough-talking local news woman had me in her sights as she crossed the room, her film crew trailing behind. Uh oh. "I don't do interviews," I muttered.

Marty blocked her before she got close, and I eavesdropped since the conversation concerned his dance partner—me.

She led with a friendly request aimed at him, not me. "Just a few words with your partner."

No, no, a thousand times no... I didn't want to talk to her or the news media because a) Maxine had sent me; b) I had day jobs; and c) my life was nobody's business.

"Sorry, Barb. We're tired. Call my office later." He stopped her from getting to me, and her tone turned spiteful.

"So, good to see you've found someone to replace Kit."

I wondered who Kit was when Marty's newly-minted

amiable expression congealed into a blank stare. He brushed her aside and steered me away from them, keeping his body between me and the camera. "We're tired. Glad the family will get some help."

"Thanks," I told him, leaning closer to keep our conversation discreet and maybe to have a final whiff of his expensive cologne. He was big, strong, taller than me, and after a night of sweaty fun, he still smelled good. What was not to like. I smiled up at him. "Who's Kit?"

His expression changed from friendly to hostile. "My wife was my last dance partner."

"You break up or something?" Go me, ever the persistent. Well, I was interested in him, and if he'd just gotten a divorce or broken it off with someone he was likely looking for a fling which I didn't do, and I thought my question appropriate.

"She died."

"Oh." I squeezed out a final, "I'm sorry." Ever the subtle me. I intended to put this example of my klutziness behind me and move on to something more on my social level like, socket wrenches and miter saws.

"You sellin' fucks this morning?"

Whoa. Shit. Damn, on so many levels. I'd completely forgotten the role I was playing. Way to cool me down fast.

"No," Marilyn said and clocked off.

To heck with the sore feet, I strode away from Maxine's client without a backward look. Except I didn't leave him behind, he walked beside me, his long legs matching my stride.

"Breakfast?"

He'd obviously not gotten my mental memo. The night

was at end. We didn't know each other. I, Holly Smith, had a life to live which didn't include widowers who used crude words to solicit paid sex. After twining with him all night, I might have succumbed to his charm if he'd asked nice. I'd been thinking about it so there was no point in getting self-righteous.

I didn't have to worry about the outcome since his asking nice hadn't happened. With my eyes focused, on where I'd left my jacket and coat, I walked toward the table and ignored him.

Common sense melted the ice in my veins. For the night, I'd been representing Maxine's Baby Doll Escort service. If he'd heard the same rumors I'd heard, Marty Jones had every reason to believe I might sell a little something on the side.

When I remained mute, he added, "At least, let me feed you. Your stomach growled in time with the music."

"Oh, you, flatterer." I murmured the silly words and batted Marilyn eyes at him instead of the nasty smack down resounding in my head. Even so, a flush of embarrassment washed over me. Or maybe it was the way he leaned closer. For whatever reason, I felt breathless, dizzy. Damn.

"You're crowding me, bozo." I snarled. And this time, it wasn't Marilyn talking. "I don't want breakfast."

"My name's Marty, not bozo. What's yours?"

"Marilyn." My brain took that moment to telegraph that certain body parts had endured enough—first and foremost, my feet. Without the artificial high of music, I wanted nothing more than to step out of the four-inch heels and slump on a chair.

Gable and Janie wore coats and waited with bad news.

"Got a problem, Marty."

The two men went into a huddle and left me with Janie.

"We'll all have to get together, again," Janie assured me, making small talk. "Marty smiled all night. Just wow."

Evidently, a smile from Marty was rare. His wrinkled brow and frowny frown earlier in the evening had given me a good indication of his usual surly mood.

Her hope of more together times surprised me. Yes, we'd bonded over home upgrades, but it was casual fill-in-the-time talk, not really bosom buddy stuff. This was a one-time date, and I liked her; but a future foursome that included Marty and me just wouldn't be happening

"I really need to get out of here," I told her. "I doubt we'll meet again, so thank you for sharing your table and remodeling tips." There, I'd done my duty. But the way she gazed anxiously at Gable, it didn't take a genius to figure something was wrong.

Something which is none of my business. I looked at the two men deep in conversation. Marty Jones had already forgotten my existence. It seemed the perfect time to slip away.

"I hope everything's all right," Janie continued as if I knew what was going on.

"I'm sure they can handle anything." I picked up my bolero jacket, shrugged into it, folded my heavy coat over my arm and started for the exit.

Marty beat me to the door and had it open waiting when I arrived. Which was good since I'd forgotten I needed cab fare.

"I'd like to borrow twenty dollars," I said quickly.

He pulled out his wallet and handed me a hundred-dollar bill.

"I don't have change." I could feel my face flame. Obviously, I didn't have change. "I'll pay you back." I was also dumping whatever money Maxine paid me into the donation fund.

"You can get change at breakfast."

I noticed his penchant for using imperative sentences. They didn't work on me. I didn't like being bossed around.

On the other hand, not being stupid, I didn't disagree. I'd found it easier to let people believe what they wanted. Regardless of his plans, I'd be peeling away the first moment possible. He'd get his change by way of Maxine.

Janie watched the exchange, with, I thought, a hint of disapproval. Since I didn't need her approval, I should have kept my mouth shut. But, I didn't. "Cab fare. I'll get change for him at breakfast."

Beside me, Marty grunted in what I assumed to be satisfaction. Okay, he thought I'd been out-maneuvered. When Marty reached for my arm, I stepped away.

"I don't need a guide to find the elevator," I muttered. I was off the clock, and *Mr. You-sellin'-fucks-this-morning* did not need to be steering me around.

"It was an interesting evening," I told him politely.

"It ain't over 'til it's over," he agreed.

"It's over," I stated.

"You owe me change," he said, and I noticed his perpetual frown had changed to a smirk.

What the heck? I fumbled with the hundred, getting ready to shove it down his throat. He was saved when a cop stepped in our path, and interrupted our conversation.

"Hey Marty. Someone took a crack at your Hummer."

"Yep. That's what I heard."

Of course, he owned a Hummer. When I would have dropped back a bit, he reached over and held my arm. Not tight, not hurting, but detaining. He continued to talk to the cop as I stood beside him, trying to tone down my desire to kick his ass.

The man-huddle subject was revealed. Marty's vehicle had been one of several vehicles parked in the reserved section of the parking garage and vandalized during the dance-a-thon. Rather than interrupting our dance, Gable had answered the license plate all-call, shut off the alarm, and taken care of initial city police business.

I hadn't heard an all-call. From Marty's surprised look, neither had he. Unfamiliar feminine pride fluttered inside me as I realized he'd been as mesmerized as me. Uh huh.

"Normally, we'd have come to get you, but no way was anyone interrupting your dance. Damn Marty. I even started calling people and getting pledges when you passed five hours." The cop tipped his chin respectfully at me as well. Evidently, our marathon dance had earned a lot of green for the cause.

All that praise didn't make my feet feel better. It was time to leave. I shrugged off Marty's hold and stepped away. The strappy sandaled four-inch heels, uncomfortable even at the beginning of the evening, scraped against a blister on top of a blister on my heel. I winced.

"We can drop you somewhere if you need a ride." Janie made an offer I couldn't refuse.

"Just downtown. That would be great." Get me downtown, and I'd go to Maxine's office and wait for Megan or Roger to pick me up. Walking at this point just wasn't going to happen. I leaned down, unstrapped my shoes, stepped out of them, and wiggled my toes.

Better. The men were still talking, their backs turned. No one else was around so I made an executive decision.

"Hold these." I handed Janie the shoes, reached under my skirt, unhooked the nylons, and began rolling the left one down and off. Maybe he heard my sigh of relief, because as I worked on the second one, Marty turned his head and watched me step barefoot on the carpeted floor.

I bared my teeth at him, daring him to make a crack. He didn't. His expression remained blank, which made me feel like an exhibitionist.

When he returned to his conversation and stopped gawking at me, I tucked the hundred-dollar bill I'd been palming into a shoe along with the balled nylons.

Normally I would have stuck it in my bra, but thanks to the Marilyn dress, I wasn't wearing one. And, I definitely didn't trust the dress's under-support to hold *me*, let alone my money.

When the male parlay ended, and we continued to the elevator, Marty again made himself my escort. I couldn't avoid noticing that the distance between us had altered. Four inches shorter and I *really* had to tilt to meet his gaze.

The cop, Gable, and Janie stepped inside the cubicle when the doors slid open. Beside me, Marty noticed my bare feet and took the shoes from me.

"I don't need help carrying—"

"Get in," he ordered me and stepped inside the elevator. I had the choice of staying in the lobby bare foot and once again broke, or following him to retrieve my shoes and money.

Or, I could wait in the manager's office and call someone. I thought of the big-eared kid and nixed that idea.

"Promise he's not an axe-murder," I muttered to Janie as I gazed at my shoes in Marty's hand. I wasn't reassured by her murmured disclaimer.

I entered the elevator and rode upstairs with Marty who stood so close to me we could have continued our dance. Once we arrived, the men took off, leaving Janie and me together to follow them across the cement floor.

"Ugh. Some cretins spray-painted nasty words on a Mercedes, keyed the side of an Audi, and slashed the tires on a Cadillac Escalade." Apparently, Janie had already seen the damage when Gable came to take care of business.

"Why?"

"Who knows," she answered and shrugged. "Guess they took pity on us peons driving the work trucks. They didn't touch Gable's F150. They did a job on Marty's Hummer though. The back window's been smashed." She stopped and pointed at the monster sized SUV before us and then at the garage floor.

Well damn. I scrunched my bare toes and stared at the broken glass, then at the tough, massive, gas guzzling, vehicle. Not new, but neither was Marty. I sneaked a quick look his way. A little gray sprinkled in the thick dark hair. He needed his eyebrows trimmed. And a shave. *Maybe not. The scruff looks good.*

I kind of wanted to reach up and run the back of my hand along his jaw. I mean, at the beginning of the night he'd been clean shaven. He had dark stubble now.

"What?" He caught me staring at him.

"I thought they quit making those," I muttered, motioning toward the Hummer. I felt a blush creep up my neck. I don't know how long I'd been ogling him.

"Lucky I got one before that happened," he said and focused his attention back on the cop. Which was fine. I went back to being nosey. I eavesdropped as much as I could since nothing else was happening and my toes were getting colder by the minute.

I don't know if he heard my teeth chattering but after a quick look my way, he wrapped things up fast. The cop couldn't have been more in awe if he'd been shaking the President's hand and agreed to whatever Marty said.

A security guard on duty had responded to the car alarm, but not fast enough. No one had been caught physically or on the camera pointing at this section of the parking area.

"Camera was okay this morning," the cop said, pointing at the smashed monitor in the corner. "The security guard called it into the police, we took pictures, and you'll have to go to the station when you can to sign some paperwork which I don't have."

I spied the security guard leaning against the wall with a broom, evidently waiting to remove the broken glass.

Marty walked around the vehicle, squatted next to it and looked underneath. When he stood again he looked at Gable and said, "Drop us off at the office."

Oh, I don't think so. I'd been too curious wondering about what was happening and indecisive about putting my stockings back on before I caught a ride downtown.

Gable lifted Janie into the waiting pickup, and I decided to take the elevator back downstairs to the main building.

Contrary to what I thought, Marty proved aware of my intentions. Before I'd taken two steps, he'd caught my arm, and stopped me. "Glass on the floor." He picked me up, carried me to the truck, and opened the backdoor.

"You're not going my way," I assured him, uncomfortably aware of his hand cradling my ass.

"Yeah, I am," he disagreed, and set me on the seat. Then he slid in close beside me and slammed the door.

He was a big man but not *that* big. He did not need to ride with his thigh pressing against my hip. But after Marty tucked my skirts closer, and buckled me in, I forgot about cold bare feet as his body heat raised my core temperature to burn. Whew.

Not being stupid, I knew where this was going. At least, where he labored to steer it.

"Janie," I leaned forward. "Just drop me anywhere downtown."

"Gable, I promised…" she paused, fumbling with a name for me since I'd asked her not to share earlier. Marty inserted himself in the discussion.

"She's got blisters on her feet, no socks to put on, and she's dressed like Marilyn Monroe, for fuck's sake." He turned to me. "I don't bite. You can use a phone in my office if you want to call for a ride. Or hell, I'll call an Uber driver to take us to breakfast before you go home."

Yeah right, and you'd have my address. Not happening that way, Mr. Jones. "Okay." I didn't need to change my plan. I checked my watch. It was eight in the morning. Baby Doll's Escort Service occupied an office on the fourth floor of the Smoke, Inc. building.

I could use Maxine's phone and at the same time make certain she charged Big Boss out the wazoo for his dance time. He could afford it. He didn't appear to give two shits about his Hummer. Maybe I'd get my fancy faucet, after all.

Marty

I HAD NO idea how Maxine worked. Did she recruit or take applications? Did she offer protection for her girls? She should. That thought made me wince. *Just what we need, hired thugs strolling in and out of the building.*

Again, I realized I might have been hasty in offering Maxine office space in Smoke's new building. But, the possibility of unwinding that contract wasn't enough to distract me from the immediate focus—my dance partner. I'd been painfully erect most of the night. Her "no" when I offered to pay her for sex should have deflated me.

Instead of embarrassed and backing off, my cock had no shame. Mild interest had changed to primitive need when I'd seen her stripping off her stockings. *Long legs. I'll start with those wrapped around me for breakfast.*

Instead of worrying about the Hummer, the business, or the bad weather, I absorbed her heat and the ice I hadn't known I carried in my veins, thawed as I sat next to her in the truck. Earlier, she'd been an uninhibited wild woman pumping rhythm through her veins. Picturing her dancing with me horizontally, had me rock hard.

But since the music had ended her sly grin had gone into hiding. I wondered about who she really was. Without the flush of exercise, her face seemed pale. I stole looks at her during the ride across town.

She sat next to me, clearly pissed-off at my maneuvering. It had been easy enough to get her in Gable's truck. I'd resisted yelling at her. Dammit, if she planned to make her living selling fucks, trusting and vulnerable were not good attributes to display.

A babe in the woods. Closer scrutiny assured me she wasn't a teenager. Still, compared to my thirty-eight years, she seemed young. That thought along with a million others popped into my head. I wondered if I was getting loopy from lack of sleep. It felt as if my brain had kicked into overdrive.

"Gettin' bad out again." Gable switched on his wipers, cranked up the heat, and turned on the radio, creating an oasis of quiet safety in the cab of the vehicle. I relaxed.

"Our twelve-hour marathon earned a lot for the family." I felt good about the night. I felt great about her. Hell, she'd worked her ass off earning money for a guy she didn't even know. I nodded my appreciation and added, "Make sure Maxine pays you accordingly."

She gave a startled jerk at my reminder. Maybe I'd been a little gruff. I tried to paste on a pleasant look. I hadn't intended to get to know my night's partner but after twelve hours of sweaty familiarity, I couldn't seem to step back into impersonal.

Paying a woman to let me screw had never been my thing. On the other hand, I now considered the possibility of doing just that. Truth. I'd not wanted to fuck for a long time.

But pressed tight against her side, with the snow outside the window cocooning us in a white veil of privacy, and her scent combining with mine in the backseat of Gable's truck, I had a prodigious hard-on, making it clear my days of abstinence were over. She'd said no. Maybe she'd change her mind.

"Before we eat, I need to stop at my office," I told her, abruptly making up *my* mind. She didn't object.

Due to it being an early Saturday morning, the company parking lot was empty when Gable pulled into his space. We had the place to ourselves.

"You want me to send over a car?"

"I'm good. Have the shop bring the Hummer over here when they replace the back glass."

It was now or never. I pasted on my *I don't give a shit whether you come with me or not* look and glanced at my dance partner.

Marilyn, huh. Costume or not, I already knew a lot more about her than she wanted to share. After she took off the jacket earlier, she'd fidgeted with the straps on her dress, making me certain she didn't usually flaunt her tits.

Her skin was as soft as a baby's. I didn't see much makeup left. No surprise since she'd been chewing the red lipstick off earlier, and it had disappeared hours before. Even without artifice, her mouth offered kissable lips. We'd touched mouths at the end of the dance. Not enough. I ached to taste her again, maybe suck on that full bottom lip before I slid my tongue...

Jesus. I fumbled for control, fighting the desire to go caveman and throw her over my shoulder, hauling her to my place. My place being my office. I stalled mentally for a moment wondering where I'd dropped my discarded dirty clothes.

She shifted on the seat next to me, and her thigh rubbed against mine. *Bare legs ready to wrap around and ride.* I stifled a groan. If she was driving up the price, I didn't care. She was a consummate artist-at-work—tease, seduce, tempt.

I opened my passenger door and stepped out, reaching back for her. She'd already unhooked her belt and grabbed her shoes. Miss Independent clearly didn't need a hand from me.

"Are you sure you don't want us to drop you somewhere else?" Janie asked her as she scrambled away from me and out the other side.

"I'm fine," she murmured.

"You got this, boss?" Gable asked, a hint of laughter in his voice.

"You know it." I closed the door, stepped back, and Gable drove away, removing the barrier between Marilyn and me.

Holly

I'D EXPECTED MORE people to be around mid-morning in parking building, even if it was a Saturday. But apparently, the weather had kept people home, and, except for my dance partner angling for another kind of dance, things were quiet. I wasted no time heading for the closest exit which happened to be the elevator going up to the ground floor.

He didn't say a word. Nor did he touch me. We walked side by side to the elevator, stood silently waiting for the doors to open, then stepped inside, and fell on each other like animals.

I don't remember who started it. I'll say he did. Geez. I did have enough sense to come up for air and hit the number four button, but unfortunately not before his finger did the walking to punch Floor Twenty.

I'd forgotten about taking off my silk stockings until he proved to be ambidextrous. The hand not claiming the elevator controls, found its way under Marilyn's skirts.

Hot fingers scorched their way up my bare thigh and straight to the thong. Before I could stop him, I stopped the elevator. For the record, I'd meant to punch button four, but hit pause. Our ride jerked to a halt, stranding us between floors.

Marty pushed aside the scrap of cloth covering me and went straight for the gold. Heat from his big paw, pressure on my clit, slippery wetness below. My common-sense circuits shorted-out at that point, and I happily let my body take charge as he worked me with his hand. At the same time, he sucked on one nipple, then the other. Oh. My. God.

I whimpered.

"Oh yeah, sweetheart," he murmured. Then he went back to worrying the bud he'd abandoned to cheer me on, scraping it with his teeth. I arched higher, giving him more breast to play with. "That's it, baby doll. Come for papa."

Honest to God his rumbled order pushed me so close to the edge, when he bit the sensitive tip he'd been sucking, I shuddered, threw back my head, and screamed my climax to the world. *Incoming...* Wow.

My God. If I'd been struck by a bolt of lightning, I couldn't have been more stunned. Literally. I slumped over his arm like a sack of potatoes.

The doors opened, he scooped me into his arms, and carried me out of the neutral zone into his lair.

The doors closed. As I began to recover from the orgasm to end all orgasms, I reconsidered our destination. He kissed me, diverting my attention back to him. I kissed him back and fumbled with his zipper, freeing the erection he'd been teasing me with all night. He growled when I touched it with my hand.

I wanted to crane my neck and look down at it, but he recaptured my mouth, and I couldn't see.

I finally came up for air long enough to sneak a quick peek at his junk. Seeing the size of the shaft, and the even thicker head, I froze.

This was reality check time. Did I really want to do this? Maybe this wasn't such a good idea.

I had no time to express my doubts. He carried me into another room, slammed, then locked the door behind us, and growled, "Rubber."

Good thinking. That interrupted things long enough for me to catch my breath.

"I don't have a condom."

He looked astonished. I suppose under the circumstances he had that right. But, I didn't carry condoms, and apparently, neither did he.

"Wrap your legs around my waist."

I obliged. He slid a finger inside me, and my body went into *I'm going to have another orgasm* mode.

He leaned me against the locked door, pushed my thong aside, rubbing his engorged flesh against my swollen clit. The only thing stopping full penetration was my inability to scale his frame and get the angle right.

"Bathroom," he mumbled, carrying me along with him as he crossed the room.

"Let me down." No way. I really hadn't lost my senses that much. My first time was not going to be in a john.

Before I could get free, he hauled me into the washroom, fumbled in a drawer, and grabbed a condom. Oh, okay. I guess in the grand scheme of things, it really didn't matter.

"Lift up."

I did, wrapping my arms around his neck and my legs higher as he covered up. And then, he sat me on the edge of the sink, and pushed inside me. I was wet and ready. But...

"Christ you're tight," he groaned, leaning his forehead against mine as he held onto my hips.

"Sorry," I muttered, in acute discomfort. It seemed like a bad time to mention he was scoring where nobody had ever scored before.

"Work it in for me, baby," he growled and moved a hand to explore my sex. When he fingered my clit, things below improved.

Not for long though. He grunted and surged forward, nailing me to the sink. Whoa. Not the most romantic way to lose my cherry. He didn't seem to notice or mind.

"Jesus," he laughed. "We can do better than this."

You think? He kept me anchored to him, his cock stretching the walls of my channel as he carried me to the couch in the office.

He pushed a blanket aside, sat down with me still straddling him, and ordered, "Ride me until I see stars, sugar."

My knees were spread wide, as were the lips of my sex. He filled me, and every time he moved, he nudged my clit.

The straps of Marilyn's halter dress fell, exposing my breasts to his gaze. "Oh, yeah. Wanted to look at these babies all night. They're real, right?"

Real what? I looked down at them, trying to see what made them so special. I must admit, I'd never appreciated their greatness before. When he again scraped a bullet-hard peak with his teeth, I lost that thread of thought, and shuddered.

"Fucking beautiful," he whispered, and covered the nipple, working it between his lips.

When my internal muscles clenched around him, sucking him deeper inside of me, he growled, "Like that don't you?"

Yes, yes, I do. I ground down, reaching for another release, which I found. I bucked against him as he thrust up, holding me in place as he buried himself deeper, ushering my ongoing orgasm into another.

"Dance for me baby. Don't stop."

I followed his lead and then made up moves of my own.

"Not gonna come, yet," he growled more than once. "Been a long time." He rolled me under him without missing a beat.

That and, "Sweet, fucking sweet," were the extent of his conversational gambits. But most of what I heard was garbled, and being otherwise occupied, I might have missed some of it.

I know at one point, me being bare up top with him not, pissed me off. I'd jerked his coat off, and managed a button or two on the shirt, before he'd ripped the rest open. Skin to skin. Flesh to flesh. Oh, my God. It was awesome. Likewise, he lost his pants someplace along the way.

He had me wasted, limp, and drooping over his chest before he growled, "Coming home, baby."

I nodded weakly when he grasped my butt, pumping me up and down as his hips jerked in an erratic rhythm.

Goose bumps spread up his arms, and he shifted his hold from my rear to my shoulders, pushing me down against his groin as he ground his flesh against the spread lips of my sex, fusing us. He exploded inside me, releasing jets of wet heat splashing against the walls of my channel.

"Fuck me, baby. You've got one more in you. Come with me." And even as I felt his cock spurt inside me, he pressed his thumb to my clit, took my mouth with a deep kiss, and pushed me into my final-final release. Oh. My. God. I passed out for a minute.

I opened my eyes, not expecting to see him in a dead slump. Then I wasn't sure it was a slump. Geez, what if I'd killed him?

Death by sex with Holly. I leaned closer. He was breathing. Okay. Things below were uncomfortably wet.

Marilyn's dress would never recover but... I scrambled off, holding my skirts high enough to try and avoid additional fluids. I was leaking.

Marty was totally out. So was his penis, though even limp it remained an impressive size. I frowned. He'd worn a condom. I could see no condom anywhere.

Where the heck is it? I visited his bathroom, and discreetly probed inside myself. I was very, *very* wet. *Gross.* I found the rubber inside me and retrieved it. *Good God, and double yuck.*

My mental faculties resumed working, and I didn't waste any time getting on my way. After I'd tidied as much as possible, I left the bathroom and headed out the door.

My dance partner woke long enough to say his version of "thank you for the dance" and "good night".

"Tell Maxine to send me the bill."

Chapter Five
Marty

I WOKE UP bewildered, but not from my location. I'd been sleeping at the office since the company bought the place. Before that, I'd slept on my couch in the building that had burned down.

Since my wife died, I hadn't had any need for a permanent location other than where I worked. I'd fixed myself a closet and made sure I had a shower in the bathroom. I'd had my pictures of Kit and me in the other place, but when it burned down, I'd lost them, too. I waited for depression to hit me. When it didn't, I stretched and realized I was naked. I don't sleep naked in my office because, well, it's my office. I buried my face against my bare arm and laughed. *Oh yeah.*

The leather I sprawled on smelled different than usual when I woke up. I inhaled the aroma of sex, green apples and sex.

My cock twitched. Whoa. What a ride. A stupid grin plastered my face. At the same time, my sense of well-being confused me. I hadn't felt so relaxed and at peace since before Kit had been diagnosed.

For the first time in years, I didn't feel empty. Giddy would be a better description, but I didn't think two hundred-forty-pound lard-asses were supposed to feel giddy.

I sat up and stretched. The sight of my gear across the room wiped the grin off my face.

I moved to the desk and inspected the equipment, needing to know what caused the malfunction. Not a mechanic myself, Gable took care of all our gear. I called him. It took him long time to answer and when he did, he didn't sound pleased to hear from me.

"Pretty early for me to be out from home, this morning. How about Janie and me stop by tomorrow and have a look." Translated, that meant Gable was holed up with his woman for the rest of the day and he wasn't moving.

"Marilyn there with you?" he drawled, not bothering to hide his nosiness.

"Was," I grunted. "She left. That's why I'm poking around this piece of shit breathing apparatus that cut out on me. We're on a job next week and I want to make sure it doesn't happen again."

"I've got the gear all scheduled for my usual clean, repair, check. I'll pay special attention to the SCBAs. I'll pick yours up tomorrow and find the problem." Gable wasn't interested in chatting and since I could hear Harley-Jane giggling in the background, I knew why. I hung up.

Business taken care of. I closed my eyes intending to re-play the moment my oxygen had cut off. Instead, the image of a wild woman giving me the elevator ride of my life filled my mind.

Have to wipe the security tapes. Shit. Still…what a night. What a dance. What a woman. *Yeah. Giddy's right.* My body felt loose and alive. My brain zinged with good vibes.

I fixed myself a cup of coffee, intending to spend the morning on paperwork and reports. The place seemed too quiet, so I flipped on the radio and tuned in some music. I ended up on my feet, practicing a couple of the moves I'd used the night before. *Next time, I need to have her cross her wrists, so I can pull her up and spin her out in one motion.*

After a few of the mental *next time* notes, I realized I didn't know my dance partner's real name. Or address. Or telephone number. Not even her hair color.

I know she didn't fake those orgasms. Smugly I looked at the couch with pride. She'd come; I'd held off as long as possible. It had been so damn good when I'd finally let go. And then... It hadn't been my finest moment. I'd passed out.

I frowned. *I'll explain that I'd been awake for over thirty-six hours when I see her next time.* That led me to the increasingly important issue of how to schedule a next time.

Holly

I'D USED THE dancing crime boss's hundred-dollar bill to get home where I'd soaked in a bath long enough to ease my aches and pains. The water was cold by the time I emerged. I then slept most of the day, until I dragged myself from bed and got ready for work. Roger's dress was a wreck. And I'd also managed to leave the bolero jacket behind. Shit.

I went to Balls & Bones in the late afternoon where I polished tables, served beer, and cleaned up after the football fans. The customers were hardcore sports enthusiasts, mostly men, none of them looking for action other than side bets on whatever game played on the eighty-five-inch big screen.

No music played all evening, for which I remained grateful. I needed a rhythm-free environment to regroup and figure out what had just happened. My feet appreciated the change from heels to sneakers, and although tips weren't in the thirteen-hundred range, they were big for a midmonth, snowy, Saturday night. I made it home by three in the morning and slept like a rock until hammering on the door woke me at ten the next day.

I came awake holding the pillow to my breast like it was Marty's head. So much for leaving memories of the evening behind. I couldn't think about anything but the sex I'd experienced.

By the time I'd staggered from bed, pulled on my flannel robe, and opened the front door, the bell ringer had departed. Instead, I found a gift bag sitting on the porch.

Huh. I stared at it suspiciously. Unexpected gifts don't show up on my doorstep. I poked at the tissue paper lining the decorative sack.

Roger's clutch purse peeked up at me. *Yes! My phone.* Ahhh…the cab company. Odd delivery method but hey, not complaining here. Replacing said phone would have been a bitch.

With that problem solved, I went online to read the newspaper, looking for pictures of Marilyn and Boss. I found us immediately, and we were dancing up a storm. I didn't expect so much attention. It must have been a slow night everywhere. We were on the front page as well as dominating the entire Entertainment Section.

The papers had stressed the amount of money raised— over twenty-five thousand dollars—not the dancers. And yes, Marty was hot, even in the grainy shots of him tossing me in the air, and another with my legs around his waist, being bent backward grinding against him.

Uh. Good thing I'd been in disguise. I suppose because it represented a more visual delivery mode, local television channels had concentrated their coverage on the dancers, primarily Smoke, Inc. Team One.

And someone had made a forty-five-minute composite of the whole thing and uploaded it to YouTube. Watching it was weird. Comments like "don't miss the tit shot at 3:34" made me scramble to find it. Thankfully, even *I* didn't recognize the woman in the wig, make-up, and Marilyn costume being thrown in the air.

Follow up news, which should have been the main story in my opinion, mentioned the fireman who'd gotten injured saving two kids and a dog from a burning building.

I was glad I'd decided to donate my dance-a-thon earnings to help the guy. I didn't want to profit from his pain. The rest wasn't that easy to erase from my thoughts. My nipples hurt where Marty had bitten them, and my core ached from…

Anyway, determined to put the incident behind me, I concentrated on filling out an application to work at Humble Homes. If I could get hired part-time there, I might get an employee discount and make a real dent in my remodeling plans.

Bitter cold kept me and most of Pittsburgh indoors the next day. I didn't mind. I got lots done and it turned into an almost perfect weekend except for the wrong number in the middle of the night.

When the sound of the phone interrupted Ray Charles singing *Georgia on My Mind* as Marty's hands slid up my hips, I reluctantly left dreamland. Picking up the offending object, I squinted at the display. *Unknown number.*

Huh. Maybe Megan's stuck somewhere like I was. Not that she'd rescued me, but just in case, I answered.

"Marilyn, is that you?" A male asked immediately, sounding frantic.

Marilyn? "Nope, no Marilyn here."

"I've been trying to get through to you. Are you mad at me?" His voice increased in volume and he seemed oblivious to the fact that I was clueless to his identity.

"Wrong number," I said, glancing at the clock. Four in the morning.

"Answer the next time I call, Marilyn or I'll have to…" As he listed in graphic detail the psycho-style punishment he'd be delivering for missed calls, I hung up. He called back, three times. I didn't answer. On the fourth, I blocked the number.

Yuck. Creepy shit. I dressed and descended to the kitchen, flipping on lights along the way. *No more sleep for me tonight.*

I turned on the music, assembled my tools, and worked all day. By six in the evening, I'd finished sanding the cupboards and vacuuming dust from the walls and hard surfaces. I'd put in a heck of a day.

On Monday, it thawed, snowed, and re-froze. I got an early call from my sometimes day job, substitute teaching. School was in, but a lot of teachers were off. I reported to a seventh-grade inner city school, thinking I'd left the dance-a-thon behind.

Wrong. One of the teachers mentioned it during lunch, and a newspaper shot of the fancy-stepping, garter-belt wearing, Marilyn Monroe draped over Marty's arm, surfaced in the teacher's lounge.

I pretended to ignore my colleagues' enthusiastic discussion about dance steps and music, hiding my interest behind a façade of indifference as they shared dance moves and I graded papers for the absent teacher.

I ended up subbing the full week. Great for my bank account, but I didn't accomplish much on my kitchen project. My thoughts were divided, between work and Marty, rendering me scatter-brained.

Had my head not been attached, I probably would have lost it. As it was, one of my gloves disappeared the second day. After the kids and I performed a fruitless but intense classroom search, I gave up and left for home without it.

It wasn't far from the school to the bus-stop, so I attached myself to the group of students walking that way and inspected their outer wear for my purloined glove. Nope.

I wasn't surprised, though. My students seemed honest enough to me. And who would steal one glove? In my mental frenzy, I'd lost it somewhere. No wonder. More than a couple of times during the following week, I stopped dead-still, blushing vividly as I recalled my recent uninhibited behavior.

Despite the clunky ending to the night, it *had* been fun. Unrepentant sinner that I'd apparently become, I laughed more than a couple of times as I remembered my dance with Marty.

On Friday, Humble Homes called. I had an interview, aced that, and ended up with a job stacking boxes in the warehouse. Not bad. I had the night shift three times a week. It came with an employee discount, and after the interview, I spent my extra time, wandering the aisles of the sales floor, mentally marking future must-haves.

I didn't think about Marty Jones at all. Well, not much. Not in the daytime, anyway. Night dreams I couldn't control, but each time I woke from a mind-blowing orgasm, I paid penance by sanding the cupboards in the kitchen and watched the project progress.

I returned Roger's dress and let Megan know I'd survived. I didn't tell either one of them about the end of the night.

"You want to meet at Maxine's and get your money?" Megan asked when I got around to calling her.

"No rush. Come over and bring it with you when you have time." No way was I going back to the building soon.

A week later, Megan stopped by to drop off my money from the dance gig.

"Wow. You've been busy." She ran her hands over the once painted, now stripped and sanded, wood. "What color will it be when you're done?"

"Like this, I hope." I handed her the pale reddish-brown chip I'd used to gauge my progress. "These are solid maple cabinets. Can you believe some ass painted them?" I patted the kitchen door, proud of my own success. "It took me hours to get all the white off."

"I like painted wood," Megan confided. When I glowered at her she hastily changed the subject. "I'll bring wine and candles for the table." She stood in the center of chaos, and I'm pleased to say, recognized the unfolding of my dream.

The house had once belonged to my grandfather, albeit mortgaged. Myriad tragedies and three bank sales later, I'd re-acquired it. I couldn't replace everything as it had once been, but when it had gone on the market as a short sale last year, I'd scraped together enough for five percent down and with Maxine's co-signature, bought it.

Megan's aunt had been helping me since I'd ventured out on my own and she'd always have a place at the table.

Because the kitchen had once been the heart of the house, as soon as I owned the place, remodeling began there. The previous tenant had apparently had a temper. Holes marked the walls where he'd lost it.

Putting up the new wallboard had been a challenge, calling for both Roger and Megan's assistance in lifting and nailing. But we'd done it.

I looked forward to finishing the huge room in time for a family dinner I'd cook for Thanksgiving. Feast versus my pride. I gazed at the envelope wistfully. The dance-a-thon payment would have really helped.

Tell Maxine to bill me. I'd choke on turkey fixed in a kitchen paid for with Marty's escort money.

It was with deep regret that I peeled one bill from the thirteen hundred dollars and put it in an envelope I'd already prepared.

"Please deliver that to Mr. Jones. Or better yet, give it to your aunt. Maxine can handle the money."

"Why?" She waved the envelope in the air, waiting expectantly for my answer.

"Because I borrowed cab fare."

"You owe Marty a hundred dollars for cab fare?"

"He didn't have change." I didn't volunteer more. I figured I'd danced with the devil to return a lot of Maxine's favors and I was now paid up. At least for a while.

I concentrated on the door I'd been sanding, resuming my work and turning the interrogation back on her. "Since

GEM SIVAD

when is he Marty, to you? I thought you barely knew him."

Megan shrugged and changed the subject to her real reason for the visit.

"Aunt Maxine said because of you, everyone made a ton of money for the dance-a-thon including Baby Dolls. And guess what? Marty Jones wants you for another gig."

"Good God, no."

Megan winced at my response. "Aunt Maxine said she's known Marty Jones for years. He's never asked to be set-up with anyone. But now he has. He wants you."

"No."

"It's for my aunt—come on Holly. This time it's at a fancy country club, billed as a *Night of Swing*. He *requested* you."

"I'll just bet he did. Grunted and pointed. Does Maxine have me on the menu, now?"

"You know this is special. You can dance. Besides, he's her landlord."

"Sorry. Not even for you would I consider an encore performance. I'm not going there, again."

"Going where?"

I focused on the cupboard, continued sanding, and tried to look nonchalant. But I couldn't control the blush rushing up my neck, flooding my face with heat, and burning a path across my scalp.

"Oh my God, Holly. You are neon red. You did *IT*. Why didn't you tell me?" It kind of surprised me that she thought it was such a big deal. I mean, hey, I hadn't had all that many offers and none of the prospects could dance.

When I didn't say anything more, she lost the big grin, took the sandpaper from my white-knuckled grip, and led me to the table.

"Did he force you? I'll kill that sonofabitch." Megan was so angry it was almost funny. I let her squirm in guilt and rage for a nanosecond before I relented.

"It was a mutual decision. Stupid, but not a big deal." I shrugged, trying to look nonchalant.

"How not a big deal?" Her fury changed to curiosity. "Not a big deal as in, he had a tiny dick?"

"No," I snapped. "Would you stop?"

"Not in this lifetime, girlfriend." Megan pounced on the information like a terrier after a rat. "Did you tell Roger? Of course, you didn't tell Roger, because Roger would have told me. You've been keeping this to yourself? After all we've shared? What was it like? Did he make it good for you? Was he sweet?"

"Enough." I held up my hands, warding off the barrage of words with a prudently censored answer. "He's big, rough, bossy; the sex was awesome, I had some orgasms, and then he, you know, did his thing, and passed out." I shivered remembering it.

"Happens." Megan rolled her eyes. "Guys just can't hang afterward. *Some* orgasms? As in more than one?"

"Yeah, kind of continuous once we got started on the way up in the elevator."

"You had elevator sex?"

"Sort of."

"And now Marty wants another dance. Holly do you know what this means?"

"Yes. He woke up long enough to tell me to have Maxine bill him." I could still feel the wash of humiliation. I had no justification. He thought I was a paid escort and sex went with the deal. I hadn't said no.

"Oh shit." Megan crossed her eyes at me.

Yeah, shit. It was just stupid dumb luck my first time would be with a sexy guy who could dance and who thought I sold sex for a living. I couldn't go out with him, again. Just thinking about the final part of the night made me crazy with embarrassment.

"I'm so sorry, Holly. I never thought he'd be like that. Aunt Maxine says he's a nice guy. Quiet."

Quiet? He never stopped mumbling the whole time we... Nice? Now that you understand that I'm the boss... You sellin' fucks? Bill me... I reined in my thoughts to deal with Megan.

"Really, it's no big deal. It was good. Like you've been saying, it was time." I'd been listening to her recount her torrid affairs for fourteen years, and she'd been waiting for me to have one. Unfortunately, mine would be a one-episode show.

"Well obviously it was good for him, too. And now he's hassling Maxine. His company owns the building where Baby Dolls leases space. It's not that easy for an escort service to get respectable digs."

I detected more than a little wheedle in her voice.

"No." I'd discovered long ago, a firm one-word answer always worked best.

"Please."

"No." Not in a million years. "Megan. I'm not seeing him again. He can hire a different escort."

"But, no one else can dance." Megan's eyes filled with tears. "Aunt Maxine may have to move."

Yes, Megan's aunt had done big favors for me in the past, but... "If there was any real danger of her losing her business, she'd be sitting in my kitchen right now, not you."

I stared back at Megan, determined to withstand the pressure. Marty Jones did not force me to have sex with him. Marty Jones would not evict Maxine because I would not have sex with him, again. I firmed my resolve. "She needs to get out of that business, anyway."

"How can you say things like that? You know how hard it is for a woman to make it on her own."

I'd heard this before, especially regarding favors for Maxine. "Don't even try that one. I am not, *not*, going out with Marty Jones again." I shoved the hundred at her and added snidely, "Have whoever goes to see him, hand him that envelope. He can use the hundred inside to tip his next escort."

"But…"

"I'm out of this fiasco. Maxine's a savvy business woman; she'll figure out something. Just make sure he gets his frigging money back."

"Shit. I feel responsible. You're first time shouldn't have been crap."

"It wasn't bad. It was…" I shrugged, pointing at the stack of newspapers I'd collected, each with a different pose. "The man can dance like nobody else."

Megan nodded as if that made sense and hugged me before she left.

And as far as I was concerned, that was the end of the discussion. But after Megan left, I found my envelope back in my pocket, her way of refusing to be my courier.

I had no plans to ever dance with Marty Jones, again. Humiliation warred with astonishment every time I remembered how my bones had melted in his embrace. Shit.

I'd been crazed in nympho mode.

I'd had enough dance partners to know he was the best. I'd have to sample several more lovers before I could grade that skill. *Escorting* Marty again, anywhere for anything wasn't an option. Returning his hundred dollars was an imperative.

After Megan's visit, I thought my head would explode. First, I still had the cab fare to return. Also, Maxine's payment should have made my piggybank smile. But I'd decided not to keep the money. But oh my, the temptation. The things I could do for my kitchen with that amount. *Sigh*.

I kept moving the envelope filled with hundred-dollar bills. First, I put it in the nightstand drawer next to my bed, then I moved it from there to the kitchen, and from there to the pocket of my coat, where it waited to be delivered to a new home.

Tuesday night was filled with erotic dreams centered around Marty. They were again interrupted by the psycho calling with threats for Marilyn.

"Give it a rest, asshole," I finally yelled at three in the morning. Damn. Money I couldn't afford would have to be spent. I needed a new number.

Which was why on Wednesday, when school was cancelled leaving me without a job for the day, instead of varnishing my kitchen cabinets as I should have, I decided it was too cold for shellac to dry correctly. Following that verdict, I also decided I needed to finalize my involvement in the dance-a-thon.

Accordingly, I decided to take care of business first and return the taxi fare to my dance partner. I'd drop off the donation to the burn victim's fund as well, and then, the dance-a-thon event could be marked *closed* in the file in my brain.

Before I could procrastinate further, I went to the Smoke, Inc. building and rode the elevator to the twentieth floor. Since it was cold outside, temperatures in the low teens, I didn't look particularly sneaky in my jeans, sneakers, heavy jacket, sunglasses, and ball cap pulled low. Nevertheless, I wore my unisex outfit in full stealth mode, determined that in no way could I be recognized.

I'd decided to deliver the hundred-dollar bill myself. For some reason, it seemed important. Like I was getting the last word. Yes, it was childish. Petty though it was, I wouldn't be able to lay that evening to rest until I returned the loan.

I'd visited Maxine's place the day she'd moved into her new suite in the building. Her previous location had burned to the ground at the end of the year. Her landlord then, also Marty Jones, had wasted no time finding a new headquarters for his company. He'd bought the building, occupied the top three floors, and leased the rest.

According to Maxine, she'd lucked out when he offered her space on the lower floors. I'd not seen much on the trip up the first time having been sucking the tongue of the Smoke Inc. head honcho.

I took the opportunity during this visit to remedy that oversight, stopping the elevator on several floors, just to check out the new digs. Or it might have been to work up my nerve.

I knew from my illicit visit to Smoke, Inc. that Marty's office was in the back. A reception desk guarded the outer door, and that was as far as I intended to go. The place really *was* ten steps higher on the nice scale. The elevator glided silently, didn't smell of mold, and never lurched once on its trip to the top floors.

I arrived and stepped into the fancy lobby, intending to hand the envelope to the person at the outer reception desk. It was empty. I couldn't decide. Would it be safe to leave the envelope containing a hundred-dollar bill on the desk? Common sense said no.

I stepped past and into the business suite of Smoke, Inc.

"May I help you?" An older woman wearing a purple tweed suit caught me before I got much further than through the door.

"Delivery for Martin Jones," I mumbled and shoved the envelope at her hand. She didn't take it.

"Wait here." She turned away from the dangling envelope and disappeared into the room she'd come out of.

That didn't bode well. Survival senses born in the wild, reared their head. *Flee.* I left the envelope lying in the middle of the desk I bumped into on the way out. I wasn't running, but my breathing had escalated into panic mode, and my steps quickened to a trot as I ducked out of the main office to the lobby.

Behind me, I sensed danger. As in Marty Jones. I knew he was there. I could *feel* his presence without turning around. Confirming my instincts, I recognized the gravelly growl that had ordered me around all one night. He roared a one-word command. "Stop."

Fat chance. I ignored the order, jumped the last three feet into the elevator, and punched the first-floor button, closing the door and beginning my descent. I opted to skip my planned visit with Maxine on the fourth floor before I left.

I reached ground floor and joined the rest of the people exiting the building. Given the fear of terrorism in the country and the nature of the company's work, I realized I might have screwed up. My abrupt departure and mysterious package might be considered suspicious.

Shit. I should have worn a hoodie. I ducked my head lower and tried to blend in with everyone else on the street. *As soon as Jones opens the envelope and gets his money, the building will settle down.*

Still. The incident left me feeling like a fool. Again. I walked across town to the building that housed the local fire station. It wasn't exactly where donations were usually made, but a dispatcher took my donation—Maxine's payment— and said he'd make certain it found its way to the right place.

Instead of feeling noble, I left feeling considerably poorer, especially after I shelled out cash for a new phone number. At this rate I'd never be able to finish my kitchen project. Feeling despondent instead of proud, I hustled to Balls & Bones to make sure the manager had me on the waitress list for Friday night. If I was lucky, I'd be serving ribs and beer this weekend at the sports bar.

Marty

PER SECURITY PROTOCOL, and because of my recent equipment failure and subsequent Hummer break-in, we emptied the building, and I called a Smoke, Inc. consultant to inspect the threat. I really didn't expect him to find an explosive device, but Elaine was insistent, and I gave into her.

Church lifted the envelope to his nose and sniffed. "It's not a bomb." He sniffed again. "Smells like green apples to me." Before he owned the bar, he'd named after himself, Church had been a demolition expert.

I pulled out my pocket knife and slit the end of the apple-scented envelope. A hundred-dollar bill fell out and the green apple aroma intensified. My cock got hard.

"Fuck." And I meant that on so many levels. Marilyn had paid me back. My smirk turned to a grimace when I remembered I'd passed out. And in spite of all my plans to make it up to her, I hadn't seen her or been able to contact her since that night. But, she'd been on my mind every waking minute.

The scent of green apples pulled me back to the envelope's contents. The hundred-dollar bill reminded me all over again of my dance partner which brought me to the end of the evening. I was only going to get a shot at next time if I could locate her.

I had Elaine keep tabs on the progress of the evacuation and re-entry. As soon as the building settled back into work mode, I took the stairs to the fourth floor, walked past the receptionist, and entered Maxine's office.

"Marty. So good to see—"

"Everything all right down here?" I gazed around, half-expecting to see my dance partner lurking in the shadows. "Did you set up my escort for *Night of Swing*?"

"Of course," she answered quickly.

"Same woman as for the dance-a-thon. I believe her name is Holly."

"Well," she paused to clear her throat. "Holly's not available."

"Maxine, I'd like you to make her available. Rearrange her schedule." I felt possessively outraged at the idea of Holly *escorting* anyone else.

"You don't understand."

"I'm listening."

"She quit." Maxine's panic came through loud and clear.

"I'll need her address."

"What?"

"Give me her address."

"I can't do that. I guarantee…"

"Maxine, we just had a bomb threat, upstairs. Your escort girl is a person of interest in the investigation. Should it turn out that you or your personnel were involved…" I let my voice deepen into menacing and watched Maxine squirm.

"I don't know her home address, and I wouldn't give it to you if I did." Maxine opened a desk drawer, pulled out a card, and shoved it at me. "She'll be working there Friday night."

I appreciated loyalty, and it was clear I wasn't getting more info from the escort agency owner.

On my way back upstairs I studied the card, recognizing the name. I didn't like the idea of competing with other men for her attention. I remembered bending her over my arm during the dance and watching her eyes light up in delight. Sort of how they'd lit up when she'd come. I didn't want anyone else making her eyes light up like that.

I'd have to go to the sports bar and convince her I would make a better client than anyone else she'd meet. I'd offer her… My thoughts dwindled to a close. I lived in my office.

Shit. I'd have to set her up in a place. I'd start looking.

First though, I had to deal with Elaine.

"Well?" My secretary hovered just inside my office door when I returned. I knew from experience that she wouldn't leave until she'd extracted every drop of information to be had.

"She quit working for Maxine, Elaine."

"Are we speaking of the Baby Doll escort woman who just left the terrorist note?"

"She's not a terrorist and evidently she's not one of Maxine's escorts any longer, either. I think her real name is Holly." I hated to admit I wasn't even sure of that. "She doesn't want to dance with me again."

"I saw the two of you on the news. You were smiling. I drove downtown just so I could watch you in person. You were both smiling. Persuade her."

"The night didn't end well."

"Well enough," she snorted. "I saw the security tapes before you wiped them."

What could I say? Elaine was Elaine.

Holly

AS DEGREES GO, mine proved my endurance if nothing else. If I could have decided on a major, I'd have finished sooner. As it was, it had taken me six and a half years, and the threat of my advisor saying, "You're close to losing everything you've earned. You've got to declare a major and get on with things."

I hated endings. I liked school. Anyway, it had been fun while it lasted. I'd sampled subject areas until I had an enormous number of hours and an impressive student loan with no degree in sight.

Finally, my advisor assembled my smorgasbord of learning into a General Studies degree.

"This doesn't certify you're qualified to do anything. But it will get you through a few doors. You'll have to take it from there."

The degree had gotten me through the substitute teacher door, where, apparently, a degree was a degree.

I always applied the money I made from teaching gigs to my student loan. But if that was all I fed the degree, it would never get paid off. Nor would my kitchen upgrade-house revitalization project continue.

Despite the fact I enjoyed being in a classroom full of hormonal, smart-ass kids, I didn't qualify for full time teaching, nor did I want a permanent spot any way.

I considered myself a mercenary—selling my skills to the highest bidder. I paid my own bills, managed my own time, and I intended to keep it that way.

I had a plan. Live cheap. Work hard. Fix up my house. And maybe someday have a kid, or go back to school to learn something else. My future plans seemed pretty vague mostly centering around paying off my student loan.

Weather issues—ice, snow, sleet, repeat for more of the same—had closed public schools most of the week. I'd had my warehouse night job and nothing else to occupy my time other than priming the kitchen cupboards. I tried turning the music on for company but found myself dancing instead of sanding every time. Worse, I practiced Marty moves from the dance-a-thon—half wishing I'd get to use them again.

Knowing that I could do it all over again was tempting.

Too many times I almost called Maxine to volunteer for dance duty. But, I didn't. Meeting Marty again would lead no place I wanted to go.

Thursday, I wiped down the cupboards prepping them for the first coat of finish. I thought I could get away with varnishing them if I opened the oven door to keep the kitchen warm enough to enhance the drying time.

Friday, I set aside my project plans to substitute teach. It was blustery cold, most of the kids had stayed home, and that afternoon, seven students and I watched the hands of the clock creep toward freedom.

The bell finally rang, and my students departed. I bundled myself into cold weather clothes, stuck my earbuds in, and boogied out the door. Thank God it was Friday.

I went home, and showered, but skipped eating when my stomach cringed at the contents of my refrigerator.

Nevertheless, I was in a pretty good mood when I started out for work that night. My happy frame of mind slipped a bit when I arrived and discovered my B&B tee gone from my locker.

I checked with the other servers to see if they'd found my missing gear, but no one knew a thing. I'd written my name in permanent marker inside the neck, but without checking shirts already on the servers, I wasn't getting mine back.

"I must have taken it home to wash," I told Ted, the manager. But I couldn't remember doing that. Anyway, I had to buy another one before I could clock on.

Marty

"YOU'VE LOST YOUR fucking mind." I stared out the window at the street below and muttered to myself. I wanted to see her again. No explanations, no apologies. I wanted to track her down and arrange another dance session with her. At least.

I'm not crazy. Crazy is being so bored and depressed I considered choking to death. Geez.

Sane was finding my dance partner. She'd pissed me off, made me laugh, fucked me unconscious, and hadn't stolen my wallet on her way out the door.

"Since you can't seem to connect with your escort through a third party, why don't you approach her yourself?" It was Elaine's idea.

Yeah, I'd blame my crazy behavior on Elaine. I didn't bar hop. Not since Kit, anyway. But there were plenty of crew members who did. I had no trouble rounding up drinking buddies for Friday night. If they thought my behavior odd, I didn't care. I didn't say why I was suddenly thirsty. And none but Jack Cahill gave a fuck, anyhow.

"Tracked down Marilyn, didn't ya?" When word got out about my outing, Jack didn't let my unusual plans go unchallenged. Since he was my father-in-law, I answered.

"Maybe. You got a problem with that?"

"Nope. Wondered when you were gonna get it out, again."

"I'm not..." The denial died on my lips and I let it lay. I was. Hell-and-damnation, I sure was. I was looking to hook up with Marilyn, again. Jesus. Just thinking of her had me hard. I wanted her back under me and this time I'd fucking stay awake.

Jack had once been my boss. He'd hired me when I was fourteen. I was a big guy, and lied about my age when I applied for my first oilrig job. Three years later, I'd married Kit, Jack's thirty-four-year-old daughter. Jack and I had kept right on working side by side.

We'd worked together for so long that no one remembered or cared who was boss. We were friends. Jack always worked at something and had an opinion about everything. He'd now appointed himself my romance coach.

"What kind of clothes you wearin'?"

"What?" What kind of a dumb-ass question was that? "Whatever I have on at the end of work, Friday. Leaving at six." I had it all planned. I'd find her fast and get her out of there early.

"Not to be disrespectful, but a suit and pants ain't gonna cut it at a sports bar. You're gonna be competin' with young studs. You need to change into what they call *casual* before we go."

We? Jesus.

By Friday, Jack had announced the dress code. At six that night, Jack, Steve Deakins, Ross McKenzie, Teague Logan, and Gable Matthews all went to the bar dressed in jeans, rugged man boots, Henley's and leather jackets. So did I.

"We look like fucking clones," I growled playfully, not really caring. I felt loose, ready for anything. When we arrived at Balls & Bones, I did a perimeter scan and left the men standing out front.

"Best to know ahead of time how to get out." Just as a precaution, I always checked out the exits before I entered a public building. This time, I paid attention to the alley, too, noting all the shadowy areas where a couple might fuck.

Satisfied that Marilyn wasn't already out plying her trade, I went back to the front sidewalk and found it empty. Jack and the rest of the men were already drinking beers when I walked inside.

By six-thirty, the place was starting to fill, and my dance partner was nowhere in sight. There was nothing to see on TV, nobody wanted to talk shop, I could see no evidence of a dance floor, the beer sucked, and I wanted to leave. Maxine had steered me wrong. I flexed my hand, wishing I could wring her neck.

"Your girl was in costume before. Maybe you just don't recognize her out of Marilyn clothes." Jack's comment had the crew eyeing the female customers. I'd already checked them out. My dance partner wasn't one of them. I spent three more hours sucking down beers and watching the front door. Twice, I went outside to check the alley, feeling like a fool, but still glad when I found it empty.

Maybe the owners thought I was vice and had put the word out. The same nothing taking place inside the Balls & Bones was happening behind the building. By nine, I'd eaten more than my share of ribs and tossed back too many beers. After I'd made my second trip through the packed room to reach the john, I decided to quit searching.

"I'm gone," I told Jack as soon as I returned to the table. I was already standing with my arm in my jacket, ready to shrug it on, as I prepared to leave. Using the advantage of my height, I let my gaze roam over the packed bar one last time.

After someone behind the bar switched the television program to an awards show, and cranked up the volume, the whole bar started jamming to the sound of Robin Thicke performing *Blurred Lines*.

The rhythm sank into my bones, and a grin froze on my lips. Across the way, a server danced through the swinging doors separating kitchen from bar. Even khaki pants with a green apron bow dangling in back, couldn't disguise the roll of those hips.

Coat hanging off my arm, I moved toward the dancing server. "I'll be back."

Chapter Six
Holly

T HE PLACE WAS rocking, the booze was flowing, tips were huge, and I was going home. Crap.

Gable Matthews, leading a posse of Neanderthals, had descended on the sports bar. Geez, it took two tall tables shoved together just to seat the five of them. Matthews didn't recognize me, and that was good.

I'd taken the food order and left another stool there when he said his boss was on his way. Boss covers a lot of territory but just in case, I traded tables with a server from the other side of the bar.

It grieved my bank account mightily to watch the waiter deliver the first round of beers, wings, ribs, and onion rings and pocket the big tip. It had been a hardship giving the table away. But when my former dance partner, entered the front door and took his seat, I was glad I'd made the switch.

I pulled on a ball cap, untucked my tee, glad that I'd bought and extra-large that hung loose over the white shirt I wore underneath, and served tables on the other side of the room.

Still, by nine o'clock I was so exhausted from dodging Marty's trips to the john, his forays to the bar where he walked up and down peering at the people on the stools, and his unexplained ventures outside, I was ready to call it quits for the night.

I told Ted, doubling as the night's bartender, I felt sick, which was true, and I was leaving. Relieved at that decision, I bounced through the kitchen doors to the music somebody turned on.

"Hey, you can't go back there." Ted's warning reached me too late for me to hide. The kitchen doors swung open behind me, and I knew without looking who lurked there.

I turned and glared. "What?"

"This guy giving you grief, Holly?" Ted along with two of his friends ready to play bouncer, followed Marty into the kitchen.

Before I could say, "Yes, beat the crap out of him," I recognized Gable Matthews as one of the men who'd followed Marty from the table. He crowded in the doorway behind Ted and his friends and brought more of Marty's posse along.

"Good to see you again, Marilyn," Gable, wearing a cowboy hat and looking damned good in it, drawled.

"That her?" The older guy next to him studied me hard.

Much as I'd like to punch Marty in the nose, I had no desire to see his crew demolish the bar's kitchen in a stupid brawl. Marty stepped closer to me. I stepped back.

"Did you want something specific or just dogging me because you've lost your mind?" I tried to be civil. Really, I did.

He crossed his arms and stared down at me. What? Was I supposed to be clairvoyant or something? I remained silent, letting my expression speak for me. If he got my "drop dead" message, he ignored it.

"Maxine says you quit."

Ahh. It has a brain. "And?"

"I need you for a dance."

"No."

"The company agreed to participate in another charity dance. I need to hire you again."

"So, I heard. And declined like I said. No thanks."

"Why?"

By this time, Ted, along with most of the wait staff and Marty's posse, all listened to the exchange.

"Look, if you two need to work something out, cool. But not in the kitchen." Realizing our drama was interfering with his business, Ted pointed at the door urging me to leave.

Ted was right. I needed to go home, and Marty needed to tie a cement block around his neck and jump into a large body of water.

"Sorry, Ted. I'll collect my tips tomorrow night." I set things in motion by retrieving my coat and purse from my locker. I intended to get out the back door while I still had a job.

Marty followed.

"Hey, you can't go there," Ted decreed. "No customers using the back exit."

Marty looked crestfallen. Really, he did. I'd never consciously used that word before, but if it meant downcast, deflated, dejected and disappointed, Marty was crestfallen. I felt bad for making him sad.

"Fine, fine. Sorry Ted." I ended up going out the front accompanied by the goon squad. Marty perked up noticeably as we left.

Once we hit the street, I tucked my head into my collar,

jammed my hands into my pockets, and peeled off to the left. I knew the area, something, I hoped, Marty didn't; but of course, he did.

"Church's place is two streets over and four blocks down," he volunteered. "We can talk there."

"We can talk here. What do you want?" I asked, plowing to a halt.

"First, let's find a place to sit and get to know each other."

While I mentally debated whether to be friendly or smack him upside the head, the dance partner from hell slid his hand through my arm and urged me across the intersection toward Church's Bar & Grill.

Megan had once described the bar as a place featuring peanut shells on the floor, the smell of old beer hanging in the air, and big men lumbering in and out morning noon and night.

I glanced behind at the crew trailing us, then back at Marty. I'd already met the animals, and they appeared not too bright, but harmless.

Marty

JESUS. I HUNG onto her arm, feeling her tensed muscles through her sleeve. I wondered if she planned to swing at me. Kit would have kicked my ass by now. I knew it and cringed inside. Nevertheless, I hung onto my dance partner's arm, ready to waltz her down the street if that's what it took to get her into my arms again.

I admit, I wasn't making good sense even to myself.

"Hungry?" I asked hopefully. Now that I'd found her and had my hands on her, I wanted to make sure I got things right this time.

She turned her head, baring her teeth at me. Shit. My cock surged to full stance.

Dear God, don't let her notice and get scared off. I suddenly had humiliatingly limited control over my body. I lengthened my stride, guiding her toward a place where I could sit her down, talk to her, and get to know her. I might have rushed us a bit. She jerked on my arm and forced a slower pace. I risked a peek at her, not surprised she was scowling at me.

"I've been on my feet all night and I don't appreciate being dragged along as if we're sprinting toward a finish line. Slow down or let loose. Come to think of it, just let go of me." She shook off my hand and continued walking, but since it was toward Church's, I stayed quiet and kept pace with her.

Behind us, I heard someone snort. I turned my head and snarled, "Get lost."

"Not a fuckin' chance in hell," Ross answered. I could hear him laughing behind us.

"Sorry about them," I told her. "They don't get out much." No doubt it seemed weird to Holly that we were being escorted to our destination. I'd dragged the crew along and now felt like a class-A fool. Not soon enough, we arrived at Church's. I could see it was quiet for a Friday night. I grabbed the end barstool for her and sat down beside her.

"Evening, Marty."

"Church, this is…"

Church polished the already clean area in front of her,

waiting for me to finish.

"Uh, this is a friend of mine." I didn't say more when I remembered I didn't know her real name. It might be Holly. That's what the sports bar's bartender had called her. Evidently tired of waiting, Church introduced himself.

"Name's Church. I own this place and make the chili. It's hot. Want a bowl?" He ignored me all together, and as he talked, he leaned over the counter, ostensibly to reach a spot on the bar.

When he got close enough to smell her hair, he inhaled, and a big grin spread over his face. "Hmmm... green apples. Seems like I caught a whiff of that earlier in the week."

"I'll have a beer." I cut the conversation off before it could develop further. I'd discuss her Wednesday envelope-dropping, alarm-sounding visit when the time was right.

Church took the hint and kept his mouth shut while he served her a bowl of chili, side order of crackers, and added two pickles. When she asked for a glass of milk, he poured that, too.

He finally got around to my order and opened a bottle, setting it in front of me, before again leaning on the counter in front of her.

"Saw you dancing with Marty at the dance-a-thon. Sweetheart, you've got the moves."

What the fuck? Church was stealing my lines. I glared at my friend, trying to warn him off. Christ, what in hell possessed the bald fool? In case he'd missed my position on the matter, I leaned closer to her and said, "She's with me."

"That so?" Church grinned, opening a beer for himself, before resting both arms on the counter as he faced us.

"I'm not with him." She spoke to Church and pretended

I didn't exist.

It had been so simple when we'd danced. We'd been in sync. Same with the sex. As much as I could remember, it had been great.

"Like I said earlier. I'd like to hire you," I said gruffly. At her incredulous glare, I added, "To dance. I need a partner who can keep up with me. You weren't bad the other night. Of course, we'd need to practice."

Her expression changed to outrage.

"I'll pay you for your time." I tried to make it clear I respected her cost, getting that part out in a rush.

"Christ, Marty. Is that the best you can do?" Church scratched his jaw and shook his head.

"Church, get the fuck out of our conversation."

"Conversation means talk between two people. That ain't happening here."

She said nothing, ignored both of us, and spooned in chili like she'd been starved.

"Fill her bowl, again," I ordered. I suspected if she got the chance, she'd slide out the door.

"Got any peanut butter sandwiches?" she asked Church, snubbing me.

But then, support arrived.

"Hey, Holly. Great seeing you again," Gable's woman said.

Janie took the stool on the other side of Holly. Hopefully, she'd help me fumble my way toward... It occurred to me, belatedly, that Harley-Jane might not be backing my play.

Janie knew her name and didn't volunteer that information. Maybe the name "Holly" wasn't real. But, she seemed comfortable with it. I watched her relax into girl talk, continuing to ignore me. I knew from my business negotiations that was untrue. She was hyper aware of me. I could feel it.

All I needed was to get her alone, without Church or Harley-Jane listening, and we'd forge a deal. Getting her alone was turning out to not be so easy. Shit, I'd brought the crew along for backup. Now, I wanted them to get lost. Instead, it seemed to me more people were arriving, and they were all eyeing Holly and me.

She'd been cute and sexy in her Marilyn outfit. In her jacket and khaki pants, she was attractive in a different way. Church's place had heated up from the number of bodies crowding inside.

Holly finally shrugged out of her coat, ignoring me and all the rest of the males staring as she got settled on the stool. I relaxed when she kept talking to Janie.

Gable had my back. He'd imported his woman to help. I ordered another beer and considered my next move as I watched Holly in the bar mirror. It occurred to me that for a man of my age, I was acting more like a teenager. Apparently, I didn't care because I kept on staring at her.

Porcelain skin, not too pale, pink cheeks. Her short hair made her ears visible. I checked them out. They hugged her head and were well shaped. Without the coat, I could see the shape of her breasts beneath her blouse. Not wanting her to consider me more uncouth than she already did, I tried not to let my gaze linger there.

Even without four-inch heels she was a tall woman, displaying good posture, straight shoulders, and walking with a no-nonsense stride. My pouty, flirty, dance partner had been replaced by a boyishly dressed young woman who smelled like green apples and wore pink lip gloss. And the more I discovered about the real her, the more attractive I found her.

Chapter Seven
Holly

MY HUNGER AND Church's chili hit it off. I sucked down the first bowl, and for the most part, ignored the man next to me. Help arrived in the form of Gable's girlfriend.

"Cowboy called and said their night-out had ended at Church's. I didn't want to miss the party."

I looked around. I didn't see a party. I saw a room filled with big men. Obviously, more had arrived since when I'd been led in. Marty remained on guard next to me, ogling my mirrored reflection.

I took off my hat and shoved it in my pocket, revealing my short hair, ala Megan.

"Oh, I like the haircut."

I preened. Megan was a beautician. She practiced her skills on Roger and me whenever we needed a trim or style. This time, she said she'd gotten it shorter than she intended, but I loved it.

I had a hard time keeping my hand from petting my own head. Janie's third-party opinion confirmed the style. I figured it looked a good deal better than the Marilyn wig she'd seen me in before.

"Are you staying long?" she asked.

"No. Did you get your floor finished?" It was good seeing her. It surprised me how much.

"Nope." She looked guilty. "I need to get a second coat on but, I work from home, and I tend to start projects that don't get finished until I'm not busy. Right now, I'm chasing myself back and forth between two jobs, and the floor is on hold."

Given my intention of saying a final goodbye to Marty, and Janie's man being Marty's friend, we probably wouldn't see much of each other in the future. That was a shame. I liked her.

Chalk-up one more demerit against Marty. I wanted to talk kitchen upgrades. Instead I had to deal with the guy loitering on the stool next to me.

"Church, could you take a break from eavesdropping with Marty long enough to get me another chili, peanut butter, and milk combo?" I felt as if I hadn't eaten in days.

I refused to turn and look at Marty, but over Church's shoulder in the mirror, I could see his sheepish grin. Neither man denied they'd been listening to our chatter. I sighed and turned back to Janie.

"I'd rather talk to you, Harley-Jane, but I need to get something settled with Marty."

"It was good seeing you again," she agreed and nodded at the clock. "I'll probably go on home. We should get together soon. You need to check out my kitchen floor. Why don't you give me your phone number?"

I stared from her face to my phone then back at her face.

"Or not," she answered herself.

"Here," I said, handing it to her.

"You sure?" Her tone might have been a tad sarcastic,

but she added her number and gave the phone back. I called her cell, let it ring once and disconnected. "All set."

Then I felt compelled to explain, even though Church and *he-who-would-not-be-named* were both leaning close again to hear.

"I left this phone in the cab the night of the dance. That left me stranded and at the mercy of the unknown." I scowled at Marty's image in the mirror and turned back to Janie. "I thought I was going to have to get a new cellphone, but the cab company returned it. I didn't realize how much information I store on this thing. And, now, I'm traumatized and almost afraid to let it out of my grip."

I slid my phone into the pocket of my jacket and picked up the food, balancing the sandwich on top of the chili bowl as I walked to an empty booth by the wall. I tried to act nonchalant but couldn't hide my grin. I don't have many friends. I kind of hoped I'd just added one. Giving Janie my number was a big deal, since I didn't share contact information with many.

Before I sat down, I checked to make sure I could see the door. Then I called Megan. As soon as she answered I said, "Church's place. Now."

My order in place, I hung up and waved at Janie who stood beside Gable, who stood beside Marty, who stood beside my booth.

"Call me," Janie said, and she and Gable left me to face Marty alone.

"Ready to talk?" he asked, ignoring everyone but me.

"You can sit if you can listen," I told him. "If not, be warned, I will not put up with being stalked."

"My apologies. I didn't know how to reach you other

than at your night job." It was interesting watching an arrogant bastard try to school his expression to benign. I had no such problem.

"You told me what you wanted. I declined. What else is there to say?" I made my question off-hand, like it didn't matter. Because, I assured myself, it really didn't.

"It's only a dance for God's sake. It's for charity." I could see him struggling with his *nice* persona. "I'd like to hire you to be my partner."

Church made good chili, and I spooned it in, eating half of the second peanut butter sandwich before I answered. "No." I didn't bother to be polite. The same rules I used when dealing with Megan seemed best used in this case, too.

"Why? We were good together."

I took my time, organizing the words in my head so I would get it right when I answered.

I cleared my throat. His eyebrow went up. Boss man's mock humility had begun to melt around the edges.

"First," I said and took a sip of water. "I do not now, nor have I ever, worked for Maxine's Baby Doll Escort Service." I mentally quibbled with that announcement even as I made the claim. Technically, I'd been working for Maxine at the dance-a-thon.

"Except for the charity event. Being your dance partner for the dance-a-thon was a one-time event. Maxine had no escorts who could keep up with you—her words. Because I am a friend of her family, she was aware that I enjoy dancing and do it well. I agreed to help her please a desperate client who needed a dance partner. Nothing else was on the table."

I wanted it clear he was a one-off, and I immediately felt better having set the record straight.

He relaxed and looked interested, almost pleased. When he opened his mouth, I shook my head, indicating it wasn't his turn. I didn't tell him it never would be, since I had no intentions of listening to anything he said. I had a feeling he already knew that. His mouth curved into a wolfish smile. I hurried on with what I had to say.

"Nothing but dancing was supposed to happen. I've treated the incident as if that and that alone is what did take place." I paused to let those words sink in.

He leaned his elbows on the table, clasped his hands in front of him, made a stand for his head and rested his chin on his thumbs. His gaze was steady, his expression blank, at least I couldn't read it. But I had his attention.

"I am not a prostitute. I don't sell sex or exchange it for favors. I don't care if others do. But, to clarify this issue, I. Don't. Maxine paid me for showing up and dancing through the night. I repaid your taxi cab fare loan and donated the rest to the burn victim's family."

And that still grated. Aside from my decision to donate to a good cause, I would have had no problem pocketing the payment if the evening hadn't ended on Marty's couch with me screaming through too many orgasms to count. But, since it did end that way, the line between when the night ended, and I went off the clock was just too blurred.

"I agree that our dance performance was outstanding. We were synchronized. I had no difficulty following your lead. If I'm in the market for another dance partner, I'll think of you. Be sure and let me know what you charge."

Score me! He winced noticeably, and delayed satisfaction warmed my insides. I was on a roll and decided to let it all hang out.

"Last. I have no idea if you are hinting, asking, or maneuvering to have sex with me, again. You were my first. It was an interesting experience. Mostly good," I hastened to add when he opened his mouth.

He growled, ready to protest, complain, or argue. Or maybe bite me. That was a bad thought, since he had bitten me before.

My breasts tingled, and my nipples turned into bullet points. *For pity's sake, behave.* I finished the speech I'd practiced while sanding my kitchen cupboards. I knew this part by heart.

"I've thought about dancing with you again, maybe even having sex. I've decided against it. If it would be for one time, it's not worth the effort. And if it would be for more than that, I don't have the time. You're a high maintenance guy. You'd want to know what I'm doing. You'd expect me to care about what you're doing. It wouldn't work, and I'm not interested in trying." *So there.* I didn't add *nana nana boo-boo*, but I'm pretty sure I telegraphed it with my expression.

"Now you've had your say, I get mine." A tide of red climbed his neck and stained his ears. He lost his patient, contrite look, and lowered his arms to the table. I didn't know if he was embarrassed or enraged.

How he feels doesn't matter. He'd dragged me out of work, cost me tips, and was messing with my time. I reminded myself why I deserved to be pissed off and glared at him. He leaned across the table and got in my face, talking low enough so no one else could hear, but so I couldn't miss it.

"Good to know you don't work for Maxine. It could get

awkward. As it is, we've just skipped over most of the in-between. I'm sorry our first fuck was bad for you. I'll do better next time as we move along."

"We're not moving anywhere except separate ways," I corrected him. I couldn't have arranged a sweeter ending. Megan came through the door, grinned, and beckoned me. "And you can pay for my food since you cost me tips tonight."

"Goodbye, Marty." I stood and called across the room, "Great chili, Church. Thanks."

"Hold up." Marty caught my arm as I started for the door. "We're not done talking."

"Yes, we are." My head suddenly felt as if it might explode. My stomach did a full roll, and goosebumps covered me in a cold sweat. It happened so fast, I didn't have time to stagger to a restroom.

With no more warning than that, I heaved, decorating the size fifteen boots next to me with the chili, milk, and sandwiches I'd just eaten.

Instead of Megan's assistance, I ended up with Marty Jones at my elbow, guiding me to what turned out to be Church's one unisex bathroom. It didn't allow for kneeling, never mind the germs swarming to grab hold of the acrobatic. I bent forward, leaning over Marty's arm, using him for support as I vomited again and again. Finally, the heaving stopped.

"I'm fine," I mumbled, clearly not. "I …" Another round of nausea hit me. I thought I'd emptied my stomach before, that proved untrue.

This time my stomach turned inside out, ridding itself of everything I'd eaten, including any stray crumbs that might have found their way to my toes.

In the throes of losing it, I appreciated the calloused hand holding me up as I aimed the stream of barf. Once I'd completely emptied my stomach I remembered the identity of my assistant. I would rather not have had Marty Jones as witness.

"Gross, gross, gross." I finished heaving at last and found the strength to stand up straight. It took all I had left to make it to the sink, two steps away. I leaned on the edge and steadied myself as I washed my hands. When Marty appeared beside me and tried to wipe my face with a damp cloth, I ripped it from his hand.

"I can handle this," I snapped. I looked past him at the open door where Church and Megan shared the view. "Megan, I want to go home."

"After you see a doctor." Marty Jones wasn't shy about offering his opinion. He clearly didn't understand how close I was to smacking him upside the head.

"If I don't feel better tomorrow, I'll go. Not tonight. I'm too tired. I'm going home."

"If it's food poisoning, you might be dead by tomorrow." Church offered his opinion and Megan decided to chime in.

"You're never sick." She turned on Church. "You must have poisoned her. She's never sick." She turned back to me. "I'll take you to the emergency room."

"Fine." I had no intentions of going to the hospital. I just wanted to go home and sleep. But I didn't feel like arguing, either. I'd change Megan's directions once we got in her car.

"She can lay down in my backseat. I'll drive. Church, call Doc Wilson."

Oh, for Pete's sake.

Marty scooped me into his arms and carried me from the bathroom, through the bar, and to the door. I weigh-in at one-fifty-eight on a good day. Even pissed off at him, I admired his brute strength. Unlike the rough tosses, and hurried lifts on the dance floor, or his swift carry across the glass covered parking garage, this time when he cradled me in his arms, it was almost sweet the way he held me.

"Let me down you, big ox," I snarled. At least, I tried to snarl. It came out more a whimper which he ignored.

Church said, "I'll drive, I'm already out front."

Megan said, "I'm following you."

"I feel fine." I'd feel a lot finer once I got home. That, I was sure of. There was nothing left of the nausea but a nasty taste in my mouth. Nobody paid attention to me.

I ended up stretched out on the seat of a very big truck with my head resting in Marty's lap, him petting my hair until I smacked his hand away and sat up.

We didn't go to a hospital. Instead, Church pulled into the parking lot of a clinic. The lights were on, and inside the front door, medical personnel, stood waiting.

Apparently, Smoke, Inc. had employed a teenager wearing jeans, a tee-shirt under his open lab coat, and a stethoscope dangling around his neck, to impersonate the company doctor. The name tag prominently displayed on the coat, said, Dr. Garret Wilson, M.D.

I did not feel reassured by the plaques on the wall, certifying the kid had graduated from medical school.

"You know, Megan. I feel fine. I think we should go home."

Megan and I stood shoulder-to-shoulder in a cage of men. Church on her side, Marty on mine, another big guy I had not yet met, but felt certain I soon would, had taken his place behind us. I had no idea from where he'd come.

The doctor, being shorter than me by at least four inches, and slighter in build, seemed the easiest exit.

Normal hours were six to six, but he'd obviously accommodated Smoke, Inc. needs by being here. He was a company man through and through. But, a *little* one. I thought if push came to shove, I could get past him.

"I don't know you from Ted's dead grandma. Megan can come into the exam room with me."

"Megan and I have words to say," the unknown giant behind me inserted himself in my plan.

"And you would be…?"

"I'm Teague Logan, Megan's man. Been hearing about you, for a while. Guess she didn't mention me."

I stared from him to her. "Sorry, Holly," she apologized. "You go on inside. I'll wait out here. If I don't have this discussion with Teague, we'll be here all night."

"Keys."

Her attempt to hand them to me was intercepted by Marty. "Will be waiting out here with me for your return."

I gave up and followed Dr. Wilson to the exam room.

"Sorry about that. I really don't have Marty kidnapping patients for me." He explained apologetically that he'd perform a rudimentary examination and I could be on my way. Okay.

"What precipitated the attack?"

I shrugged. "I left work, stopped in at Church's for some chili, got sick. I'm only here because I threw-up on Marty Jones' shoes. Any other man would have cussed me out. Marty hustles me to an emergency room."

"Have you known Marty long?"

"Barely know him at all."

"Marty's a take charge kind of guy. As you've just found out."

"Well he can take charge of someone else. I just need to get this exam over, and by the way, how much will this cost?"

I might as well start the torture, now. My deductible was sky high, I never used my insurance, and if I could persuade the doctor to take direct payment as in cash up front, it would be even better.

"Don't worry about that. Marty brought you here, so the company is covering it."

"Smoke, Inc.?"

"Yes."

I looked around. Nice office. Nice building. "Are you really a doctor? No offense, but you look about eighteen."

He laughed. "I'm older than I look. There's a nasty strain of flu going around. Did you have your shot this season?" When I'd turned the tables, and asked *him* questions, he hustled back to being a doctor.

"No." I never get the flu, and the shot seemed a waste.

"Are you allergic to any…?"

His questions were routine. I answered them as he took my blood pressure, temperature, listened to my lungs, my heart.

"What about birth control?" he asked casually as he looked into my left ear. "Do you know your prescription?"

My head was tilted to accommodate the light shining instrument he held. I mumbled, "No."

"That's okay. I can look it up. It might be the cause of

your nausea if you've recently made a change."

"I don't take pills other than aspirin."

"Diaphragm, patch, IUD, Depo shot."

After I shook my head indicating no for each, he finally added weakly, "Rhythm method?"

The last brought a snort of laughter I couldn't suppress.

"So, no birth control." His gruff voice telegraphed his disapproval.

"No, but it's highly unlikely that..." My stomach lurched, and I felt the blood drain from my head. I honestly thought I might faint as a horrible possibility presented itself.

"I'll visit my own doctor if I'm not better tomorrow. Thanks for coming in to accommodate Marty's late-night demand."

"Church is waiting to find out if he poisoned you."

Basically, Dr. Wilson guilted me into submitting to a few more tests, finally establishing it wasn't food poisoning causing my upset stomach. It was the baby Marty Jones had planted inside me.

"How can that be? It only happened once. I orgasmed many times during the once, does that count as more than once?" Stunned didn't cover my emotional response. All rational thought departed.

"Did you use any form of prevention?" Young though he was, the doctor's tone had become gruff and disapproving.

"Condom—it came off during. I guess it did. I had to fish it out afterward. Gross."

It was his turn to look embarrassed and very young again. I think I gave him too much information.

"Wow. I hope you like this guy because—you do like this guy, right? It wasn't forced?"

Oddly, the child doctor's anxious concern steadied me into reassuring him. "Hey," I said, and reached out to pat his arm. "It's cool. I'm in the middle of remodeling, and my kitchen project is going to have to go on hold while I get a nursery finished." My extraordinary stretch from reality to wonderland made him relax.

"Good. That's good," he muttered.

That of course remained to be seen, but I wasn't one for sharing drama.

"This is private, right? I'm not interested in telling the peanut gallery outside." I insisted the doctor keep my diagnosis to himself, laying on all kinds of reasons. "Church can make a fresh batch of chili after he scrubs his kitchen. His business won't suffer from either outcome." I finally piddled to a halt, returning his glare. Evidently, I'd insulted him.

"Of course, what I want to do more than anything is run out in the middle of the street and start telling your business. But, thankfully for you, I can't divulge patient information. I'm bound by the HIPPA laws and the AMA," he answered stiffly.

"Of course," I muttered as if I'd known that. Well I did sort of, but who knows what information goes anywhere these days. I shrugged and asked, "We finished?" I hoped so. I needed to get home and think.

"You need to see a doctor. Get some vitamins. Tell the father."

"Your bedside manner sucks. But thanks." I headed for the door, he followed.

"Probably a touch of flu," I told them all when I stepped into the waiting room. The child doctor walked out behind me and didn't contradict my story.

"Sorry I ruined your shoes," I told Marty on my way past him to the door.

"Don't worry about it. They'll clean up. Meanwhile, your girlfriend had a change in plans. I'm taking you home." During my examination, he'd been busy. He'd had clothes and his vehicle delivered and now wore sweats and sneakers.

While I wondered what was up with Megan and the giant claiming to be *her man*, Marty guided me to the Hummer I'd almost ridden in once before.

Tell the father. After a quick peek at said sire, I slouched on the front seat of the Hummer and concentrated on my shoes.

"You going to be okay?" Marty's voice was anxious.

You think you're worried. Hah. His presence was both infuriating and reassuring. "I'm tired, my stomach is still upset, and I want to get home and rest."

All my answer was true. He didn't push me for more, and I didn't offer. When he pulled into the narrow drive way, I didn't invite him in. I hopped out and scurried into the house, locking the door behind me.

After the sound of the Hummer died away, I walked to the closet under the stairs and stepped inside. Door shut, I crouched amid the shoes and boxes on the floor, trying to get a grip on my new reality as I stared into the darkness.

Chapter Eight
Marty

S OMETHING WAS WRONG, really, wrong. I knew it, but she wouldn't tell me a thing. She'd walked into see the doc sassing and sarcastic. She was quiet when she came out. Too quiet. I intended to find out why.

I drove back to the clinic. The lights were out, but junior's Jeep sat out back. I let myself in. He had his coat on, ready to make a run for it.

"There are rules. I'm not telling you a thing, so go home, Marty."

What an attitude. And I helped put the ingrate through school. "Did I ask you to tell me anything?"

I wandered around the office, giving him time to marinate in guilt and gratitude. It usually worked. This time not.

"Look, just tell me that she's going to be okay."

"So, who is she to you? Did she apply for a job or something?"

I saw an angle here. "She's done some work for Smoke in the past. I was going to hire her again, but hell, if she's sick..." I let my voice trail off. "So, did she pass the physical?"

"What kind of work?" he asked suspiciously. "She won't be jumping out of airplanes and helicopters that's for sure."

"Why not?" *Like I would put a woman in that kind of...* Well if the right one came in and applied, maybe, but not my dance queen. "She's a big strong girl. Why not? You turning sexist? Think she can't handle the equipment?"

"Marty, let it rest. I'm not telling you anything other than if that was a pre-job physical, which we both know it wasn't, she didn't pass."

He walked out of the place with me trailing behind him and I was still whining for answers. I knew better. I didn't want to bully the kid. But dammit. "Look, Garret. She's kind of a girlfriend." The look of horror he gave me let me know she was doomed. I froze. "Jesus. What's wrong with her? Is it, is it...? God dammit, tell me."

I was in full panic mode. "The earlier we get her into treatment, the better her chances. Who should we see? Give me a name. A doctor specializing in her condition."

"Are you saying that you and my patient are a couple?" By this time, we were standing by his Jeep.

"Yes," I lied.

"Since when? I thought you didn't date." The little ass seemed way too interested in my life, suddenly. "Was that Marilyn?"

"Yes. We met, we danced... What the hell difference does that make? We're a couple. And couples share each other's troubles. So, what's wrong with her?" I'd started out reasonably enough, but I didn't do so well keeping the snarl from my final burst of words. I might have also been standing a little too close to him.

He maneuvered enough to crack his door and exited our close encounter by sliding into the Jeep. He wasn't intimidated. That was good. But shit, I still didn't know what was wrong with her and… I glared at him, not sure how much of my concerned boyfriend act had been an act.

There wasn't enough sun to warrant them, but, pointedly he put on his sunglasses before he rolled down his window. "She's not sick like Aunt Kit, Marty. I'm not a specialist in…" It was his turn to glare. "You, sneaky bastard." The window started back up. He threw the last words out the one inch opening he left at the top. "If you want to know what's wrong with her, ask her."

I heard the locks click on his door, his final insult before he backed up, barely missing my toes. Then he revved the motor and peeled out of the parking lot.

In the sixth year of our marriage, Kit had decided she wanted us to be parents. I was twenty-three, working alongside Jack. He'd gone out on his own and rounded up enough oil jockeys, and skilled wild men, to call it a crew. We were hustling twenty-four hours a day, trying to stay alive long enough to build the business, and I was away from home a lot.

"Marty, I want a kid but it doesn't look like it's going to happen for us without a boost. What do you think?"

What I'd thought was *shit, damn, fuck, I'm a loser who can't even give his woman a baby.* What I'd said was, "Sure. Whatever you want." I'd pretty much always said yes to what Kit wanted. I expected us to go through some kind of fertility ritual. Or maybe an adoption process where she'd bring home a baby, preferably a boy, and I'd watch her raise him until he was old enough for me to teach him the business.

It didn't happen that way. I came home from a job in South America and found Garret living with us. He was eleven. Not an unknown at all since he'd already been hanging at the house a lot. His father, Bud Wilson, lived down the street. Bud was a drunk. Kit decided Garret would do better with us. Nobody objected. The kid moved his stuff into a room, and she bought him some video games. When he got old enough, she enrolled him in college.

Now and then, Bud would come down to check on him. As Garret got older, the situation reversed, and he'd go down and check on Bud. It was good all around. Kit had been like that, seeing need, and reaching out to fix what was broken while others stood on the sidelines.

I'd worked really, really, hard in our marriage to not be needy. I'd wanted Kit to *need* me. But she'd needed me to give her a baby, and when that didn't happen, she'd settled for the drunk's kid from down the block. I stood in the parking lot watching the kid, now all grown up, drive away, knowing in my gut something big had just happened without knowing exactly what.

She's not sick like Aunt Kit, Marty. My thoughts swung from Kit and Garret to holding Holly as she retched over the toilet bowl.

What's wrong with her? Jesus God, I couldn't go through that again. *That* being sickness and death. Though I judged myself a coward, part of me wanted to go back to my office, bury myself in the paperwork Elaine had stacked on my desk, and forget I'd ever met Holly Smith.

But damn, I couldn't do that. I only knew one way to find out what was wrong with Holly. I was sorry for the way I'd discovered her address, but glad I'd been smart enough to get my ride to the clinic in time to take her home.

I knew where she lived, I'd take Garret's advice. I'd ask

her what was wrong with her. One way or another, I'd get it out of her. And then we'd figure out what to do next. I wasn't sure how she'd feel about my being part of her get-well team.

That wasn't true. I was sure she'd tell me to fuck off. She didn't take orders well. Maybe bribes would work. Breakfast seemed a good way to start.

I stopped for coffee, bought some donuts to go along with it, debated over sugared or filled, and finally drove to her house. And then remembered she'd puked her guts out the night before. The coffee and donuts suddenly seemed like a poor idea. The entire ludicrous conversation running in my head had been masking the anxiety pounding in my veins. It came back full force.

I didn't question any of my actions until I pulled into her driveway and shut down my ride. It was eight thirty in the morning. She ought to have been up. She didn't seem like the kind of person who'd be a late sleeper. *Maybe she's still sick. She could be in there unconscious.*

I was still in my vehicle, trying to decide if I would be justified in breaking in to check on her, when she came walking down the street. She looked fine. Brisk walk, long stride, no obvious health issues or pain on display. She spied me sitting in her drive and scowled. I relaxed. She was better.

I grabbed the box of donuts and scooped up the coffee. Breakfast time.

Holly

THERE ARE TIMES I enjoy getting out for exercise. I'm not a

jogger. Too much work. But, I love to walk in early morning when there's little traffic and no people cluttering the world. Well usually I do. This morning not so much. I had an unpleasant creepy feeling making me secure the packages in my arms and hurry.

As I approached my place I spotted a vehicle parked in my drive. I lengthened my stride, replacing one anxiety with another.

Did I miss something? I tried to remember if I'd paid all the utility bills. I'd forgotten once, they'd shut off the water on a Friday, and I'd had to go without for a weekend. I groaned in relief and exasperation when I recognized my visitor.

"And there he is, again." Good God, Marty Jones was sitting in his monster truck in my driveway. *Gah.* I shifted my bag of groceries to my left side and fumbled for my key.

As soon as I'd gotten home earlier, I'd retreated to my closet to have a panic attack. I could pretty much take root in any dark closed space and not come out until I got my mind back. I'd been using this method of dealing with stress for a long time. The possibility that I might be pregnant seemed like a good enough reason to make like a mushroom.

But, as soon as I'd gotten comfortable on the floor, most of my thoughts had centered on disbelief rather than panic. I'm not sure how long I mumbled to myself in my therapy cubicle, but when I came out, I felt better. And I had a plan of action.

First, the doctor said he could be wrong. I agreed. He was probably wrong. *He told me to see a specialist.* I agreed with that, too. I needed to know what was what before I gave up on my fancy faucets and invested in a crib.

I couldn't afford doctors any better at seven o'clock in the morning than I could three hours before. So, I decided to visit another kind of specialist. Someplace close that sold pregnancy tests.

I'd been hungry when I came out of the closet. So, after I'd showered, pulled on some sweats, and shrugged into my coat, I'd walked to the 24/7 grocery that had a pharmacy as well.

Breakfast food had looked good to me—all of it. I carried bacon, eggs, bread, milk, and a frozen box of hash browns in my arms.

I'd also picked up three Home Pregnancy Kits. Feeling surprisingly good for a chick who'd barfed her brains out the night before, I'd headed home. That changed when I saw my unwelcome guest.

No doubt, planning to head me off before I could get inside and call the cops, Marty stepped out of his huge, gas guzzling, environmentally shocking, albeit comfortable, vehicle, and watched my approach.

"You are like a frigging bad headache that goes away then reappears with no warning. What is it about 'get lost' you don't understand?" Maybe I could *rude* him into leaving.

"Thought you might want breakfast." He held up his box of donuts, my favorite kind. My stomach rumbled. I knew he heard it because his frigging eyebrow went up, and he grinned. What was I supposed to do?

"All right. Bring the donuts, and come in." As a matter of fact, I was about to do eggs, hash browns, bacon, and toast. The donuts would be dessert. To say I was hungry would be an understatement.

As I have a right to be. After all, my last meal of chili and peanut butter sandwiches hadn't stayed down long enough to digest. Of course, I was famished.

I went straight through the miniscule foyer, passed the couch in the living room through the opening to the kitchen. He followed.

"Nice place."

"Thank you." I set my groceries on the counter and watched him pull out a kitchen chair and sit down. After I unloaded the breakfast supplies, I left the pregnancy detectors in the sack, and pushed it to the back of the counter. I'd take it up to the master bathroom and use it after Marty was gone. "Make yourself at home."

He grinned, not missing my sarcasm.

I wondered why I found him attractive. Marty wasn't cute, or handsome in a conventional way. He was big, but more than just being size extra-extra-large, his personality filled the room even when he kept his mouth shut. His gaze lingered on my chest and without looking down, I knew my nipples were puckered nubs tenting the thin material of my tee.

"How you feeling?" His grin got down right wolfish.

Oh, for Pete's sake. "Did you come to check on my health or fool around?"

"Is option two on the table?" he growled.

"The only fooling around I'm doing is making myself breakfast. Drink your coffee. Have a donut. I'll eat one, too. Then you can leave."

"Seriously, how do you feel?"

"I feel like breakfast." I pulled a skillet from my oven. With sawdust swirling around and half the doors off the cupboards, it was currently the best place to store my cooking tools.

"Nice kitchen. Beautiful wood." He clearly knew how to romance me. The solid cherry I'd uncovered gave me incentive to continue sanding but it was a lot of work. Marty's spontaneous admiration made me smile. While I set out my ingredients, preparing to cook, he got off the chair and inspected my cabinets.

"Some dumb ass painted them white. Tell me it wasn't you."

"Would I be sanding the paint off, if I'd slapped it on?"

"Tedious work," he grunted, then picked up a tack rag and began wiping down the upper cupboards. From where I was standing, facing the stove, I could see him from the corner of my eye.

Like me, he had on gray sweats. The drawstring pants rested on his hips, and when he reached high, the gesture hiked up his sweatshirt, displaying a line of black hair, arrowing down his stomach, a road map to what lay below. And what went below, suddenly went up.

I will not laugh, I will not laugh, I will not... I focused on the stove and pretended interest in frying the hash browns. Once they were crispy and golden brown, I broke a dozen eggs in the skillet and scrambled them, sprinkled grated cheese across the top to melt, while I nuked a pound of bacon, and toasted half a loaf of bread. Like I said, I was hungry, and my hulking visitor didn't look like he was leaving before he at least got some food.

"Eat up. Then you can leave." My manners seemed to have deteriorated in direct proportion to my lust as if I tried to drive him away because I wanted him. *Okay, I'm nuts.*

After I laid cutlery on the table, I handed him a plate and

served myself eggs and hash browns from the skillet, added a couple of slices of bacon, stacked two pieces of toast on the side, poured myself a glass of milk, and slid into my chair at the table.

He set a coffee in front of me, kept the other for himself, and sat facing me across his own loaded plate. Very loaded, falling off the edges, loaded. At my round-eyed blink, he said gruffly, "I'm a man with a big appetite."

He gave me a knowing look and smirked, making me blush, and that pissed me off. But my face got red just the same. I pushed the coffee in its carry cup back across the table at him.

"You don't like coffee?"

"Not in the mood," I answered.

"You drank milk last night."

"Yes, I did. And?"

"You have an ulcer?"

"No ulcer and I don't think milk is a cure for ulcers anyway," I said and began making my way through the food on my own plate. Then embarrassed at my own churlishness, I added, "Help yourself. I've got all I want."

I ignored him and ate.

He took me at my word, plowed through the first plate, then finished off the eggs, the hash browns, and wrapped the last piece of bacon into the last piece of toast before he stood and began clearing the table. "Great breakfast. Got a dishwasher?"

"Soon. Sink for now."

"You own this place?"

"Me and the bank," I told him.

"Mind if I look around out back?"

Whether I cared or not, he piled the breakfast dishes in the sink and used the door off the mudroom to get to my backyard.

I smiled to myself while I did the dishes and watched him wander around the yard. It was my version of paradise. My grandma had been a gardener. She'd passed away before I was born. Grandpa had kept the bushes trimmed and didn't bother the flowers that returned every year. After I'd reclaimed the house, I'd been identifying the flowers from the weeds, by carrying my laptop out back and making comparisons between cyber pictures and what was growing in the neglected jungle.

Last fall I'd bought a package of gladiola bulbs and planted them. I was looking forward to seeing if my grandma had passed down her green thumb.

That thought startled me. I found myself staring at my stomach, my wet hands splayed protectively over my belly. *Oh, my gosh.* I needed to go sit in my closet again. And dunderhead was still out back.

Breathe in, breathe out... I gripped the edge of the sink and focused my gaze out the window on Marty, now gently rocking back and forth in my backyard swing. He looked relaxed. I calmed down a little.

My gaze switched from him to the grocery sack and its contents. While Marty was otherwise occupied, I'd just get it over with.

"Ready or not, here I come," I muttered and grabbed up the bag, carrying it to the bathroom.

Chapter Nine
Marty

I COULDN'T REMEMBER when I'd last felt so peaceful. Tired too. I'd been putting in some hours lately.

The dance-a-thon had brought in more than good will. Smoke, had reaped a few local contracts that wouldn't have happened before the fund raiser. Last week we'd assisted in a Coast Guard rescue and I'd chalked it down to PR, too.

I yawned. My office couch seemed far away now. I considered sprawling sideways for a nap in the great outdoors.

She has a great place going on here. The weather had been fucking nuts. Thirty-four degrees and ice one day, sunshine and seventy the next. Her yard was already showing green but in the corner where fence met gate, a pile of snow hadn't completely melted.

I'd left her kitchen and headed for the back yard rather than leave after eating breakfast. I knew I should get out, but, when I'd spotted the swing, it had drawn me like a distress beacon. I suspected she'd adjusted the drop to accommodate her own tall frame. And though it was still a little low for me, it worked.

The day had turned out to be warm and after I closed my eyes and leaned against the cushion in the two-seater, I'd lost myself in the pleasure of mindlessly gliding back and forth.

Okay, not mindlessly. I analyzed the Holly situation as I enjoyed the feel of sun on my face. She was fine. She'd eaten almost as much as me and kept it down. At least, I thought she had.

Having a company physician kept Smoke's insurance premiums from eating us alive. So far it was working and was worth every penny of our investment. Garret had been damned handy last night.

Okay, I overreacted. Having resolved my concern for her health, my thoughts meandered back to our final conversation the night before. When we were in the booth. Before she puked all over my shoes.

I hadn't had time to think about our *talk* as I'd been busy right after that, holding her over the toilet while she made me certain I'd never eat Church's chili again. But I had time, now.

Point one. She's not a Baby Doll escort and doesn't work for Maxine. Good. Like I'd told her, it could have gotten awkward.

Point two and three went together. The gist of them being, Maxine needed a dance partner for a desperate client, or maybe desperately needed a dancer for a client. I couldn't remember the exact words.

But I got the important part. Holly did someone a favor and showed up and danced with desperate client—me.

Point four, ditto. She wasn't for sale. *Well, how the hell was I supposed to know that?* My bad that after six years of not having the urge to fuck anyone, I'd wanted her.

I pushed the swing a little harder as my dick twitched indicating that that want hadn't disappeared.

Point Five. She'd never fucked before. Was that possible?

I'm thirty-eight, I don't know how old she is, but she's too old to be a virgin. That whole concept kept my mind churning for a bit. I mean, if it was true, what had she been saving it for? Not me, that was for damned sure. She treated me like gum she'd found stuck to her shoe.

You're a high maintenance kind of guy. Belatedly, her insult landed. Huh? I picked up my own clothes, ironed my own shirts, washed my own vehicle, paid my own bills. Whatever else there was in my life needing done, I did.

You'd want to know what I'm doing. She'd lost me on that one. What was to know? *You'd expect me to care about what you're doing.* Not really. Half the shit I did, I wouldn't tell anyone. The other half got sanitized—a lot. So, not talking was safer than talking, texting, or whatever fucking way men communicated with their women these days.

My woman. I mulled over that thought. She'd been eyeing me when I wiped down her cabinets. She'd looked away, but not before big john had decided to stand tall. I'd seen her grin, even if she'd been trying to hide it. Her tits had perked up, too. I was sure underneath her sweats she'd gone commando, at least up top.

I'd showered in Garret's office bathroom; glad I hadn't stinted on that addition when we built. We were all big men and Garret kept sweats on hand for when one of us came in wearing torn clothes from whatever encounter had caused us to need bandaged or stitched.

Underwear wasn't a clothing accommodation Garret kept on hand, hence beneath my gray pants, there was nothing holding me down. I swung harder. Inside my sweats, my cock stretched, pointing the way to the house and the woman I'd like to be inside.

Every once in a while, I opened my eyes and peered at the house. At first, she was there doing dishes and watching me swing. I waved at her, wanting to expand the playground to include her. When she disappeared from sight, I knew it was time to go.

Haul ass, Jones. But, we hadn't had any of the donuts, yet. The thought of two different kinds of dessert got me out of the swing.

Holly got me out of the house even faster. Shit. All I said was, "Wanna...?" Dammit, I didn't even get 'donut' out of my mouth before she snarled at me and said, "Get out."

What the fuck? "Did you throw up?" Her illness must have kicked back in.

"None of your business. Leave." She had a ball bat in her hand, and though I was sure I could take her, it didn't seem like a good idea. Reason seemed better.

"Calm down, and tell me what's wrong."

"You're still here." Looked like she knew how to handle a bat. Good for her.

I stepped back and continued talking and backing as she stalked toward me. "Do you need me to drive you somewhere, back to the clinic maybe? I can call Garret, he'll be there and ready."

I mumbled suggestions across the floor and out the entrance. She followed me, catching the thick inside door in her hand and bringing it along with her until she stood in the doorway, set the end of the bat on the floor, and leaned on it.

"Your company doctor said I had to let my sex partners know about my illness. Call him, tell him you're one of my victims and you need the cure. He said the problem would go away, but it's going to be a bitch for months. Maybe for years. The treatment includes weekly anal probes." Having gotten the last word, she shut the door.

I thought about knocking and asking for my donuts back just to piss her off. But, I took the high road and left them for her. She'd been lying through her teeth, but I'd call Garret anyway. Hell, if there was any chance I'd encountered dick rot, he'd have already told me.

But, something was up. Maybe she wasn't sick-sick. But she'd looked a little green around the gills when she'd been throwing me out. Garret knew all about her problem.

I climbed in my Hummer with a frown on my face. Oh yeah. Dr. Wilson knew all about her problem, and she'd told me to call him. Okay. I was damned sure with that order in hand, I could finesse some answers from the kid. I voice dialed. I loved this technology. He answered on the first ring.

"Unless you're dying, leave me the fuck alone."

"She told me."

"Good."

He was going to hang up if I didn't come up with something fast. "She said she gave me something."

"Marty, I don't want to hear any of this. But if I must, I should tell you, I put you on speakerphone, so I could finish my steak."

"Where the hell are you? And who's ..."

"Church's fixing breakfast for the crew at his place. Surprised you don't know about it. Oh. And you pretty much just told everyone we know that you got a case of something from a hookup." Too late, the tinny echo of his voice, as well as the raucous sound of the Smoke, Inc. maniacs in the background, confirmed what he said. Shit.

"You, sonofabitch," I snarled.

"Dr. Sonofabitch, to you. If you're bleeding, need bones set, or an x-ray, come see me. I don't know anything about Trichomoniasis issues. You'll have to see a specialist." He hung up.

That had been way too easy. I drove to Church's place trying to piece together the information I had. One, Garret wasn't worried about Holly at all, so basically, I extrapolated that she wasn't bad sick, and whatever was wrong was neither life threatening nor my business. I disagreed about the last part, but I didn't have a strong case for why, so I'd leave it at that.

I parked in back, used my phone to Google Garret's diagnosis, and then went inside. As usual, most of the crew had ended up at Church's place. Garret sat a table with Jack. Both were eating steaks. I pulled the phone out and read aloud.

"*Trichomoniasis*, a bovine venereal disease, specifically targeting male cattle." Jack snorted but kept on eating. Garret grinned.

Dick rot for bulls. Cute.

I sat at the bar. Mistake number two.

"Good looking woman," Church said.

I nodded. "Give me a beer." Yeah, it was early. But I'd already had coffee and breakfast.

He sat one in front of me, opened another for himself and asked, "You care if I ask her out?"

What the fuck? "Shit, yes I care. Stay away from her. And if she's with me in here, or anywhere, stay away from both of us. And if by pure bad luck we run into each other, for fuck's sake don't go sniffing her hair, again."

"Smelled good," Church answered. He tipped his beer, drank deep, and belched before he added, "I'd like to bury my face in…"

"My fist." I set my beer on the counter and left.

Shit. Once back inside my vehicle I didn't know where to go. I should go back to the office. The same pile of paperwork that had been waiting before still waited. I could nap on the couch and watch something on the tube this afternoon.

But it was a nice day. I closed my eyes for a moment, remembering the breeze, the sway of the swing, the sky overhead, Holly at the window pretending to not watch me while I watched her through half-closed eyes.

Okay, I'd go back to her place. Based on the fact her nipples had pebbled a couple of times when I'd been with her earlier, I didn't think she'd use the ball bat on me. I couldn't think of anywhere else to go and going there felt right.

And that was fucking stupid since I'd danced with her once. Okay, all night long ending in a magnificent fuck that I could be remembering as great because it had been so fucking long since I'd fucked who the hell knew whether it had been fantastic or fair to middling. She hadn't been impressed.

I wanted a do-over.

I made a couple stops, picked up some condoms in case I got lucky, and headed her way.

Holly

UNFORTUNATELY FOR MARTY after I'd used two of the three pregnancy kits I'd purchased, my first encounter out of the bathroom was with the dancing sperm donor. I'd felt a panic attack coming on, grabbed my bat, backed Marty out the door, and retreated to my closet.

What if it's true? What if I'm pregnant? I did not want to face that possibility. I almost left the closet to avoid it. But I sat, trying to fathom how it had happened again, how my world could shift, changing everything with no warning.

I sat with head bowed, surrounded by darkness… My lifestyle was not conducive to having a child. I worked a lot of the time to afford the things I had. And I could only afford the things I had, because I worked a lot of the time. I couldn't stand the idea of selling my house. But a baby cost money. A baby needed lots of things I didn't have…

My chaotic thoughts paused as I strained to identify a new concern. I'd just heard the backdoor open and close. I'd locked the front door when I'd escorted Marty out. I'd neglected the back.

The floor boards creaked, and the building shifted slightly. Someone was in my house. I held tight to the bat, hoping I wouldn't have to use it.

The closet door swung open. I froze. I hadn't expected it. While my eyes adjusted to the light, Marty peered inside. I'd moved the shoes and boxes, but I hadn't cleared the entire area, yet. His gaze focused on the vacuum cleaner then shifted to me, sitting on the floor.

"What the fuck are you doing in here?"

"What the heck are you doing in my house?" I scrambled

to my feet, belatedly remembering the bat I still held.

"If that's your security, I think you need an upgrade."

Smart ass.

"How about I upgrade to a 911 call and report a burglary. Then I can beat you over the head until they arrive and still claim self-defense." And yet, as I lobbed threats and insults at Marty, I felt so much better. "You broke into my house."

"Technically, no. I rang your doorbell, it doesn't work by the way. I knocked, you didn't answer. I was worried about you. I went around back and came through the kitchen door."

"I received unsettling news. I needed to think."

"You think in the closet?"

"Pretty much," I answered and shrugged. "We all have different ways of dealing with stress. This happens to be mine." I had no idea why I shared evidence of my craziness with him.

"Well, next time, lock up before you crawl into your think tank," he growled, evidently not finding my meditation spot odd. Which was nice but left my own question unanswered.

"What do you want?" I repeated.

"How about sex?" Seeing my eye-roll, he said, "Hungry? I brought chicken. And I've got some music I want you to hear."

"Why would I be hungry? We just ate breakfast not long ago. And I doubt we listen to the same sounds."

"Need some help sanding your cupboards?"

"No."

"Want me to work on your swing? It's a little low."

"No. Honest to God, I'd say you're like a stray dog begging for scraps only you brought the meal. What do you really want?"

"Female company, yours specifically."

"Company as in…?"

He nodded.

"Aren't you past the age where you want it all the time?" I kind of hoped he wasn't.

"I would have said yes to that until we danced." He delivered that line with one of his wolfish leers.

Heat pooled low in my belly, my breasts ached, my nipples pebbled, and I told myself I was simply curious to see what he'd offer. Incapable of stopping myself, I opened my mouth and asked, "What music did you bring?"

I did not expect him to carry in a Harmon/Kardon speaker, set it on my living room mantle, and fiddle with his phone getting the song he wanted me to hear.

Rhinestone Eyes started playing, my hips swayed, my shoulders shifted, and my body absorbed the sound. Marty's gaze held mine as he took my hands, caught the beat I'd already started moving to, and mirrored my actions. When the music segued into *Stylo*, he reduced the space between us, turning me in his arms to hold me from behind.

One of his arms wrapped around my front, palm resting on my stomach. The other delved under my sweatshirt to find bare skin. I arched my back, pressing into him.

His fingers, traveling upward as they were, plus the heavy beat of the music, made my blood heat and my body pulse to the rhythm. As warnings of overload echoed through the song, my butt rubbed sinuously against my partner's arousal. Oh wow.

There could only be one place this was going. I edged us toward the steps, closer to my bed upstairs. He turned me in his arms, again. No playing around now, or I should have said, a lot more playing around now. His hand went for gold and slid beneath my sweats to cup my wet heat. His erection, confined by his pants, stood tall between us and pressed against my belly.

Damn. My sex clenched, squeezing hard on nothing, eloquently showing me a better place for his hard length. I yanked up his sweatshirt, hiked up my own, pressed my breasts to his chest, and pulled his head down to capture his lips.

Behind us, *Glitter Freeze's* high-pitched squall provided counter point to its bass beat, and I sucked on Marty's tongue, rode his fingers, and desperately reached for an orgasm. Apparently, he was just as greedy to come. He pulled his mouth from mine and growled, "Where?"

"Up." I no sooner croaked the word than he lifted me, again as if I were weightless, and held me in his arms as he carried me upstairs. Just call me Scarlet.

I was impressed. He was impressed when he saw my bed.

"Whoa." He slowed down to admire the giant, pedestaled, mahogany creation I slept in each night. It came with the house. I grinned. My grandpa was a big man. He'd built it before beds came in king-size. Evidently, no one had wanted to move it between the time he'd lived here and the time I'd reclaimed it.

But now was not the time to digress. I shifted in Marty's grip and slid my hand under his waistband. Yep. He was a big man, too. I didn't have practice at this kind of thing, but, when I wrapped my fingers around his hardness, he grunted,

"Oh yeah," and became more interested in using it, than staring at the bed.

I laughed when he dropped me on the mattress and started peeling his clothes off until he growled, "Get naked."

Okay.

I started with my sweatshirt, but he was already baring me down below by the time I got my shirt over my head. My arms were still tangled when he propelled me backward and came down on top of me.

"I'm covered," he assured me.

I looked down at his too late to matter condom covered cock, poised for action. I wrestled with the arms of my sweatshirt as he nudged apart my thighs, and almost casually, reached for my top. I thought he was going to help me out of the tangle of material.

Instead, he leaned his forearm across my trapped limbs.

"Hey," I twisted and arched, instinctively trying to throw him off. Oh. My. God. He thrust home. I didn't even have time to draw breath before the first climax rocketed through me.

He moved with it, timing his thrusts to the rhythmic clenching of my insides. Round one over, he freed my arms and grinned wickedly down at me. Oh yeah. Two could play that game. Using a move I'd learned in a self-defense class, I rolled him to his back and held his arms above his head, his wrists cuffed by my hands.

Of course, that meant I had to lean across his face to hold him down. He latched onto my nipple and sucked like he'd planned it that way. Every time he pulled with his mouth above, my sex clenched below. I was going to come, again. No, I was going to ignite and incinerate in less than sixty seconds.

I fleetingly tried to think of some way to reciprocate but gave into gluttonous pleasure when he stopped sucking my nipples and kissed his way lower. Much lower.

My slippery wet state didn't put him off a bit. He separated my lower lips and licked. I would have cringed. I was embarrassed. But *ohmygod* it felt good, and I wanted him to lick again. And again.

He paid special attention to my clit. It felt swollen, needy, sensitive beyond belief, the zone of pleasure I'd underexplored in my limited experience. He used his finger inside me to appease my sexual core that screamed *fill me* even as another orgasm rolled over me.

Apparently, Marty heard. He slid up my frame, until his mouth reached mine, his chest covered my breasts, and his cock found its home inside me.

"Oh yeah," I sighed.

He grinned, slid his hand under my rump, and growled, "Hang on sugar, daddy's gonna take you for a ride."

I'd thought myself to be in pretty good shape. I walked a lot. Sometimes jogged. Heck, stacking boxes at my warehouse job should have prepared me to match Marty's endurance.

Not so. A blur of orgasms later, he finally came. He didn't pass out this time. I thought I might. Before I could, he nibbled on my ear.

"How was that for a do-over, hotshot?" he whispered in my ear, making me want to do it all over again.

"Good. It was good," I managed to answer.

He laughed, gave my butt a friendly pat, and got up.

Worn out and unbelievably content, I lay on the bed,

eyes closed, thinking about nothing. I drifted awhile. Marty's music still played downstairs, and I recognized Snoop Dogg talking revolution.

I dozed a little. Not much because the same song continued downstairs when I became aware of a change in the room's atmosphere. I swear, it felt as if someone had thrown a switch and blasted cold air on me. I opened my eyes.

Marty stood beside the bed. In his hands, he held three boxes. Two were opened. One, of course, not.

"You want to explain this?"

So much for sex softening his personality. I grabbed and put on the first sweatshirt that came to hand, which happened to be his.

Covered, I rolled to the other side and stood facing him across the wide mattress.

"No," I answered. "First of all, don't snoop through my trash."

"You will explain this right now. Do you hear me?"

Really? "Here you go. How's this for an explanation?" I guess sex hadn't softened my rough edges that much, either. "You're the frigging moron who wore a condom and didn't put it on right. The darned thing came off inside me. I should sue you for that, alone. Don't stand there and glare at me. Your sperm got loose. My eggs came out to play. They tangoed. Or *maybe* they did. Whatever you call it, *shit, happened…*"

He held up the box and squinted at the fine print. "Says here 99.97% accurate. How many times did it—"

"Twice, three times if you count your on-call doctor's test." I crossed my arms defensively. I shouldn't be feeling apologetic. Screw him. Well, no, we did that and look how that worked out. "You can go now."

"What? I don't think I heard you just tell me to get out after I've just found out you're…" His lips seemed to grope for the term, but it escaped him.

"Pregnant. I think that's the word you're searching for," I muttered, putting him out of his inarticulate misery. He grabbed sweats off the floor, his shoes, and left.

Well, that went well. I lay back down on the bed, listening for him to leave. The music abruptly switched off. Guess he didn't feel the beat, anymore. Sadly, I tracked his footsteps to the door. *Uh huh, open. Close. Goodbye Marty.* I waited for the sound of his Hummer starting. All remained quiet.

I should go down and lock up behind him. Instead, I wandered into the bathroom and showered. It felt good, geez, wonderful. I probably ran all the hot water out of the tank I stood there so long. I might have cried some, too.

Silly, sloppy sentimental me put his sweatshirt back on once I was clean and dry. It smelled good, and I liked the illusion of strong arms wrapped around me. My stomach growled. *For heavens sakes give it a rest.* If I kept eating like this, I'd weigh four hundred pounds soon. Still…

I went down stairs and directly to the kitchen, hoping Marty had left the bucket of chicken behind. He had. He'd also helped himself to my kitchen scissors and the arms of my sweatshirt lay on the counter. Revenge? I could only wonder.

I shrugged, picked up a drumstick and shuffled to the sink, prepared to stare mournfully at my empty backyard. Except it wasn't empty. Though it was only mid-March, the early warm days had already produced budding trees and grass beginning to green. And evidently a permanent resident in my swing. Marty wore my sleeveless sweatshirt. No doubt the slashed neck was so he could get his big head through the opening. His eyes were closed, and he sat in the swing, gliding back and forth.

Chapter Ten
Marty

J ESUS. I'D GONE to a dance to do a good deed and ended up... I didn't need to open my eyes. I could feel the sway of Holly's swing beneath me. After I'd fled the bedroom, I'd found myself standing naked in the middle of her kitchen. *Befuddled.* That's what Elaine would call it. I'd managed to get my head together enough to dress. Sort of.

I'd pulled on my pants for the sake of any neighbor who might come by, but, I'd left my sweatshirt with Holly upstairs. I'd thought about going back up and claiming it. Instead, I'd made-do with hers before stumbling outside to her backyard swing, where I collapsed when my feet wouldn't prop me up any longer.

I'd thought I needed fresh air to clear my head. Nope. My head was still in a far-away place. I still couldn't quite believe it. *Shit, I knocked her up.* I had sense enough to understand that didn't sound right. *I put a bun in the oven.* No. *She's increasing.* I didn't understand that one. *Expecting.* Hmmm. *Holly's expecting...* Maybe. None of my descriptions matched the reality. *Jesus, she's having my kid.*

I wondered if she'd planned on me finding out this way. She'd pointed us upstairs. The pregnancy test kits had been in her bathroom. But, I didn't think any of our fuck had been calculated on her part. She seemed like an innocent caught up in…

I swallowed, and pushed the swing harder. I'd wanted a do-over and had come loaded with bait. Music, food, charm. *What a fuck.* Lust squashed paternity thoughts and my cock stirred, remembering. *Now, that, was a do-over.*

I didn't waste time wondering if it had been as good for her. She'd been sprawled, limp, satisfied, and smiling when I left her bed. I'd been pretty damn satisfied myself, taking a piss and staring down at the wastebasket, grinning like a loon.

My mind had been in *I don't give a shit what I'm looking at, I just want to get back to bed*, mode, when I kind of focused on the box. I couldn't see what it was; I thought it might be beauty shit. I was not snooping. Well maybe a little bit.

Kit had colored her hair from a box and I was curious if Holly's blonde color was natural. I'd even made plans to check her lower curls after I climbed back into that magnificent bed.

I'd leaned closer, trying to figure out what had come in the box, without actually touching it. I mean, that would fall into the snooping zone. I could see that. But, still.

I'd nudged the can with my bare foot, shaking it enough to get a better look. There had been two boxes. And after I read the label, I shut the shit about nosiness down, and examined the box, read the instructions, checked for wands, and found a third kit unopened.

I'm having a kid. Holly and I are having a kid. Hell. The full implications of her pregnant state settled over me. I needed to tell Jack, call Garret and get medical instructions, set up a trust for the kid. Excitement zipped through my veins.

I opened my eyes and gazed at the house. Holly stood where she had earlier, watching me from the kitchen window. *There stands the mother of my child.*

I realized this could get complicated. I mean, I wanted the kid, my progeny, a son I hoped, but hey, a girl would be okay, too. I frowned. I'd need a lot of help with a girl baby. Not so much with a boy.

But that was a dumb thought. I'd have Holly to help. But would I? Did she want the baby? My baby? Women didn't always feel maternal or want to commit to raising a kid. My mom hadn't. She'd left me with my grandma and took off right after I'd been born.

I needed to let Holly know I'd be responsible for everything if she wanted to just hand the baby to me after she'd delivered. We needed to talk. But, my penchant for opening my mouth and pissing her off kept my ass parked in the swing.

I was afraid if I went into the house, she'd make me leave. I didn't want to leave. I wanted to go back upstairs with her, crawl into her grandpa's bed, and enjoy it with her for a long time.

My thoughts seemed to be lingering a disproportionate amount of time on having sex considering that this new development should have captured all my attention. And that led me to questions about fucking during pregnancy. Could we? Should we? Would she?

While I'd mulled over the possibilities of when and how to get into her pants again, Holly had been busy. She was dressed in khakis and a green shirt. Different clothes from the night before, but same combo.

"I'm going to work. I need to lock up."

She didn't tell me to get out, but she didn't invite me to stay, either.

"I'll drive you there." I expected her to tell me to go to hell.

"Okay." Her answer had me out of the swing and scrambling to be her chauffeur.

"Why don't I leave that here?" I said casually, as she handed me my sweatshirt when I went back inside. I guess she wanted hers back. I'd decided I'd keep it. Who knows why because the neck was too tight even with the slit I'd cut in the front.

"No." She shoved the shirt at me like it was hot.

"Fine. Ready to go?"

She nodded. I escorted her to my Hummer. She was very quiet. She didn't object when I buckled her into her seat. Another sign all was not well. I cleared my throat, delicately, I thought.

"What?" her snarled question assured me she was getting back to her old self.

"Can I tell anyone?" It might seem like a dumb question, but I didn't know how this was going to play out.

"Huh?" Her startled look informed me that was an unexpected question.

"I'm not comfortable with maybes. Either I'm going to be a dad, or I'm not. If it's happening, I've got to tell Jack, and," I added in a mumble, "a couple other people."

Elaine, my secretary, administrative assistant, motherish in a bizarre kind of way, and friend. Church, because he was still worried about the chili, and it was only fair to share the news. Besides, Church might poach on another man's woman but not his pregnant woman.

Then I needed to talk to Garret and let him know I knew. He could recommend a specialist for Holly, one who would share medical information with him, and he in turn would share it with me. Jack, being a man who didn't hold back on happy, would tell the crew. So, if Holly intended to keep the news secret, it wasn't happening.

Unless she'd decided she wasn't into having a family yet or at all. In which case…

"The test could be wrong," she said.

"The stats indicate otherwise." Pretty accurate outcomes. A 99.97% probability, in fact. "But either way, am I allowed to talk about it?"

"You want to tell people I might be expecting?"

"Yeah." I did. I was proud. "Hell, yeah."

"And if I'm not?"

I shrugged. "Then I'll tell 'em you're not. It's a big deal to me. You've got your friends you'll share with. I've got mine. But, I want to know if *maybe* is real, because if I can do anything to sway your decision into *a yes it's real*, tell me, and I'll do it."

"That made no sense at all."

She was right I'd garbled that explanation.

"I want you to tell me that *if* you're pregnant, you're going to stay pregnant." I'd pretty much worked out all the details while I'd been swinging in the backyard. Holly was the only part I couldn't control.

"Yes, if the test was right, I'm having the kid." She remained silent the rest of the ride to the sports bar.

Not wanting to push my luck, I kept my mouth shut.

When we arrived, I blocked traffic and let the cretin behind me blow his horn while I pulled her into my arms for a goodbye kiss.

"I'll pick you up. What time do you get off?"

"I'm meeting Megan after work tonight. She's picking me up. See you around. Thanks for the ride." And out she went and on her way.

Message received. Leave her alone. Okay. For now.

I returned to my office, sweatshirt in hand, and wondered when I got there how I'd managed to live in the cramped space so long.

I'd struck out on getting laid again tonight. I wouldn't be sleeping with Holly in a bed obviously built for me. But in the grand scheme of things, I'd scored big. I'd left my H/K speaker on her mantle, giving myself a reason to return to her home.

I'd also put a baby in her belly. I was going to be a father. I needed to tell someone. I called Jack.

"Meet me at Church's place. I have news."

"This about Marilyn?"

"If you get there first, order me a steak. Rare." I avoided his question, knowing that if I mentioned Holly at all, I'd spill my guts over the phone. And I wanted to deliver the news personally.

He was the only dad I'd ever known. And he'd been a damned good one. He'd be shocked, I knew. Hey, I was. But he'd get accustomed to the idea of being a grandpa. I smirked. Grandpa Jack. Yeah. Still, I'd hold off on pushing that idea until the little fellow arrived.

As soon as I walked into the bar, I knew something was up. Church had his best Scotch on the bar and glasses lined up, and Jack, grinning from ear to ear, held a handful of Cubans in his fist.

"Congratulations, son," he said, and pounded me on the back.

"Your woman's saved from my planned advance," Church assured me and filled the glasses.

"Marty, I'm so happy for you," Elaine said, and handed me a drink. At my astonished stare, she said, "Jack called me. And it's a good thing he did. Do you think I wanted to hear news like this through the grapevine?"

I turned my gaze from Elaine back to Jack, the grapevine. "I didn't know. How could you? Did that little shit, Garret, tell you when he wouldn't tell me a thing?" I looked around for said shit. He was lurking behind Church at the bar. Jack came to his rescue, though.

"Knew the minute I saw her throw-up all over your shoes. Kit's mama puked just like that when she was carrying."

"Nausea, referred to as morning sickness, although it can strike any time during the day," Garret shared, coming out of hiding.

"And you didn't think I should know that I'm having a kid?"

"There are rules," he reminded me. "Besides, how was I to know you were the dork who'd fouled-up using a rubber?"

Jack lifted his glass and waited. I lifted my glass and clinked against his, Elaine's, Church's, and Garret's. We all threw back together, celebrating the coming of my soon to be born son. At least, I hoped it would be a boy. Not that I had anything against girl babies. But since this kid would no doubt be my only child, if I could choose the sex, I'd choose a boy.

I swallowed the twenty-year-old Scotch, savoring the mellow burn as it slid down my throat.

"Ahh…" Jack slammed his glass down first. "Great booze. Fill me up again, Church."

I started drinking at 6:00 p.m. and continued until I was beyond drunk when we closed down the place at 2:00 a.m. I didn't want to stretch out in a booth. I didn't want to go back to my office and sleep on my couch. I wanted Holly's bed, with her in it beside me. I conveyed that wish to my drinking partners.

"Let's go. We'll tuck you in." Church's offer had me thinking of that giant bed, again.

"She said she had plans after work."

"Maybe you should call her before we deliver you to her house," Garret suggested.

I didn't want to admit that I didn't have her number. She'd already brushed me off once today, well really, yesterday. But before that, we'd had mind-altering sex. At least, my mind had been blown wide-open. And then I'd found out about the baby, I'd taken her to work, and she'd declined my offer to pick her up.

"Hey, she's your baby's mama. You don't schedule an appointment with her. You show up and crawl in bed with her." Jack's version of courtship resonated with the drunks celebrating with me.

Garret, not drunk, drove. I sprawled on the passenger side of his Jeep giving him directions to Holly's place. Jack sat in the backseat. It was a harebrained idea, but like I said, we were drunk.

Doubts arose about my welcome as soon as I saw the car

occupying her driveway and the other car parked on the street in front of her house.

"Maybe this is a bad idea." There were lights on. And music played inside. She had company. Nevertheless, I climbed out of the Jeep and checked out the black Mercedes SUV in front before I walked past the dark sedan in her drive.

I already knew the bell didn't work, so when I stood in front of her door, moron that I was, I hammered on it. I had a grin plastered on my face when it swung open.

My smile froze in place when a man greeted me. "Can I help you?"

I noted the tailored slacks, red suspenders holding them up over a white tee shirt, bare feet and tousled hair. Shit.

"Sorry, sorry," I mumbled, reeling backward. Too late, Jack was already on the porch and at my elbow.

"Who the hell are you?" he demanded. "And where the hell is Marty's woman?"

"Check the time guys. It's 3:00 in the morning. What the fuck do you want?" And there stood Holly's friend, I thought her name was Megan.

Not one to back down, Jack said, "We want Holly. Marty wants to talk to his woman."

Megan's gaze swung my way.

"What?" Holly appeared behind her guests. I noticed that she stood a couple inches taller than the guy. It shouldn't have given me smug satisfaction, but it did.

I couldn't think of anything to say. Confronted with my reason for being there, I muttered, "I forgot my speaker when I left earlier."

It was the booze talking. Honestly, I hadn't intended to

take it back. Even if she'd already moved on from me to the short guy, she'd need music for the baby in the next few months. Then I wondered if it was really my baby and not his. I couldn't help it. My glare focused on him.

"I'm sorry. You can't have it yet. We're using it."

What the fuck? Behind her, bass notes rumbled, and a saxophone sang.

"Using it for what?" As someone had already pointed out, it was three in the morning.

"Dancing." She had the nerve to use my speaker to dance with her new guy.

"I want it back," I growled. "Now."

"Well, you can't have it, now. You'll have to wait until we're done practicing. All of you, come in and quit scaring the neighbors." As soon as we stepped through the door she introduced us.

"Roger, these three stooges are Marty Jones, the dance partner who made Marilyn famous, and also boss man at Smoke, Inc.; Dr. Garret Wilson, Smoke Inc. physician; and Church, owner and bartender of Smoke Inc.'s watering hole, Church's Bar & Grill. You three already know Megan, and Megan knows everybody." Holly then turned to me. "Marty and crew, this is Dr. Roger Valentine." She didn't elaborate, leaving a slew of unanswered questions about her *new* dance partner.

I hadn't gotten a tour of the house, before, so the basement was a total surprise. A wet bar with my H/K sitting on the counter, filled one end of the thirty-foot room.

"Sit," she ordered me, pointing at a bar stool. "Megan, make them some coffee. Roger, we'll do this one more time."

I sat. Jack, Garret and I watched Holly guide her dance

partner through a tango into a pulse pounding rumba.

"No wonder she tried to lead when we danced," I muttered aloud.

The rumba ended with her spinning her partner around, draping him over her arm, and bending him backward with a flourish.

"Coffee coming up, regular unless anyone's got a preference," Megan said, pointing at the Keurig and selection of coffee pods on hand.

"Black, plain." I needed to sober up and figure out what was going on. I had a feeling I'd royally screwed up. The H/K was my ticket back into the house. But if I took my speaker with me, Holly might permanently bar her door.

Pressure beat a drum in my head. My coffee arrived, and I took a sip. The music ended. Holly threw a towel at her partner. He walked to the bar. I stood, ready to leave.

"Play it again, Megan. I know I didn't get that last spin right." Holly's friend wiped his brow, drank from a bottle of water, and sat on a stool next to Garret. "Holly, why don't you partner with Marty and demonstrate how it should look."

I didn't know Holly well enough to interpret her shrug. Not knowing what else to do to save the night and maybe get back into her good graces, assuming I'd ever been there, I shuffled to where she stood in the middle of the floor.

"You smell like a brewery," she said, wrinkling her nose in distaste.

"You got a shower to loan me, I'll take care of that. You can wash my back if you want." I leered suggestively at her, ready to dodge the punch she looked ready to throw. But then magic happened. The music started.

Holly lifted her arms, I stepped closer, settled my hand on her hip, and we danced. A long time. With no words between us, we communicated with the greatest of ease. I didn't know why she'd been dancing with the other guy, but it no longer mattered. She matched my steps, moved to my beat. We had rhythm.

Much, much later, I remembered that she was carrying my baby, or at least, she was potentially carrying my baby, and I danced us to a stop and pulled her closer.

"You need to get some sleep."

"Yes, I do," she agreed.

"Want company?" I asked hopefully.

"No."

But it was okay. It didn't seem like a rejection as much as a slap down for over-stepping into her world. And after her dancing friend walked me to the door, I didn't worry about him anymore, either.

"I believe Holly left my bolero at your office the morning after the dance."

"What's a bolero?" I asked cautiously.

"My jacket. She wore it with my Marilyn Monroe outfit. Did me proud. You looked good, too. If you get a chance, see if you can find it, and send it over to me." He gave me his card which I tucked into my pocket without looking at it.

Okay. I again left my speaker behind, but just to make sure she understood it wasn't an accidental oversight, I kissed her forehead and told her, "Don't break the H/K."

Chapter Eleven
Holly

"WOW, HE'S HOT." Roger voiced his opinion as soon as the three stooges departed.

"You crushing on Marty?" I asked.

"No. But I wouldn't mind playing doctor with Garret."

"The kid?"

"He can't be all that young. He's a licensed physician and it takes a long time to become a medical doctor," Megan said thoughtfully.

"Roger, you think he might have noticed you?" I asked casually.

"Not in this lifetime." He surprised me with his wistful stare.

"Want me to try and hook you up?" Megan asked.

"Your last date arranging didn't turn out so well." I glared at Megan. "What are you, a matchmaker now? Keep this up and Maxine will go out of business."

"You and Marty seemed pretty cozy during your dance. He's not a womanizer like some of the crew. And he's got money. You could do worse." Megan's mercenary tendencies were urging my kitchen upgrade designer genes to take advantage of a man who could afford any faucets I chose.

"Just how do you know so much about Marty?" I asked.

Her knowledge of the Smoke, Inc. building I could understand. But her information about the owner, I didn't quite follow.

"Teague," she muttered. "And no, I don't want to talk about him."

I assumed Teague to be the man who'd claimed Megan as his woman, the night of my puke-a-thon.

Because it had been an eventful day, an interesting evening, and a crazier night, I hadn't gotten around to my announcement to either one of them. I used the moment to rectify that.

"I'm pregnant."

Megan didn't look surprised making me wonder if she'd gotten her information via her caveman. Evidently Marty had sent a memo to the entire Smoke, Inc. crew.

"What?" Roger looked totally confused. "How can you be having a baby? You're still a virgin. Aren't you?"

"That would be, no." I didn't tell him when I returned the dress I'd borrowed for the dance-a-thon. "Sorry, a lot happened since I talked to you last and most of it's been too weird to share." I'd had the Marilyn outfit dry-cleaned, hustled it back, and decided to put the incident behind me.

"I had sex and now I'm pregnant."

"Did I just meet the dad?" Roger asked.

I nodded.

"Marty?"

"Good guess," Megan answered before I could. "Garret's gay, and Jack's ancient, who else could it be? You saw them dance."

"How do you know Garret's gay? You keep coming up with this stuff. Are you a Smoke, Inc. groupie or something?" I couldn't keep the exasperation from my voice.

"Maybe," Megan answered and shrugged. "They have great parties."

"So, is it a good thing happening or a bad? Do you want the baby? Is Marty onboard?" Roger's questions wiped away my irritation at Megan and eliminated the momentary calm I'd gained while dancing.

"I don't know. Yes. I think so," I answered his questions in the order he'd asked. "I'm tired," I told them both. "Beat. I must work tomorrow, so it's lights out. If you're staying, find a spot to sprawl. If you're going, lock the door on your way out."

"It'll be okay. We'll deal together. Let me know what I can do." Roger smiled, kissed my cheek, and left. Megan lingered.

"Marty will take care of things. With him stopping by tonight, it's obvious he's not upset about the baby."

I didn't know what Marty would do and was too tired to care.

"He was surprised at finding Roger here," Megan said.

"You mean jealous," I corrected her.

"Most people would be upset if they arrived at their lover's place and found said significant other having a private party."

"In case you haven't noticed, Marty is *not* my significant other. I am not looking for a relationship. I told him he'd be high maintenance. I was right."

"In case you haven't noticed, girlfriend, things have changed. Sticking your head in the sand won't make you not pregnant."

"I want you to go home, Megan. I need some time to

myself." If I said more it wouldn't be pretty. I left her standing in the kitchen and went upstairs. I didn't sleep, though. As soon as I heard the outside door open and close, and her car start and drive away, I went back downstairs, checked the front and back doors, then went to sit in my closet.

I didn't know what to think about. Too much had happened, burying me under so much emotion I could only try to numb myself to keep from feeling anything.

I wanted to cry, but I refused to give into the urge. My head ached from lack of sleep, and yet I sat staring into the dark, eyes wide open. The back door clicked as it opened and closed. The floorboards creaked outside my closet, as footsteps approached.

"Is there room in here for me?" Marty asked as soon as he opened the door.

"Yes, if we both stand." I stood. I'd moved the sweeper from the closet the day before for unexplained reasons. The same reasons had dictated that I leave the backdoor unlocked and the porch light on.

He stepped into my space and pulled the door shut behind him. I put my hands on his shoulders and turned him so we faced each other. Then I stepped into his embrace, wrapping my arms around his waist as I closed my eyes and rested my head against his chest.

I didn't know how to explain it other than he made me feel safe.

He didn't say a word. He held me, stroked my hair, and rubbed my back, no funny business, just comfort. He'd done the same thing when we'd danced earlier. I'd gone from head-exploding anxiety to composed calm. I wondered how he'd learned such a thing. Marty had hidden depths.

"My dad was a silent comforter," I whispered when I finally let go of him and stepped back. "He'd hold me and pat my back when I got upset."

"He build that bed upstairs?"

"My grandpa. My dad's dad." I laughed. The bed was unique. Too big to move, but what a treasure if you were tall and liked to stretch out when you slept.

"You going to invite me into it again?"

"Right now, I need sleep."

"I can do that."

"Just sleep?"

He nodded and followed me from the closet up the stairs. "I took the liberty of locking your backdoor."

I had enough energy left to tilt my head in approval.

"The right side is mine," I told him, then went into the bathroom, brushed my teeth and pulled on my sleep shirt.

Whether pretend or real I couldn't tell, but when I climbed into the bed he was already snoring. I don't know if I snored or not, but I fell asleep.

I half-woke to bands of steel wrapping me in a tight embrace.

"Promise me you won't leave, again," Marty muttered against my neck. "Promise me."

Huh. Even my sleep fuzzy brain knew that didn't sound right and his hold on me felt frantic, not romantic. While my mind coasted trying to decide whether to sink back into oblivion or switch on for the day, his touch changed from clutching to caressing.

One of his hands cupped my breast, the other left a trail of heat as it slid across my belly. *Oh, my.* I let my body do the thinking, writhing in his arms as his thumb and fingers tweaked my nipple. His erection pressed against my rump as he held me tighter and nibbled my neck.

"Kitten, sweetheart, I love you so much," he whispered in my ear.

Kitten, I smiled, rubbing against him, loving the way his big hand petted my belly, making me purr. His lips lingered on a spot behind my ear that had me hot and steaming. *Oh yeah.* He rumbled stuff, who knows what, as he made love to me. Who knew I liked sex talk. I tuned in for more.

"Oh, baby," he growled in my ear. "I've missed you, Kit."

Kitten. Kit, as in his wife had been named Kit. Kit as in *my wife died, Kit.* I ripped myself out of his arms, out of the bed, and into the bathroom. I didn't need an explanation or a bucket of cold water. I'd been iced down. I shivered and tried to warm myself under a hot shower, but it didn't help much.

I wanted him to be gone when I came out of the bathroom. He'd dressed and made the bed, but instead of departing, I could hear him downstairs.

My thoughts were scrambled as I hurried to pull on clothes. Before he left, I wanted to tell him not to come back. Shit. My life was so messed up right now.

What kind of inept moron puts the condom on wrong? It wasn't hard to work up anger at Marty since the whole damned thing was his fault. The thought finally occurred to me that I could have caught more than a baby from him.

On top of everything else, and maybe what pissed me off the most, was, I'd really been getting into the warm and cozy vibes and I'd left myself vulnerable.

Won't be making that mistake again. I was going to have to find a new closet. Since Marty had occupied mine, it wouldn't be the same.

I hurried downstairs, hoping he'd gone to the backyard. He seemed fascinated by the swing, undoubtedly it called to his not very inner child.

But no, there he was sitting at my table. He had a notepad in front of him. I recognized it as mine. The one I used to make lists and write down measurements and stuff. I kept it in my side drawer next to the sink. He'd helped himself.

I don't know why I'd expected him to be embarrassed that he'd called me by his wife's name. He clearly hadn't been affected. Maybe he didn't even realize it had happened. I leaned in the doorway of the kitchen trying to decide what issue to address. I chose one I could handle.

"Stop rummaging through my drawers."

His eyebrow went up. I detected a smirk on his lips.

"What is wrong with you?" I asked. "You don't get to take over my life. Are you nuts? What do I have to do to see the last of you?"

He slid the notepad he'd been using across the table to the far edge. I still had to enter the room and walk across the floor to pick it up, which irritated me. He'd made a list. *Number one*, what a surprise, *See a doctor.*

Marty

SHIT HAPPENS ALRIGHT. HELL. I'd been in deep clover, dreaming about making love to Kit. We'd been together, she'd been real, in my arms, her heat warming the last of the frozen particles from my heart. And then…

I stared at the woman who'd sucked the ice from my veins and apparently into her own. She did not appear happy, sort of like the *Road Warrior* chick right before she made a kill. I guess I should be grateful Holly was only leaning against the doorframe and glaring at me. She *did* look sexy.

Yes, no doubt a shrink would point out that I felt conflicted. The dream had been so real, but the real part of it stood in front of me.

Her wet hair hugged tight to her skull outlining the attractive shape of her head. I wondered if she knew a cowlick had sprouted at the back. The way her jeans hung from her hips and tee shirt clung to her tits, it seemed evident she'd still been damp from her shower when she rushed downstairs to have her say before I left. I was glad I'd made my list.

She opened her mouth to speak. I held up my hand, halting her. "First, I have a few issues to discuss concerning the baby."

At least I got her into the room. When she picked up my list I considered that progress. I don't like explanations, but it was possible I owed her one.

"I was seventeen when I married Kit Cahill. She was thirty-four. She was pissed off at the cheating sonofabitch she was engaged to and promised him she'd marry the first guy she saw." I paused, savoring the same smug satisfaction I'd felt then. "I made sure that guy was me."

Of course, I'd been hard to miss. I stood six feet two by the time I turned fourteen, quit school, and had gone to work for an Alabama oil rigger named Jack Cahill, Kit's father. I'd developed serious lust for Kit when I saw her the day I was hired. During the next three years, I'd kept growing and so had my crush. I was six feet five by the time Kit made her infamous vow, and I'd already been trying to figure out how to get her attention.

"When I heard Kit, spouting off to Jack, I stepped in front of her and said, 'I'd be pleased to make you my wife.' We drove one county over to get married, returned the next day." Every time Kit had told the story she'd laughed, but it had always been a soft sound of pleasure.

I ached, wishing I could relive that time again, until my glance landed on the woman carrying the baby I hadn't been able to give Kit. My voice was harsh even to my own ears as I ended my nostalgic reminiscing and told Holly the truth.

"Kit and I were married fifteen years and still would be if she hadn't died of cancer. Sometimes good things turn to shit."

"Yeah," Holly agreed and shrugged. "And your point is?"

"About upstairs. Sorry. I've had sex with one woman before you. I've slept with one woman before you, the same woman. Before today, the last time I occupied a bed, Kit was in it with me."

"How long ago was that? How old was she? How old are you, for that matter?"

"She was forty-nine when we lost the battle with cancer. I'm thirty-eight." The usual feeling of despair threatened to overwhelm me until Miss Sarcastic interrupted my reverie.

"Well if you haven't been using a bed, where have you been sleeping? A tree? A cave? And for how long?"

"My office." It was my turn to shrug. "It's been six years since Kit died." I crossed my arms on the table and leaned

Holly

WELL IF THAT'S TRUE, I guess I don't have to worry about catching more than I already caught. Relief made me feel dizzy again. At the same time, I had so many things to say, I thought I'd strangle as they all tried to spew from my mouth.

"I looked outside. Your mammoth vehicle is not there. How did you get here?"

"I never left. I was still too drunk to think straight so I sent Garret and Jack on their way. I sat in your swing. Didn't want to go back to my office."

"And then you came inside."

"After your friends left, you turned on the porchlight and unlocked the door. I took that as an invitation."

Which it had been, even though I'd not known he was already here. It had been more a wistful longing. Darn it, I could feel the edge of my righteous anger slipping away.

I glanced at the list again. Doctor, insurance, income, exercise. The first three items left my stomach in knots and my earlier serenity blown all to hell.

"I get a lot of exercise," I told him, starting at number four since it didn't cost anything.

"What, aside from walking and waiting tables which you will not be able to do soon? Which leads us back to income. What is yours?"

"None of your business. And of course, I'll be able to work." Anxiety morphed to anger quickly, and I embraced it.

"What else besides waitressing," he persisted, ignoring

my need to fight.

"I work nights, too." I didn't miss his beady-eyed stare as he waited for me to explain further. I didn't. He leaned forward, his jaw jutting aggressively, his posture poised for combat.

"Humble Homes," I muttered. "Satisfied? Now go away."

"What the hell do you do there?" Obviously not okay with my answer, he demanded explanation.

"None of your fucking business, you cretin. Stop badgering me and get out."

"And insurance?" It seemed he wasn't leaving until we worked our way through his list. Since he was too big for me to evict, I sighed and sat down.

"I don't have a regular doctor which doesn't matter because I'll have to go to a specialist for a baby."

"A perinatologist," he inserted.

"What the heck is that?" I really hadn't heard of that kind of doctor.

"I researched it. It's a doctor with additional training for high-risk pregnancies."

"Why would I need a high-risk doctor? I'm fine."

"We don't know that until you've been to the doctor which we're arranging right now. We'll begin with the best; someone with training ready to handle anything. That way we don't have to break-in a new guy if things develop."

"First, there won't be *any* guys poking around on me. I'll make an appointment with a female doctor."

"See, we're already making progress. You want a woman tending you. Fine."

"Number two," I continued without acknowledging his

input. "I have insurance. It sucks. I don't get sick much which is good because the deductible is horrific." He opened his mouth. Before he could chime in, I cut off his. "Number three. I have three jobs that keep my bills paid. I wait tables, monitor inventory at the HH building and supply company, and substitute teach. Number four. All of the above plus my house renovations give me plenty of exercise."

I don't know what I expected. Certainly, not for him to put on a pair of glasses and start scribbling on a piece of paper in front of him.

When he finished, he slid one big hand across the table, pushing a check toward me. Without touching it I leaned forward to see the amount.

Hmmm... Fifteen hundred dollars. "And this would be for...?" Not enough to raise a child alone. Too much for take-out dinner.

"I called a realtor friend. The houses in this area lease for twice that amount per month. I'll pay you that much to rent a room, so I can be here while you gestate."

Gestate? "Where the hell do you come up with this stuff? Farm animals gestate. Humans..." Okay, I didn't know the term for a woman carrying a baby, but gestation just sounded wrong.

"Look it up, baby doll. You'll find it in the dictionary."

"I'm not a baby doll," I snapped, side-stepping the real issue. *Fifteen hundred freaking dollars. Each month.* Marty rooming with me wasn't without precedent since he'd rented from Harley-Jane when his first office building burned down.

"Concentrate on what's important. You're *gestating.* You're the mother of my kid. I planted the seed and one way or another I'm watching him grow." Marty had reverted to being the overbearing ass I was reluctantly coming to know.

"No." I stared at the check, itching to grab it up and stuff it in my pocket. Instead, I kept my twitchy fingers away from the money, and fixed my gaze on his chin.

"Yes." He didn't even ask me why. Two could play that game.

"No."

"Look," he said. "I didn't force you. We both consented to sex. I personally thought it was great. I've done what I can to rectify your first disappointment. If you didn't like the second taste of me, okay. I can live with never fucking you again. But," he paused and leaned forward even more. "You don't get the kid all to yourself. He's half mine. I'm claiming him. Besides, you need my money to make it happen right."

I bristled at his tone. It didn't matter that what he said was mostly true. I felt aggrieved, put-upon.

"I don't know the gender and neither do you. Stop calling what may be *her*, a *he*."

"A girl's okay," he conceded. "I'll get used to pink."

"Pink? Stop with the stereotypes. Your age is showing."

"Just call me Big Daddy," he grinned and waggled his eyebrows at me.

Jeez, while I wrestled with the image of me curled up on his lap calling him daddy, heat blossomed in my lower regions and lust clouded my mind.

"I won't be here all that much," he assured me, adding a bonus to his proposition.

"How much?" The firm *hell no* resounding in my mind started tipping more toward *maybe*.

"I'll be gone on a job next week. That's why I want to

get things worked out now."

Somehow, we'd gone from *no* to *working things out* in less time than it had taken for me to get pregnant. I made a mental note to remember Marty's negotiating tactics. Bully, coax, bribe.

"I'll think about it. When you get back, I'll give you an answer."

"Not good enough," he answered immediately.

"Hey, we had sex but I don't know a darned thing about you other than you're bossy. And since you're not my employer, an older relative, or my significant other, you are not my boss." I paused to think if I'd overlooked anything and added quickly, "And if you were my significant other you still wouldn't be my boss." Statement made, I crossed my arms and glared at him.

He gave me his patient, long suffering expression and said, "You're making this a lot more complicated than it needs to be. Rent me a room, for fuck's sake. What are you afraid of? You're virtue's safe with me." Okay, so now he'd introduced the scaredy-cat challenge.

I couldn't help myself. My glance shifted back to the check. It would cover my mortgage payment. My resolve began to crumble which pissed me off even more. Marty was making me see one big fact I'd been trying to avoid. I really wanted this baby and without some frigging miracle, I couldn't afford it. I assessed the frigging miracle staring at me and made up my mind.

"You are not to stick your nose in my business."

"Agreed."

"You cannot hang around where I work and cause trouble."

"Not a problem."

"You buy your own food and keep your own messes cleaned up."

"Of course." He agreed to every condition I put before him. He was maneuvering me, herding me and I didn't like it. I couldn't escape reality though. The baby was made of parts of him as well as me. Poor little thing.

Before either of us could change our minds, I snatched the check from the table and shoved it in my pocket. "Okay. The spare room's all yours."

"I don't get the king size?" He gave me a cocky grin. I bared my teeth at him and he muttered, "Okay, okay, I'll make do. Baby needs a place to stretch out and grow so I'm not complaining. Still, it's big enough for two—"

"You talk in your sleep. Not doing that again." I at least wiped the smug expression from his face. "Going to work, now. Knock yourself out moving your things into the room across the hall."

"Need a ride? I can call someone to bring the Hummer."

"No. I need exercise, remember?"

"Do I get a key? Or do you prefer that I climb through a window or slide down the chimney?"

I retraced the mental footsteps that had led to him moving in, wondering if I'd officially gone nuts. Hard as I tried, I could not think of Marty as a stranger. I didn't know him, but, he and I were going to share a kid. His moving in made as much sense as anything else in my life.

"Do you negotiate contracts for your company?" I asked, handing him a key to my house.

"Yes," he grunted, giving me a look of disapproval. "You didn't even haggle. You could have gotten more out of me for the room."

He pocketed the key and followed me to the door. I expected him to ask when I'd be back. He didn't. Instead he pulled out his phone and said, "What's your number?"

"Why do you need my number?"

"I'm a tenant. You're my landlord. I have a right to be able to contact you if something goes wrong with the plumbing."

"Nothing is wrong with the plumbing." I threatened him with my stare, wondering if I should take the key back and kick him out. "Don't touch my tools or the cupboards. Don't mess with the house. Just don't." But I pulled my phone from my pocket and handed it to him.

He looked at the blank screen than at me.

"Push the button on the side," I told him impatiently.

"Don't you have to unlock it?"

"No. Just key in your number and give it back."

"Done," he grinned, plugging in his number and calling it. As I listened, his phone chimed, and I realized he'd out-maneuvered me again.

Part of me wanted to lock into hunker-down mode, climb in my closet, bar the door, and not come out for a week, maybe more. I needed some serious head time. Too much had happened too quickly, changing my reality overnight.

And yet, I'd given Marty a key to the front door, and his check rode in my pocket. We hadn't discussed its disbursements because that was none of his business. I bristled at the idea of him monitoring my expenditures and yet, I braced myself for the coming event.

Marty

THE MOTHER OF my kid didn't have a bit of common sense. What was she thinking letting an unknown male shack up with her? It had taken me less than a minute to get Holly to give up her cell phone number and hand over a key, confirming my first opinion.

On the other hand, it simplified everything and her readiness to be practical boded well for the future…our future.

I knew I was rushing things, but dammit, having discovered I was going to be a dad, I wanted this with the ferocity of a lion. I refused to slow down for fear I'd lose hold of this miracle.

As soon as my landlord left, I called Jack. "Pick me up at Holly's." I puttered around, checked out the bedroom upstairs she'd granted me, and explored the outside more until he arrived in the Hummer. I liked the place. It needed a lot of work. I found a push mower in the utility shed in the corner of her yard. Like the shed, the mower was old but well kept.

It being early spring, the grass was barely long enough, but I'd mowed half the yard anyway by the time Jack arrived. He sat in the swing while I finished and put the mower away.

"What's up?" he asked as I brushed green clippings from my pants.

"I'm moving in here today."

"Fast work. Yours or hers?" He frowned as he studied me.

"Mine. Renting a room from her. I intend to be part of

my kid's life from the get-go."

"Do you want to know more about your landlord; what she's been doing and who she's been doing it with? I can call Hack and ask him to put a rush on this. He owes us a favor."

Hack was just what his name implied. In a digital/cyber world, Hack could go anywhere. In the real-time space our bodies occupy, his minions served his will.

Last year, the company had been one such minion. We'd extracted Hack's nephew from a dicey situation. The kid had been wandering through Europe, nosing around where he shouldn't. He was caught when he'd crossed the wrong border.

Hack orchestrated a rescue without leaving his chair. He'd helped the parents negotiate with the guards turned kidnappers, packed a bag full of money, and paid Smoke, Inc. for a fast, quiet, exchange.

I'd headed the extraction crew. Though the guards had aimed weapons at the helicopter, they hadn't fired. We'd returned the college boy back to the states for a happy ending.

That, plus the big check we'd all split, had made the job seem easy. But I'd bent more than a few international laws in the process. I felt queasy thinking about that job, so yeah, Hatch owed us. Frankly, he scared the shit out of me.

"How far back you want him to go?" Jack asked, interrupting my thoughts.

"I'd rather keep Hack's favor unused for now. And what the fuck does it matter where Holly's been and what she's done? She's the mother of my kid."

I'd seen no sign of drug use, she claimed I was her first fuck, and she wasn't one of Maxine's regular escorts. I believed her. But if she'd cut corners on the story of her life, it was up to her to share her truth.

"Whatever Holly wants me to know, she'll share." I pointed at the house. "I already know her grandfather lived here." I thought of the giant bed upstairs and added. "I know he was a big guy. Think about that. My size genes plus Holly's height genes equal…"

"Equal we better find an extra-long crib before the kid arrives," Jack answered and grinned.

Jack stayed put for most of the afternoon and though he was not ready to embrace Holly into the fold, I could see he liked her house. He helped me move my clothes from the office before we went shopping.

"So, your rent covers use of the main room?" Jack asked slyly.

"Yep."

"Do you say that, or does she say that?"

"She can use the chair when I'm not here." Why the fuck would she care if I stuck a chair in the front room?

I tested the recliners in the furniture store and only found one where my feet didn't hang over the end when I powered back. It made the choice easy.

"Maybe I should get her one to match," I'd offered.

"Son. What you don't want to do is try to redecorate a woman's space. You won't like the outcome."

With that advice in my head, I settled on just the one recliner for the living room. We carted it home and carried it in, angling it, so I could see her front door.

That was when I realized she needed a serious upgrade in the television department. Unless she had it hidden away, she didn't have one. We remedied that with a 70" curved

4K.

I admit, I enjoyed pretending I belonged in the house. Just being in the place gave me a sense of home I hadn't experienced since Kit died. I knew the Jack felt it too. We slouched at the kitchen table, drinking coffee and conducting business like we had a right to be here. That was a stretch, and we both knew that too.

"I don't want to take piss her off and have her kick me out," I told Jack at one point. Really, it had more to do with fear of being locked out of her life than her house. I didn't want to fight with the mother of my kid. I wanted to see the day to day progress as the baby developed. Living in the house this way, I'd get to be part of that.

"You're not gonna be around enough for her to realize what a pain in the ass you are. Quit worrying." Favoring that advice, after I set aside guilt over making myself comfortable in Holly's home, we made calls, arranging a company powwow the next day.

"Might as well meet here," Jack drawled. "Might make the schedule change go down better." He'd quit testing the limits of my lease when we installed the TV.

Here or somewhere else, the meeting had to happen. While TV shopping, a New Mexico state official caught up with me via phone, requesting Smoke, Inc. travel asap to the out of control fire, raging there, rather than deploying midweek as planned. I'd promised them we'd be there and working the fire by Monday.

Now I had to break the news to the crew. We'd expected the job to keep us busy until the end of the month. But, they wouldn't be happy they only had until the end of the weekend to take care of business.

Realizing during the afternoon I had my own personal business to tend, I called the company lawyer and made sure if anything happened to me on this job, my kid and his mama would always be taken care of.

Jack left, and as I wandered around Holly's yard, I got the attention of one of her neighbors.

"Is Holly moving?"

I studied the old guy leaning on the adjoining fence, trolling for information. When I didn't volunteer any, he continued. "New furniture? You her boyfriend?" He'd obviously been spying on her for a while.

"Security detail," I answered and left him standing there to chew on that.

Ten-foot privacy fence, I mentally added to my backyard wish list and retreated to the great indoors to doze in my new chair. I expected Holly to eventually come home from her waitressing job. But, when she hadn't shown by midnight, I started to worry and made some calls.

Holly

AFTER THE SPORTS bar, I still had an eleven-to-seven at my warehouse job, stocking shelves at Humble Homes. After I clocked off at Balls & Bones at 10:30, with a pocketful of tips to add to Marty's check, I hustled to catch a bus for the ride across town.

I didn't want to hurt the baby doing something stupid, so I called Garret from the bar. I figured he'd give me some information I could trust, he was free, and I had a card with the clinic's number on it. I expected an answering service to patch me through. But, he answered immediately.

"Hi, Garret. Sorry to bother you but there's stuff I need to know about my condition."

"Are you asking me as a friend or a doctor?" he fired back rapidly. "Because it's not my specialty."

"A knowledgeable friend." Never mind that it was late at night and my behavior rude, I shamelessly used Garret. It was called *networking*. He'd been in my basement and he was a friend of Marty's. Marty was more than a friend, but not in a known category. While I pondered our connection, Garret grunted, which I accepted as encouragement.

"How much weight can I lift?"

"Please tell me you're not getting ready to bench press a hundred pounds."

"Nope. Have to do some lifting at my job and just wanted to make sure I—"

"No throwing your partner in the air. Do you perform with him?"

"No. I help him rehearse for his Regina routine." I grinned, sensing interest on the other end of the conversation. "Roger's a best friend."

"Who's his partner when he performs?" Garret's voice dropped to a low rumble and I swear I could *hear* his pheromones calling.

"He chooses someone from the audience."

"That could be disastrous," Garret's sharp response had me grinning. Yep, he was interested.

"You'll have to tell him so. I've pointed that out, but Roger does things his way. Meanwhile, what weight limit would you put on my lifting?"

"Nothing heavier than a tray of glasses," he answered. "A

light tray of glasses."

"Thank you, Garret. Sorry I called so late." Not good news but Garret didn't seem to mind at all that I'd called.

"I was going to call you anyway. Marty ask me to schedule an appointment for you with a pre-natal specialist. Do you have a preference?" His answer confirmed Marty had already begun *arranging* things.

"Yes. I prefer to choose my own doctor. Thanks for the offer, but your assistance isn't needed." I started to hang up.

"Wait," Garret said, his voice a low, demanding growl.

"What?"

"Your friend, Roger. Can I have his number?"

"No. But, I'll tell him you asked about him. I'll give him your number if you want. He gets busy. If he doesn't call, you should check out his show some Friday night." I hung up quickly and called Roger.

"What's up?"

"Garret's interested." My matchmaking skills didn't go any further. "Good luck, Roger. It would be nice to have a doctor in the family."

I returned to my own problems.

I didn't know Marty's end game. Sheesh, I didn't even know mine. My stomach knotted on thoughts of going home. Though I'd given Marty a key, I hadn't willingly cohabited with anyone since I was fifteen and departed the group home where I'd lived.

Given Garret's medical advice, once I arrived at the next job, I told the floor manager that I had a touch of the flu.

"I don't feel so hot. Kind of ache all over. I hope I'm not infectious. I don't think I can lift much tonight." My story must have resonated true, because he stepped back, not wanting to catch whatever I had.

"Use the barcode scanner to track inventory instead of shelving boxes for the night. That way you can get in your hours but not give whatever you've got to anyone else." Not that I could, but hey, my excuse worked.

He pulled out his pen, made notes on the duty roster he kept pinned next to the timeclock and said, "Not a problem. I'll give Richards the lift and stack detail this time. She loves the crow's nest."

I hid my disappointment. I liked riding the lifter and looking over the warehouse from the top shelving.

However, the barcode scanner was an easy job and I wasn't complaining. I wouldn't be able to ask for preferential treatment again without saying why. I had a sinking feeling my part time work at Humble Homes would end shortly. I also faced the imminent loss of teaching jobs during the summer months.

With panic nibbling at the edge of my mind, I walked miles through the warehouse, exercising my legs and my thumb. Unfortunately, the mindless task, left my fertile imagination time to revisit sleeping with Marty. My mind probably went there because my body wanted to. My yearning ache to cuddle with him again, translated into some vivid images that kept my mind totally occupied while I worked.

When a row of shelving across the warehouse collapsed, I was jarred from my illicit imaginings. I sprinted down the aisles and across the floor to see what was what. Shit. It was a mess. I arrived in time to help extricate two employees from the wreckage. Neither was dead, both were banged up. Someone called for an ambulance which arrived right before

I clocked off at seven.

I left the building exhausted. The adrenaline rush I'd experienced as I'd raced to the rescue, had fizzled to an end. Marty's Hummer sitting in the parking lot should have pissed me off. Instead, I was profoundly grateful for its presence and for the man leaning against the driver's side, arms crossed, waiting for me.

"Hey, I could have caught a bus for home," I said when I reached the SUV.

"Figured I'd kill two birds with one stone," he drawled. "Came to see if I can use your employee discount to buy a grill. What the hell happened in there?"

"Huh?"

He motioned toward the ambulance, the two stretchers, and the EMT's loading one of them.

"Oh. Shelving collapsed. I was on the other side of the warehouse." I felt immediately defensive as he frowned, studying me.

"Yes, you can use my discount." I agreed quickly to change the subject, then wondered if I'd been maneuvered again. "You're rich. You don't need my discount to buy a grill," I muttered.

"A penny saved is a penny spent elsewhere," he disagreed. "I already picked out the grill. You need to go pay so I can get my discount."

I opened my mouth to tell him I couldn't afford a grill right now but closed it when he handed me a credit card.

"Which grill?" I asked as he drove around to the front of the store.

"They're holding it for us. Smoke already gets a company discount. Add in your employee discount and we're saving eighty bucks on this bad boy."

I'd been working since three the afternoon before. I was hungry, and most of all tired. I wanted to punch him. Instead, I went back into the store, used his card, got the discount, returned with the sales receipt in my hand. "Paid for it."

"I'll take care of business. You rest." He pointed at the Hummer, tailgate open, waiting. I climbed into my ride home, closed my eyes and dozed while he loaded his new toy. At some point, I slept because I woke up when he backed into my driveway and shut the Hummer off.

His arm was around me, my head resting on his chest, my arm around his waist. I'd drooled on his shirt. I saw the wet spot when I sat up.

"Sorry," I murmured, scooting over the seat to get out. I headed for my bed and left him dealing with the box protruding from the back of his vehicle.

Chapter Twelve

Marty

"BOUGHT AN OUTDOOR cooker," I told Jack as soon as he picked up his phone. But I had other things on my mind as I assembled the grill.

"Is that right? What kind? Gas, charcoal, or wood?"

"One side uses charcoal or wood, the other side cooks with gas. The clerk sold me a tank of propane to go with it." I'd arrived at the employee entrance too early, so I'd driven around the building and filled in the time checking out the store front wares—a long row of grills, every shape and size.

I'd needed an excuse for being at Holly's place of employment, and grills offered a perfect reason. I'd already made my choice and had my card out ready for the buy when an ambulance streaked through the parking lot and circled to the back of the store. I'd left the clerk holding the sales ticket and promised to come back.

"What's on the menu?" Jack's question called me back to the immediate.

"Steaks. Buy a pile of thick cut. See if you can get some wholesale from Church."

"He'll cry."

"Yeah. Invite him. Tell him I'll wait till I see his bald head before I grill the first piece of meat."

The truth was, I didn't want to leave here. I'd had one of my paranoia fits when I'd seen the ambulance at her job. I'd driven around the building and jumped out of my ride, ready to infiltrate the E.M.T.'s before I'd spotted her coming out a different door.

"Had a scare. Before we go out of town, I need to get things settled. Bring some beer. Some food. We'll talk."

"I'll call the guys. Are you telling your girl, or is this a surprise?"

My girl. I wish. I snorted at the idea. Before he ended the conversation, he managed to remind me I didn't call the shots here. Guess it was time to test the limits of my lease.

I planned to tell her we were having company when she woke. The way she was under, I could see she was exhausted. No way was I waking her up. For a while I sat in the chair next to the bed and watched her sleep. I knew it broke several of her rules.

But, checking on her health was different. I wanted to make certain she wasn't in a coma or unconscious. Her skin had a rosy bloom. Her lips were pursed in a half smile as if her dreams were sweet. She didn't look sick. She looked asleep.

After I made sure she was breathing I noticed she barely moved under the light bedcovers. I mean her position didn't shift at all. Since I floundered all over a mattress like a drowning whale, her stillness fascinated me.

Anyway, Jack arrived with supplies and I quit guarding her rest while we set up outside. When seating became a problem, we had to adjust, and the Hummer made a few trips in and out of the drive. It was a good thing she slept soundly. I'm guessing it was the music blaring that finally brought her awake.

Holly

MY HOUSE HAD been invaded while I slept. I woke to the sound of voices, the smell of barbecued meat drifting in the air, and the startling realization that I wasn't alone. I'd been totally wiped when I'd crashed. I vaguely remembered Marty's grill purchase which seemed to answer the question of who'd taken over my backyard.

I lay in the bed, trying to decide my mood. Without question my renter was pushing the boundaries of our agreement. On the other hand, I wondered if he'd feed his landlord. My stomach growled to the beat of the music playing below.

I slid out of bed, smoothed the sheet and comforter, plumped the pillow, and headed for the shower. Clean, hair dried, and dressed, I followed the aroma of charcoal and steak downstairs and to the kitchen where I paused to peer out the window.

Yep, I had company. Besides Marty, I counted six more big men plus Jack, Marty's father-in-law, and Garret all standing around an ice filled barrel holding bottles of beer. Maybe because Megan sat next to her *friend* on a picnic bench attached to a long table holding covered bowls, plastic cutlery, napkins, and assorted two-liter bottles of soda, I didn't freak.

I felt remarkably calm as I surveyed my backyard. A few new Adirondack chairs had been arranged in a semi-circle around the grill, and Harley-Jane occupied one of them.

Several other unknown females sat in the others. I recognized Gable Matthews as one of the men drinking beer and talking to Marty.

While I watched, Church, a.k.a. the bartender from Church's Bar & Grill, carried a large platter filled with steaks and set it in the middle of the table.

Two children and a woman I'd never seen before had been swinging. When the main course arrived, the mom hopped from the swing and led the boy and girl toward the men. One of the big guys met them, lifted the boy onto his shoulders, and picked up the girl. Slinging an arm around the woman, he herded her toward the table. The crowd converged.

I wondered if there'd be anything left if I decided to fight my way to the food. When Marty looked at the window and caught me peering outside, he motioned me to join them.

Huh, nice of him to invite me to the party. When I remained fixed in front of the window, he left the group of men and strode toward the backdoor.

"I've got a plate with your name on it," he growled as soon as he entered the kitchen.

If I intended to complain, now was the time. I turned to face him, casually leaning against the sink as I met his gaze. His expression changed.

"Come here," he said gruffly.

Geez. My nipples went on point. *What the hell is this?* "Why?" I stalled. So much for my aloof indifference. Lust instead of blood pumped through my veins, heat pooled low in my belly, and my womb literally clenched.

"We need to talk."

Shit. Talking was not on my agenda.

"About what?"

"Us. Work. Your schedule. My schedule. Us."

I opened my mouth to tell him there was no *us,* but couldn't quite choke out the lie. Oh yeah, there was a Marty, there was a Holly, and, growing in my tummy, there was the conjunction tying us together.

I didn't feel pregnant. I felt horny as hell. I wanted to jump his bones. Instead, I shrugged and, turning my back on him, walked to the refrigerator. The weight of his stare blanketed me, made me breathless, and I resisted the urge to run. The question in my mind though was, should I run toward or away from him.

I reached for the fridge handle. He moved, the floor shifted under him. It was no surprise when his body heat and scent announced his presence before he wrapped an arm around my waist, drawing me back. My butt fit against his groin perfectly. It was difficult, but I resisted the urge to grind against his package.

I'd pulled on a pair of running shorts and an oversized tee. He slid his hand under my top and up my torso, cupping my breast, kneading it while he pressed his hard-on against my behind.

"You listening?" he growled in my ear and pinched my nipple. Well that got my attention, but not the kind he was after.

"No fair," I panted.

"Fair," he muttered, nibbling on my ear lobe before he sucked on it. When he turned me, so my back rested against the refrigerator door, I resisted the urge to jump up and wrap my legs around his waist.

I focused on his mouth instead of meeting his gaze.

"I think we should rewrite the lease agreement to include the master bedroom, specifically me *and* you in the bed." He stated his opinion in one long growl that didn't end when his lips covered mine. Only the growl became a rumble that vibrated through me by way of the chest plastered to my breasts.

I tore my mouth away long enough to mutter, "Fat chance."

He huffed in laughter, stretched my wrists above my head, and proceeded to nuzzle my neck.

"What the crap *is happening?*" I gave up asking nicely. My garbled question ended when he took my mouth again, and this time he used his tongue. He went so deep, I thought I'd strangle on it. No, I was choking on the pheromones resonating inside me.

Oh God. He pressed against me and nudged my thighs apart, sharing his *real* reason for our conversation. His stance shifted, he held my wrists in one hand, and cupped my breast with the other. Liquid heat gathered between my legs. This was ridiculous.

He slid his hand down to my crotch and I struggled to release myself from his grip.

"There are people outside." My snarl sounded more like a whimper. My nipples were completely stiff, topping already sensitive breasts. They itched, and I *needed* to rub them against his chest. Lower on my body, his hand lazily stroked between my legs, feeding the ache growing there.

He didn't free me, though he dropped his hold on my arms and used his extra hand to cradle the back of my head as he deepened his kiss.

Someplace along the line I wound my arms around his

neck as my body took control, absorbing pleasure through every pore. I leaned into his touch, grinding against his fingers…

"Harder," I moaned into his mouth, willing him to obey.

"Oh yeah," he muttered, and his gruff voice only made me hotter. As if he knew I teetered on the precipice, he renewed pressure on my clit, releasing my mouth long enough to whisper, "Come for me baby."

Skyrockets went off. I mean I flew apart. Thanks to his pressing, and rubbing, and groaning into my mouth, I had an off-the-charts orgasm that left me sated, pliant in his arms and totally vulnerable.

While my legs threatened collapse, he held me against his body, rested his chin on the top of my head, cuddling me against his chest while I caught my breath and waited for my legs to stop trembling. He stroked my hair, patted my back, and hummed, making this deep sound of contentment that rumbled under my ear.

I don't know how long we stood that way. It was long enough for me to gather my senses. Back in my right mind, I stood in his embrace, breathed his scent, and felt his hard length pressing against my mound. Not nudging, pushing, or insisting. But he was big and ready.

"Marty. You're needed outside."

Whoa. I didn't know which crew member stood in the doorway, but Marty sighed and gave me a squeeze.

"Busted."

"I need to use the bathroom," I managed through lips puffy from his kisses.

He leaned his forehead against mine. "You all right?"

"Yeah," I lied. "Just need to uh, refresh, you know."

He kissed my forehead and stepped aside. I rushed into the downstairs john, put the lid down on the toilet, and sat. I felt a little dizzy, embarrassed, and really tired which was stupid since I'd just slept nine hours.

I needed to cry but I wasn't sure why. I stood and peered at my reflection. I looked pretty much the same. No scarlet *A* stamped on my forehead from having sex against a refrigerator. Well not full sex. But sex. *Geez, I came.*

"And he's going," I muttered, splashing water on my face to get my brain firing. Our arrangement wasn't going to work. This was way too personal for me.

I intended to refund his rent and send him on his way when I reentered the kitchen. But he'd left the room, and his go-bag sat on the table, suggesting his imminent departure. Before I joined him in the great outdoors, I inspected the bag's contents.

Hmmm… Clothes. My stomach growled, announcing its disinterest, and that seemed as good an excuse as any to follow him to the backyard.

"Hey, I like your place." Harley-Jane waved me over to her and handed me a plate as soon as she saw me. "Marty says he rented a room from you. You'll be amazed at how much work you can get out of him while he's bunking here." Janie's easy acceptance made my weird situation seem almost normal.

"How do you take your steak?" Church manned the grill while Marty and the other men, huddled up for a meeting.

"Medium."

Harley-Jane nudged me toward the assorted bowls which proved to be potato salad in an iced down bowl, baked beans in a pan covered in tin foil, and a heap of roasted corn on the cob.

"Better eat dessert first if you're going to have any," Janie suggested eyeing the last piece of apple pie and an almost empty bowl of crushed strawberries.

While I hesitated, she darted forward, claimed the pie, cut a piece of golden sponge cake, drizzled the remaining strawberries over the top, and paused by the whipped cream. "Yes?"

Embarrassed at my own gluttony, I nodded approval as she piled on the sweet topping. "Midnight snack," I told her, wrapping the plate in plastic wrap. "I'll put this in the fridge and be right back."

The steak and fixings were great. Megan slid in beside me, I introduced her to Harley-Jane, and they talked while I ate.

Most of their discussion centered on speculation about the meeting taking place.

"They might be leaving early for New Mexico. I hope not."

"Gable said it's a government job," Harley Jane offered.

"They'll be on the ground fighting fire where ever they are," Megan said. Both women frowned.

I decided to listen in on the meeting. I stood, grabbed the back of an unoccupied chair, and dragged it toward the crew's powwow zone.

"Did you need something, Holly?" Marty asked.

"I'm good," I answered and plopped myself down. He nodded, continued talking to the men, and pretty much ignored me. I studied him as much as I eavesdropped.

The upshot of the whole thing was, I didn't have to evict Marty; he was leaving today. Janie had been right about their destination. New Mexico. Twelve thousand acres of forested area on fire, with a hundred men already on the ground, and less than ten percent containment.

Their plans had been moved forward and a government plane awaited their departure. The men were grim-faced, the women tense.

I understood enough to know Smoke, Inc. had been hired to penetrate the interior of the fire zone. According to Marty's plan, they'd use explosives and foam to create a control line. Then they'd parachute into the cleared zone and fight the fire from the inside moving toward the firefighters already on the outer perimeter. It sounded dangerous. Janie's expression telegraphed her terror.

The afternoon picnic ended with crew and families leaving. Gable and Janie were first to go. Everyone else followed quickly. I half-expected Megan to stay, but she said, "I'll call you later," before she left with Teague.

As the charcoal turned to ash, Marty tidied the backyard then went into the house. When he re-emerged, he carried the duffel bag in one hand and an envelope in the other.

"Take care of yourself, Little Bit," he growled, pulling me close.

Little Bit? What kind of a nickname was that for someone my size? Did he have me confused with Kit again? I didn't have time to ask before he tilted my head and kissed me silly. When he let me, I came up for air, and of course, he had orders ready.

"Instructions inside. Behave." He wore his bossy frown as he shoved the envelope in my hand.

Behave? I felt an aching emptiness as I watched him walk through the gate, climb into his Hummer, and drive away, leaving me wondering how he'd managed to become such a huge part of my world in such a short period of time.

I sat in the swing and surveyed my kingdom. Except for the new lawn furniture and grill, the backyard showed no evidence of the gathering. Not so much as a napkin or plastic fork had been left behind.

The swing creaked as I pushed higher, closing my eyes, enjoying the breeze on my face. I still held the envelope in my hand. I opened my eyes and stared at it. As if he had a hidden spy camera monitoring my activities, which given Marty's controlling instincts seemed possible, my cell phone rang.

Marty

"WHAT?" SHE ANSWERED on the first ring like she'd been expecting me.

"Did you read through the contents of the envelope yet?" I asked. Long pause. I could almost see her looking at the sealed envelope. No surprise in her answer.

"No."

"Well open it." It had occurred to me as I'd readied to leave, that I needed to secure my kid's future before I jumped again. I didn't intend to die, but if I did, the little fellow would be taken care of.

"Do you have a spy-cam on me, for Pete's sake? Monitoring me somehow?"

"No. Why, someone bothering you?"

"You are. What do you want? You just left here. I thought you were going out of town."

"I'm getting ready to depart. Knew you'd sit on that envelope and do nothing with it. Read through it. Elaine expects to hear from you tonight. She'll give you your schedule." I've found that telling people what to do works well. Most would rather get along than argue. Holly demonstrated loudly she wasn't most people.

"You have clearly lost your mind. I have my own schedule, thank you. And why would Elaine try to give me one? Never mind. I don't want to know."

"Insurance. Yours sucks. You said so yourself. Mine doesn't. I can't insure the kid without insuring the mother he's gestating in. So, you work for Smoke Inc., now. After Junior's born we'll figure out something else."

"You're claiming me on your insurance?"

"I hired you. Elaine's cutting the papers now. She'll tell you when to report and what documents she needs—"

She hung up on me.

That went well.

Chapter Thirteen
Holly

*H*IGH MAINTENANCE. I'D called it the first time we met. Marty required a lot of attention. After I hung up on him, he tried to call back. I didn't answer. Then another number popped up.

"What?" I asked, half laughing.

"You've been avoiding me, Marilyn." I almost dropped my phone as I hurried to block the caller. *Geez-Louise, how did he get this new number?*

I shut the phone off and pulled out the dessert tray I'd stashed earlier in the day. After gorging on apple pie and strawberry shortcake, I went to bed.

Maybe it was the late dessert, the forty winks earlier, or all the changes Marty intended to foist on me. Or maybe it was the idea of some creepy guy getting my new number.

For whatever reason, I couldn't sleep and suddenly had a love hate relationship with my phone, fearful of getting a call at the same time, unreasonably disappointed when Marty didn't try again.

He's working, idiot. Get real. I lighted a scented candle and stood in front of my kitchen window, drinking a cup of morning brew and studiously ignoring Marty's sealed envelope on my counter.

The force of his personality was such, I felt his will, urging me to get on with things and open it; at the same time, I considered using the candle to burn it without reading the contents.

Who knows how long my schizoid-duel would have lasted if a knock on my front door hadn't interrupted my meditations. I had no idea who could be visiting me that early.

I went from alarmed to pissed-off when I peered through the spy-hole and recognized Marty's employee.

I'd never officially met the older woman waiting on the porch, but we'd encountered each other when I'd gone to Marty's office to return his hundred dollars. She'd been the woman wearing purple tweed.

"Good morning," she said as soon as I opened the door a crack. I decided, playing dumb was my best option, so I pretended to not recognize her.

"I don't donate to religious solicitations," I answered politely and edged the crack closer to closed.

"I'm Elaine, Marty's personal assistant and your ride to the office. Marty suggested that I pick you up since you don't drive." Her smile didn't reach her eyes as she studied me. I didn't bother to hide my scowl.

"I told Mr. Jones when we last spoke that I appreciate his job offer but I'm already employed. I'm sorry you've made a trip for nothing." I started to close the door the final inch when she stopped me.

"May I use your restroom?" Cagy lady, she'd decided to prolong the agony. Nodding, I stepped back, inviting her to enter and then led the way to the bathroom off the kitchen.

Moments later, I heard her emerge from the bathroom,

but remained at the window with my back turned, hoping she'd take the hint and just leave.

"Coffee isn't good for the baby," she said behind me, her voice laden with disapproval.

How old is too old to sass? My mother would have washed my mouth out for disrespecting an elderly woman. Elaine didn't really come off as elderly, but I remained silent in Mom's memory. Nevertheless, words fought to get past my lips.

"Before I make the trip back to the office, we need to talk." She seemed intent on making me feel guilty. Not happening. I'd allowed her use of my lavatory. I didn't invite her to spend the day with me.

"I've gone ahead and made an appointment for you to see Dr. Lily Spencer this week. It would have been better had I been able to speak to you first to confirm your availability. Since you're now working for Smoke, Inc., we can adjust your schedule to fit your medical needs."

I glared at her image in the window glass.

"I tried to call. You didn't answer so I'm here." She set her briefcase on the table and pulled a laptop from it. Reluctantly, I turned to face her.

"How did you get my number?"

"Marty, of course."

"Did you give my number to anyone else?" My phone stalker had jarred me more than I realized.

"Of course not. Personnel information is strictly privileged."

"I don't work for Marty's company so I'm not personnel," I corrected her. "Thank you for your concern but I'll make an appointment with a doctor I choose. I'd like you to go now."

The truth was, I'd been stalling. I couldn't even say why. I knew I needed to find a doctor and… Everything was just so complicated now. I could feel panic welling from the pit of my stomach. As soon as Marty's quarterback left the field, I'd go to my closet. But she didn't leave.

Instead, she shrugged off her jacket, draped it over the back of a kitchen chair, removed a cup from my mug tree, popped a pod into my Keurig, made herself a cup of coffee, and took a seat at the table.

"Marty's paternity rights allow him to cover the baby's healthcare needs, i.e. he's covering yours." Dragon-lady stared me in the eyes, daring me to argue.

Since I didn't know whether I was being bullied with legal authority or just bluff, I kept my mouth shut. What I didn't need was sued on top of everything else.

When I didn't tell her to get out, she nodded and opened her laptop. "I'll just go ahead and fill out your paperwork while I'm here today," While I fidgeted, trying to decide what to do next, she focused on a form on the screen.

"All right," I said. "What's it going to take to get you to leave?"

"Birth date, name of parents, medical history, work history, number of siblings, social security number." She rattled off those items quickly, flipped screens on her laptop, and waited expectantly.

"Birthday, October 20, 1988. No parents. No siblings. No medical history because I'm healthy. My work history isn't pertinent." I gave her the answers I wanted to share and reeled off my social security number before adding, "Now you can go." My personal history didn't belong to anyone but me.

Even so long after I'd lost everyone, I had to steel myself to keep from blubbering at the memory. I clenched my teeth and willed my eyes to remain dry as I stared at the woman demanding information.

"You're an orphan?" Elaine had the finesse of a rhinoceros.

"Yes." I most definitely was, and having been on my own since I was fourteen, I didn't take to being interrogated by anyone, especially Marty's secretary.

"How pregnant are you?" Her suspicious look spoke volumes.

"One hundred percent," I answered pertly. Technically the possibility was a smidgen lower, but not by much. Elaine glowered at me.

Ah hah. Not my fan. Hmm... I had to think a moment. "Okay, two months, five days, three hours," I looked at the clock, "and ten seconds."

"Are you really? Do not do this to him if it's not true. I won't allow it."

"You're his personal security detail, right?"

"His office assistant. I've been with him for years," she said stiffly. "He's like a son to me. I..." She teared up. "Please don't be stubborn and make me worry about you, which makes him worry about you, which takes his mind off what he needs to be doing—staying alive while he and the rest of the crew fight the fire."

Well, okay, putting it like that I suppose that makes her a grandma of sorts. I sat across from her, gazing at this addition to the baby's family. I was not inclined to like her.

Oh boy, the kid isn't even here, and I already have surrogate in-law problems. "I wasn't wrong. Marty is high maintenance." I answered because I didn't want Elaine crying in my kitchen.

"I only know what Garret, wearing his doctor hat, said, plus two pregnancy kits confirmed. I'm operating on the assumption that they were right."

"Then you should already be following a healthy diet," she answered, glancing at the mug next to me.

"I am," I muttered sounding defensive. Then I remembered I was twenty-nine, she was a guest in my house, and I didn't owe her any courtesy beyond what I'd already extended.

"Coffee is not..." Her words stuttered to a halt as she peered into the mug I pushed across the table. "That's milk."

"Yes, it is. You smelled coffee when you barged in because, before you helped yourself to a cup of what I can't have, I'd already lit the java scented candle to supplement my morning milk break."

"I'm sorry." She stood, tendering her apology. I nodded my acceptance and silently willed her to be gone.

"The appointment with Dr. Spencer is tomorrow. Call the number on the back to confirm." She handed me a card and added, "I'll pick you up in the morning."

If she'd offered instead of going all commando on me, I might have agreed. Also, her smug expression made me question her earlier teary-eyed look. She'd obviously learned her manipulation skills from Marty.

"I have transportation covered," I told her. Which I did. I intended to catch the city bus.

"Who's taking you?"

"I'll walk to the corner and ride the bus. I want and need

exercise and if you show up, you'll be sitting in a car by yourself. Elaine, get a grip. Whatever you usually do for Marty, go back to doing it."

She made unhappy noises, but I remained firm. I'd take myself to the physician Marty had chosen, and if I didn't like that doctor, I'd find my own.

When she finally left, I locked the front door behind her and then for added protection from an ambush attack, locked the back door as well.

Between the poor sleep the night before and her conversation I was worn out again. But more than that, I was distraught. I could feel the pressure building inside me. I headed for the closet and opened the door. Things had been shifted around. I flipped on the light.

"I don't believe this." The closet had been fitted with a bench. It had a note pinned to the seat.

Holly, I'm not trying to intrude. I just want you to be comfortable when you come here to think. ~ Respectfully, Marty.

I retreated to the kitchen, grabbed my phone, dialed Marty's number, and walked toward the closet.

"You've invaded my personal space. You had a party in my backyard while I slept, your secretary showed up this morning to nag me about seeing a doctor, and now I find out you've even redecorated my..." I fumbled for the right term. Sacred retreat? Hiding spot? Mental therapy zone? "Stop. Just stop."

"You found the bench," he said as soon as I shut up. "I shouldn't have messed with your think tank. I'm sorry. Won't happen again."

All the sizzle went out of me and I deflated like a punctured balloon. I should have hung up, but I could hear a lot of noise with an overlay of male voices in the background. "Where are you?"

"Helicopter transport."

"Transporting as in, taking you to the fire?" I asked.

"Yep. You won't be able to reach me soon. If you need anything, call Elaine."

Great, one more thing to worry about. I frowned at the phone.

"So, do you like the bench?" He reminded me of the reason why I'd called him.

I stepped into the closet, closed the door, pulled the dangling cord to shut off the light, and sat on the padded bench. I couldn't help myself, I giggled.

"You like it, right?" he growled in my ear.

"Where did you get the cushion?"

"Picked it up while I was waiting for… when I was grill shopping."

I heard him switch gears. Okay, he'd been there waiting for me to get off work. I'd already surmised that. Marty wasn't exactly subtle. But, since I'd rented him a room and he was currently flying away from me, the home invasion scenario didn't really apply.

"So how dangerous is this job you're on?" I drew up my legs and leaned my back against the side wall, squirming to make myself comfortable.

"On a scale of one-to-ten, with *one* being the least dangerous and *ten* being an inferno, this is a fifteen," he answered casually. While I was digesting that, he attacked.

"Elaine said she had to pry answers out of you for the insurance upgrade. What the hell is the big deal? You need better insurance to cover the cost of that woman doctor I found for you. I don't want you cutting corners on healthcare. That's my kid you're gestating." Obviously, Elaine kept Marty informed via speed dial.

"You're ruining the calming closet effect. All I want to do is reach through the phone and smack you upside the head. And I'm seriously rethinking our rental agreement."

"What the hell is wrong now?" he asked gruffly.

"Are you related to Elaine? Because frankly, you share the same bossy gene."

"No blood kin." His rough laughter followed his admission. "But yeah, she's a cross you'll have to bear. And Jack is too. He'll be by before long to stake his claim. The kid won't be shy of babysitters and places to stay."

"My baby will not be staying with anyone I don't approve." I didn't want to quarrel but enough with the pushing.

"Elaine says your people are dead. That so?"

I blanched at his question. When I didn't answer, he said, "Well are they?"

"Yes. I don't talk about it so drop the subject."

"Not before I get your promise to go see the new doctor and share any pertinent information needed." Marty's technique of getting what he wanted, kept me teetering on the edge of indecision. As he downplayed the dangerous nature of his work, he also focused his interrogation skills on me.

I fielded his subtle and not so subtle suggestions bordering on orders concerning the doctor. I considered telling him about my phone stalker, but, remembering Elaine's reference to his dangerous work, I figured he didn't need me yammering negatives in his ear since he was about to jump into a raging forest fire.

"I'll see your suggested physician. But, if I don't like the doctor, I'll find someone else." Having stated my position, I changed the subject. I'd tried not to think about Marty's work. But, remembering Harley-Jane's terror, I asked, "Is Gable okay?"

"Landed on his target and got us set up. Tell Janie he's in the safety zone." He laughed again, and I wondered if there was such a thing where they were.

"Take care," I told him, eager to sign off and *not* think about Marty. But he had other ideas.

"Hey, I'll call you tomorrow after your appointment. And I'll see you when I get home," he growled. "Meanwhile…" The deep timbre of his voice sent shivers up my spine. "Think about us in the kitchen, me touching you, and taking you to heaven."

"Why?" I whispered as a blush heated my cheeks and a twist of desire pulsed in my core.

"Because when I get home, baby doll, I'd like to visit heaven again." His gruff words made my insides clench remembering, or anticipating, I wasn't sure which, probably both. "You going to think of me when you curl up alone in that big bed tonight?"

"Hmmm," I managed as I headed upstairs, ready for *later* now.

Chapter Fourteen
Marty

WHEN COWBOY SHOVED his box of equipment toward the door, I realized I'd gotten so caught up in my conversation with Holly, we were circling the drop area already. A couple of the guys smirked knowingly at me, and Gable gave me a thumbs-up, then jumped. I watched him land, then said my goodbyes, ready for my own launch. As it was, I'd almost enjoyed the hurly-bird ride that preceded our jump into hell.

I hadn't pushed my luck and nagged at her about working for Smoke, Inc. *I'll do that later when I call.* Cowboy had our equipment out of the boxes and setup in the clearing he'd targeted by the time the rest of us landed. We'd been slated to relieve a hotshot crew, but they stayed on the ground with us when the fucking wind shifted, threatening to obliterate all their work.

We spelled the local team while they took a much-needed break. The Smoke crew fought side-by-side. Drought conditions had left the underbrush nothing more than dried tinder; heat lightning set off new patches of flames as thirty mile-an-hour gusts kept the blaze from being contained.

It was easy to lose track of time as we fought the flames. But every moment of the battle, I thought about the call I'd make to Holly when I took a break at the end of the second day. *Am I going to be a dad?*

Holly

I WOKE EARLY, showered, dressed, and left the house to avoid any of Marty's crew. I made it to the bus stop unscathed and hopped off at the corner next to the correct medical building.

With an hour to kill before my doctor's appointment, I found a coffee shop for breakfast. I didn't eat much since my stomach was too full of *what-ifs* and anxiety flutters to allow for hunger. I stalled as long as I could, and finally made my way into the building.

Plush carpet, soothing music, and a receptionist whose main concern seemed to be to make me comfortable, greeted me when I stepped into the physician's office. She ushered me to a private room, and got the blood pressure, weight, and paperwork out of the way.

I needn't have worried about paying. Elaine had sent ahead the insurance information, and all I had to do was confirm and sign. This I did, feeling queasy as I shared information again.

"Remove everything and slip into this for your exam. Dr. Spencer will be right with you." The receptionist handed me a soft, terrycloth robe, and left.

"Well, la dee da," I muttered. The robe, the kind expensive spas and five-star hotels provide for their guests, impressed me more than the office.

As soon as I removed my clothes and put on the robe,

the receptionist returned. Evidently, she was also a nurse.

"The doctor will be with you in a moment. I'm just going to draw some blood for your preliminary lab work." She whipped out her equipment, slid my sleeve above my elbow, found a vein, and took her sample before I could muster a squeak of surprise.

Dr. Spencer arrived, introduced herself, and proceeded with the examination. She asked me questions about my diet, work habits, sleep patterns, menstrual cycle, sexual activity, and feelings about having a baby.

"What was your first thought when you found out?"

Really, that was a tough question. I'd had a lot of incoherent thoughts but…

"I wondered if my baby would inherit my grandmother's green thumb."

She smiled at my answer and pointed at the examination table. "Time for the dreaded probe," she announced. But I must admit, the cringe part of the appointment didn't turn out to be that bad.

"So, what do you see?" I asked when she'd donned her head lamp and peered up inside me.

"We'll talk in my office," she answered, patted my hip, handed the nurse the swabbed material she'd collected, and left. After I redressed, the nurse/receptionist ushered me into an elegant sitting room circa 1800.

Oak floor, heavy drapes open on each side of high mullioned windows, velvet covered reclining couch, and a mahogany table with three chairs. A basket holding a variety of rolls adorned the middle of the table. A tray of cookies and a silver urn sat beside it.

"I hope you like hot chocolate," the nurse said and invited me to sit. My earlier scanty breakfast betrayed me as I stared at the delicate cup decorated with whipped cream and a cherry on top.

"Make yourself comfortable. Dr. Spencer will join you as soon as your lab work is complete."

"Oh. I didn't plan to stay for hours." I didn't mean to be churlish but my shift at the sports bar started at four, and I had other things to do before I went to work. "You can call me with the results." I gave the hot chocolate a regretful last look and started to turn away.

"We have our own lab. Fifteen minutes. Have a cookie," the nurse urged.

I was on my third crescent when the doctor arrived, diagnosis in hand.

She sat in the chair across from me, poured herself a cup of hot chocolate from the silver urn, and smiled with pleasure as she sipped from the dainty cup.

"You're going to have a baby."

In spite of my warning them away, both Jack and Elaine were waiting when I came out of the building.

"Well?" Elaine asked when I approached the car on her side.

"What Dr. Spencer had to say is my business and Marty's," I told her.

"He'll be in the field. Doubt you can raise him on the phone tonight," Jack offered.

"He said he'd call me. If he doesn't, he won't know whether he's gonna be a dad or not until he does." I glared at them and turned toward the bus stop.

"Aw, for fuck's sake," Jack snarled. "Get in the car and we'll drive you home."

Geez, I barely knew Marty, but his family had already adopted me—whether I wanted them or not.

✦ ✦ ✦

"I CAN'T TALK long, baby doll. What's the verdict?" Marty asked when he called that night.

"I'm pregnant," I told him, feeling unexpectedly breathless. Silence greeted my announcement, and my inner warmth began to chill. I guess it had been easy for him to be supportive when the baby was theoretical.

"Okay," he finally said, his voice raspy. "I don't want to be pushy, but I'm laying down some rules."

What now? I braced myself for an argument.

"I'm going to take care of you. That means you're giving up working three jobs, starting with the manual labor gig at Humble Homes."

Well, the fierce words I'd been about to spew, withered on my lips. "Uhh, I already did that."

"Did you get your vitamins?"

"Yes."

"How are you feeling?"

"Tyrannized. Explain to me how to rid myself of your office pest." Marty's laughter was my answer.

"Elaine is my personal assistant. She organizes all the company's information into nice manageable bites a dunderhead like me can comprehend."

"She doesn't take direction well."

"Funny, she said the same thing about you. Don't scare her off. I couldn't run the company without her. I know she's a royal pain in the ass; nevertheless, she's necessary."

"I don't need her organizing my life."

"I don't know. She signed you up for company insurance and nagged you into seeing a doctor. So, how do you feel?"

I'd forgotten how single tracked and focused Marty could be. When his focus was keeping me comfortable, it was almost endearing.

"First off, I found out pretty fast that morning sickness isn't restricted to mornings," I grumbled. "And your family, as in Jack and Elaine, are both…" I couldn't find the words to describe the unrepentant busy-bodies.

"Yeah, they're all that," Marty agreed and laughed. "Welcome to my world." Then he added, "Wish I could be there to hold you while you puke." His unromantic offer made me grin.

"What's that noise?" I asked as the dull roar became a loud roar in the background.

"That's why I've got to go, sweet cheeks. Breaks over. Behave."

"Be safe," I whispered after he disconnected.

✧   ✧   ✧

THERE WERE SO many changes going on in my life, I couldn't keep up with them all.

After my condition was confirmed, Elaine began showing up at my house every day like clockwork. At first, I resented her presence. But, after the first barfing event, it didn't take long for me to understand Marty's loyalty to her.

"If men had to go through this, humans would be extinct," she'd said grimly when I hadn't made it to the bathroom in time and had puked all over the kitchen floor. She'd cleaned up my mess while I'd been sitting on the closed lid of the commode, too weak to do more than rinse my mouth and wipe off my face.

After I'd staggered back to the kitchen, she'd *mothered* me. It was hard to get uppity with someone who rubbed my back.

Not that Elaine and I were suddenly sisters under the skin. But, after that, we managed detente. Unfortunately, having let down my barriers allowing Marty's secretary access to my life, my unfettered existence quickly became entangled.

For the first visit, when I'd accepted Jack's ride from the doctor's office to the house, I'd sat in the back and left Elaine and Jack to talk to each other. After that, though, I'd rejected his regular chauffeur services when they were offered.

"No. Just no. I prefer walking to the bus stop." And when Marty gave me flack in one of his calls, I said, "Medically speaking, I need the physical activity since I've had to quit most of my jobs where I got plenty of exercise."

I'd not yet made peace with Jack. Him being Marty's father-in-law, I felt awkward around him. It wasn't exactly like Marty was stepping out on the old guy's daughter, but I still felt like a scarlet woman when he was near.

Having turned down a ride for the second visit to the doctor's office, I thought that was the end of the matter.

Not so. I took the bus on the day of my appointment and arrived without a problem. Afterward, when I left the medical building, I walked to the light at the crosswalk and waited for the light to change. I was thinking about baby stuff, Marty stuff, work stuff, and stuff in general, instead of paying attention. *Okay, sue me.*

Anyway, the light changed, I started to cross the street, and the next thing I knew, someone grabbed the neck of my shirt and hauled me back onto the sidewalk.

Being assaulted that way scared the bejesus out of me. I reacted by pivoting and plowing my fist into my attacker's face. Jack's face.

I couldn't believe he'd been following me and I hadn't even known he was there.

"What do you think you're doing?" I yelled. I'd been in the path of the vehicle and I had that hollow feeling in the pit of my stomach a near death experience tends to bring. So, my voice reflected my panic as well as my being pissed.

"Damned minivan almost got you," he'd snarled back, rubbing his jaw.

He didn't like it that I'd caught him off guard and popped him in the face. I didn't like it that he'd grabbed me, and I hadn't even known he was there.

I let him drive me home because we were both shaken. But I told him I'd be walking in the future, just the same. I didn't realize Jack spent his day loitering outside the edge of my property until the first time I took an Elaine-break to walk to the store.

"Want a lift?" There he was, leaning against his Ford Explorer.

"No thank you. I need the exercise."

He nodded. Instead, he crept along in the SUV, driving at a snail's pace beside me and speeding up to remain parallel when I jogged.

I finally walked to the vehicle and knocked on the window. He rolled it down.

"Why are you following me?"

"Security detail." And he said that with a straight face. "You're accident prone."

"I don't need a bodyguard.'"

"I'm not guarding you." He glared at me.

"Then go home, wherever that is. Not back to my house."

"You almost got run over," he reminded me. "I'm not guarding you. I'm babysitting Marty's kid."

"I can't believe you just said that." I gave him the evil-eye, guaranteed to make the meanest seventh grade hoodlum squirm in his seat. Jack's face got red.

"Aww, come on. Get in. If you don't let me give you a ride, Elaine will report to Marty I'm not earning my keep."

I seriously doubted that Elaine would tattle on Jack. Then again, I glanced over my shoulder at the house. Even from this far up the street I could see her staring out the window at us.

"I'll ride back with you," I promised, then turned to jog up the street at a faster clip than I'd been going. It felt wonderful. I'd really been slacking off and this was my wake-up call to get in shape before…

I slowed down. Dr. Spencer had recommended exercise, I'd have to check with her to find out how much was allowed. Still… I rested my hand on my belly hoping the baby would feel the excitement and not the jarring as I jogged. I cut through the park to lose my tail and arrived at the store long before Jack arrived. I'd already picked up bread, milk, and Elaine's lottery tickets when he pulled up.

I slid into the SUV, set the bags on the floorboards, and buckled up. He backed out of the parking spot and nodded.

"I knew your granddad," he said without warning.

"You don't know who my grandfather was, so I doubt that."

He gave me a sideways look. "You told Marty your granddad owned the house before you. Being curious, I did a title search and bingo. Took me a while because that house is fifty-two years old and it's been through a lot of hands. But, as soon as I saw the original owner, I knew. You're Cap Carpenter's grandkid."

Yep, that was me. I didn't say anything. I didn't share my personal business. Jack on the other hand, didn't mind discussing it with me. He'd been digging all right.

"Holly Anna Carpenter. Only child of William and Anna Smith Carpenter. Parents deceased, killed when a tractor-trailer jackknifed and crushed their car."

I closed my eyes, trying not to think about that time.

"You were nine. Tough time for a kid to be orphaned."

"Well actually Jack, any age is a tough one to be orphaned."

"Happened to you twice, didn't it?"

"You seem to know everything. You're welcome to my memories. I don't visit them often."

"Well that's the thing, Holly. You should. I knew Cap when he worked for the Pittsburgh Fire Dept. Hell, Elaine knew him. She used to sit in on the firehouse poker games."

I snorted, trying to suppress my laugh.

"I lost track of Cap. He retired, I found work outside the state. We lost touch. But, he was a good man. You should be proud of him."

"I *am* proud of him. Granddad was a wonderful man. I lived with him for five years until he had a heart attack. He was walking out of the bank up town. People forgot I lived with him. It was a couple of days before anyone remembered and thought to tell me why he hadn't come home."

"How old were you?"

"Jack, I've put the past behind me and I'm happy to let it remain there."

He pulled into the driveway and parked before answering me.

"The way I see it, you've got the same problem as Marty. You lost everybody who you loved, and decided you weren't going to go down that road again."

"Works for me," I told him. I hopped out, grabbed my bags, and walked into the house before he could deliver some more opinions.

✧   ✧   ✧

JACK HAD THE street covered and Elaine sat in my kitchen running the company and barking orders over the phone like a drill sergeant. Twice a day, she paused in Smoke business, long enough to roll out a spreadsheet, study the odds, and place a call.

From my eavesdropping, it became clear the other party on the line was Elaine's bookie. Her mood usually depended on the news delivered during the afternoon conversation.

"Organize these." That was Elaine's directions one afternoon, after she'd scowled through her bookie call. When I half-heartedly protested, she said, "You're on the clock. I need this done, you need insurance."

I'm not a weepy woman. But, her remark reminded me that I'd lost control of my life. I teared up so much I had to leave the room. I didn't feel comfortable climbing into my closet with Elaine so nearby, so I opted for the backyard and the swing.

My life has been hijacked. The thing is, I knew that I

needed better insurance to cover the cost of the baby. I squirmed on the seat of the swing, embarrassed, as I considered, all the belligerent antagonism I'd heaped on Marty.

At the same time, I wanted to march into my kitchen and unload on Elaine. Accustomed to being out and about, the switch to homebody left me feeling smothered.

Count your blessings, numb-nut, I told myself. *This is for the baby. Marty could have said, 'tough shit' and 'goodbye,' Instead, he's... super-pain-in-the-ass-expectant-dad.*

"I should be grateful for all his help." Inevitably my mind returned to my grievance. *He's a bulldozer disguised as a man. Elaine isn't even disguised. Geez. How did I get myself into this?*

Oh yeah. I had sex with a virtual stranger. Now said stranger's entourage was taking over my life. I wanted to scream at everyone to leave me the fuck alone, at the same time, day by day, I shared more parts of my life.

Both the weather and my condition limited my freedom these days. Even before Marty's edict, I'd given up my Humble Home job because of the lifting part. Sadly, I hadn't earned enough to make a dent in my kitchen remodeling plan. The school holidays as well as the mostly good weather with spring sunshine, albeit, occasionally offset by snow flurries, reduced my substitute teaching time.

Fuming at Elaine from the comfort of my backyard swing, I acknowledged the incredible dent Marty's rent check had made in my financial worries. So much so that I switched from being panicked at a looming money crunch, to being concerned about developing dependence on him.

Yeah, the after part just loomed bigger in my mind all

the time. I mean, I wanted the baby to have a mom and dad. I just didn't want to lean so much on dad right now that I wouldn't be able to survive later on without him.

For having only been here a brief time, Marty had already marked his territory outside as well as in. He'd mown the grass before he left, but it had begun to look shaggy again. I debated mowing it, or nagging him about it when we next talked. The potential opportunity to scold Marty made me grin. *I'll give him a reason to come back.*

I skittered past that thought, and examined the flowers struggling in the corner of the yard. Not much to see yet. I left the swing to investigate what I remembered to be grandma's tulip bed.

I squatted on my heels to get a better look. Green tendrils were pushing through the soil, and a hint of yellow crocuses had already appeared. The trees had buds showing but leaves hadn't unfurled yet. Mother Nature seemed to be as indecisive as me this year.

My sojourn in the yard turned into a great therapy session. After I had my temper under control, I did what I should have done from the beginning—went back inside and sorted.

If I ever got fed up with Marty's spy, I'd evict her. As it was, any time we had weather fit enough for me to be outside, I escaped Elaine to spend time in my flower garden, watching the plants grow. *Gestating. Gah...*

But after Marty had been gone almost two weeks, it became apparent that Elaine heard from the crew before anyone else did. I'd had three brief calls from him, each bordering on contentious as he requested detailed updates on my health.

"What was your blood pressure?" he'd led off with.

"One fifteen over seventy-five," I answered. "Why?"

"Just checking," he answered. "What about your blood work? Did it all come back normal?"

"Yes. No problems there."

"You're sleeping and eating okay? No indigestion? Insomnia?" Marty continued, pausing after each question as if recording my answers.

"Did Garret supply your list of questions," I finally asked.

"It pays to have a doctor in the family." His answer neither admitted nor denied his long-distance health monitoring. The first time it happened, I thought, okay, he's the baby's father and of course he has a right to know this stuff.

The second call repeated the same questions. As did the third. No time for conversation other than one clinical health check after another.

"He's overdue taking a break," Elaine groused at me on Thursday morning of the second week. "Tired men make mistakes," she continued, glaring at me as if I had some power to make him behave.

"Well, tell him to come home," I answered.

"Hah. Like he'd listen to me." Her meaningful stare suggested I had some power to make Marty mind. "You should ask him to come home."

I laughed out loud. "Elaine, I don't think you understand. My association with Marty is strictly business. He's a tenant in my house, we don't have a relationship."

"Yes, you do." Her gaze shifted to my stomach. "Use it."

My name didn't have to be Sherlock for me to deduce

Elaine's responsibility when Megan and Harley-Jane descended on me that afternoon. My friends shared Elaine's opinion. Both had fire in their eyes.

"She's right. The Smoke, Inc. crew should come home," Harley-Jane agreed immediately. "They've got to be exhausted. Tired men make mistakes."

"It was Teague's turn on the SAT-phone last night. He said Marty's been talking to a local agency about extending the Smoke, Inc. contract." Megan studied her nails and added, "Teague says with the baby on the way, Marty's suddenly all about making money."

Why is this my fault? I whined mentally. My closet called to me as I faced them. I told myself that I wanted to veg and think. I needed the darkness to calm my nerves. I craved quiet time alone.

"I may have misremembered the date and told him you were going to see the doctor today," Elaine murmured innocently.

"You lied to Marty?"

"Whatever. He'll call."

"And he'll ask me my blood pressure, if I'm retaining any fluids, last time he asked if I'd started to gain weight yet. I can't wait to hear–"

"Promise him sex," Elaine interrupted.

Reluctantly or not, in a totally weird way, I'd been pulled into the Smoke, Inc. family. And as the *boss's-baby's-gestating-mama*, they expected me to make him mind and reward him with sex.

"You know," I drawled, grinning at them. "I'm not promising Marty squat. He's driving me nuts. Because of him, I'm under-exercised. And, and no offense, Elaine, but

I'm totally, freaking-bored out of my mind."

I had their attention. "We need an intervention," I announced. "I'll call Roger."

Chapter Fifteen
Marty

THOUGHTS ABOUT THE baby stayed in my head as the Smoke, Inc. crew plunged straight into fortifying the firebreak. I usually did well separating personal from business, but not this time.

Me, fathering a kid, seemed impossible. Kit and I had tried... *Maybe Kit had been sick longer than we'd known.* Holly, on the other hand... One time and bam. Like I said, I just couldn't wrap my head around it.

I feared the tests had been wrong and she'd come back from the doctor with a different diagnosis. God forbid it was anything serious. I calmed myself by thinking about the woman herself. Holly looked fit, more than fit, blooming.

I admit, conversations with Holly were difficult. If she wasn't my baby's mother, I'd pass on knowing her. Too much... I pictured her in my mind and swallowed a groan.

Too much, my ass, I sneered at myself. I thought about how it had felt curled around her in that big bed. Baby or not I wanted more of her. But, she didn't want more of me.

She claimed I was being nosey. Fuck that. *It's my right to follow the progress of my seed as it gestates.* She said I was a pompous ass.

I laughed at that one, because, yeah, sometimes I am.

But, I can take a hint. Not wanting to set her blood pressure sky rocketing, I decided it best to focus strictly on my kid. That meant eliminating all the personal blathering I wanted to share with his mama.

Because she didn't want personal. That was being nosey. So, instead, I timed my calls to coincide with her doctor's visits which she had each week. When I called in between, to hear her voice and make sure she sounded okay, I focused the conversation on her health since that was an acceptable topic.

She had a doctor's visit scheduled each week. Garret explained that Holly had been designated a high-risk pregnancy because of her age and her first-time birthing status.

"Marty, it doesn't mean Holly's sick or that there's anything wrong with the kid. Most first pregnancies in women her age are watched more closely."

"Christ. You act like she's an old woman. She's only..." Shit, I didn't even know her age. And that pissed me off all over again.

"Holly's twenty-nine, Marty," Garret had supplied information I should have already known.

Even out on the job, if I contemplated Holly long enough, I ended up grinding my teeth. So, I thought about our kid instead, and prepared questions for when I called. I figured out fast that if I let her take the lead, I got more conversation time with her. It surprised me when she seemed worried about me.

"Are you okay? I'm following the news and it looks bad from here." Hearing Holly's concern for me made me happy though I didn't want her worrying about anything.

The last thing I intended to do was tell her it was a god-damned nightmare here. Jesus. Hell couldn't be any hotter and the changing wind patterns, well...

"Lost my eyebrows when the wind shifted," I told her. "Otherwise, I'm good." I thought that was probably too much information, so I backed up to the topic of weather. "What we really need is heavy rain." I couldn't think of anything else to say after that.

"I don't know when I'll get a call through again. Don't give Elaine fits. Take care of yourself. Keep a spot in Grandpa's bed warm for me." I added the last to remind her of my proprietary interest in her sleeping arrangement.

Her laughter broke through all the stilted bull shit we'd been shoveling at each other. I knew I had a smile plastered on my face, and I suspected she did too. Mission accomplished. My next call from Jack wiped the grin right off.

"Girlfriend almost bought the dust the other day. Had I not pulled her ass out of the way, she'd be roadkill under a van's front tire."

What the hell? "Explain." He did. I told him to stick close to her from now on. Christ. Along with every other quirk, she appeared to be accident prone.

"At least she's got quick reflexes," he'd reported, explaining that she'd punched him in the face when he'd grabbed her.

"Jack says you almost got run over the other day," I said as soon as I reached Holly again.

"Jack exaggerates," she answered, supplying no other explanation.

"Says you clipped him a good one," I added.

"He'll live. I didn't hurt him much. It wasn't a big deal."

"Did you or did you not almost step into the path of van?" I demanded, getting irritated.

"I did not."

"So, what the hell is Jack talking about?"

She sighed, irritating me even more. "I was waiting at the bus stop. Standing on the edge of the curb so I could be first in line to get on. A vehicle swerved too close, Jack, who I did not even know was lurking behind me, grabbed me by the collar and jerked me backward. It startled me, and I swung around and punched him. No big drama. End of story."

"Why the hell don't you just let Jack drive you to and from?"

"Because I don't want to," she answered, sounding belligerent. "And furthermore, stay out of my business."

I knew Jack wouldn't have mentioned the incident if Holly hadn't had a *very* close encounter with a metal monster. But her version made it sound as though Jack had overreacted. Since I couldn't be there, I asked Jack to continue his bodyguarding, discreetly of course. Meanwhile, I limited my conversations with Holly to her medical updates.

I held to my part of the bargain and focused on pregnancy issues. Holly seemed a bit testy when I asked details about her health, but when I pointed out it was under the purview of what could be considered *our business* she kept me abreast of her gestation progress.

Assured that things were fine at home, I concentrated on the job, limiting phone calls. Smoke, Inc. got an offer to stay on site, and the contract tempted me. I talked it over with the crew; the money was top-dollar and even though we were all tired, I'd made up my mind to accept the job when I heard from Elaine.

"What do you mean Holly's going clubbing? She's pregnant, she can't do that."

I'd expected my personal assistant to assist, as in, be my eyes and ears while I wasn't home. As with Jack, I had included in her job description, keeping a watchful eye on my future progeny.

I thought Elaine had managed my baby's mama into a sensible lifestyle. She'd scored touchdowns in getting Holly to agree to the insurance, the baby doctor, and even company employment.

I'd been sprawled on my blanket, SAT-phone in hand, ready to tell Elaine to fax one of our extended contract forms to the appropriate local agency. I didn't get a chance to give my order before my unflappable secretary revealed she'd lost control of her charge.

"Can't make your woman stay at home?" Teague and Cowboy both smirked at me from where they lurked, openly eavesdropping.

"Seems like it's going around," I drawled. "Harley-Jane and Megan are planning to party with her as well." That wiped the smile off their faces.

I called Garret. As soon as he answered, I began. "I need you to call Holly and tell her she can't go out clubbing with a bunch of women." Even to my own ears I sounded like a petulant child.

"She's not," he answered immediately. Good. Someone had my back. "I'm going with them. She'll be fine." And he hung up before I could even ask what club they intended to start at.

Holly

I'D BEEN ANTICIPATING the conversation with Marty when he called to review the results from my nonexistent Thursday medical appointment. I didn't get to use any of my rehearsed sassy remarks because the phone remained silent that night. I felt cheated. I'd intended to tell him that the consensus of four Smoke, Inc. women was that the crew needed to come home.

When he didn't call at all, I focused on life without him, because, really when all was said and done, my life and Marty's life were separate entities. I had to keep reminding myself of that immutable fact.

Sheesh. I'd only started the whole, *I'm going out thing*, to demonstrate I could do whatever I wanted. I'd also assumed Elaine would tattle on me and Marty would tell me to stay home.

From that conversation I'd intended to work my way to telling him to come home...based on the will of the Smoke, Inc. women, etc. However, our imaginary conversation never happened.

Though I had no desire to go clubbing anywhere with anyone, my idea snowballed, and my rebellion gathered supporters along the way. Not being much of a party-goer, and never a bar-hopper, I yearned for rescue.

I'd fully expected Marty to find some obscure reason I shouldn't go out and I'd blame him when I weaseled out of going. When I didn't hear from him at all Thursday night, I worried something might have happened at the burn site.

Elaine stayed at the office on Friday. I called to find out what was going on with the crew, specifically was Marty okay, and she said she'd talked to him and he was fine.

She didn't seem surprised he hadn't called me, and it definitely showed me my place in the grand scheme of things. I was embarrassed that I'd let myself get comfortable in Marty's world.

I had to follow through on going out, or lose face with my friends, numbering three now. But, my heart wasn't in it. Since I couldn't drink, and had no desire to sit in a bar and watch others have fun, that left a night with Roger.

I secured Garret's escort by baiting my hook with Roger. Megan and Harley-Jane decided they were accompanying us to the CZ Club Friday night where we'd watch Roger's alter-ego performing as Regina.

When the night arrived, Garret picked us up at my house and drove all of us to the club. As promised, we had a reserved table waiting for us. Roger was nowhere in sight, and I didn't want to interrupt his pre-performance prep time, so I sat at our table and waited for the show to start.

"Staying out of trouble, I hope," Maxine, the owner of Baby Dolls, greeted me when she strolled into CZ a bit later.

"I didn't know you two knew each other," I sputtered, shocked to see Elaine behind her.

"Poker Tuesday nights," Maxine answered.

"Mind if we share your table?" Elaine asked, already pulling chairs from other tables to accommodate their addition to our group.

✧ ✧ ✧

"HAD A VISIT from a spurious member of the city today," Maxine announced as soon as she sat down. "Said he'd been told that Baby Dolls Escort Service was really a stable of high class hookers."

"It is, isn't it?" I'd meant it as a tease, but her frown indicated she didn't see the humor.

"Might want to rethink that opinion since it was my dancing Marilyn he wanted to know better. He wanted an introduction. He was quite insistent."

"So?" I didn't see much of a problem. Maxine had handled a lot worse.

"He threatened to go to the media and cause a stink if I didn't give him what he wanted."

"So, what did you do?"

"I told him business was booming since Marilyn's dance, but a reminder to the public that she'd helped a disabled firefighter would be fine. Anything else would be libelous and my attorneys would see him in court."

"And?"

"He scuttled away. But," she paused and shook her head. "Something about the guy was off. I wouldn't have booked him for any of my girls."

"You trying to recruit my dancing mama, Maxine?" Marty's question rumbled in my ear.

"Marty," I gasped. "What are you doing here?" I'd been so focused on Maxine's story I hadn't seen him arrive.

"You should be thanking me for the introduction, stud," Maxine answered, grinning up at Marty.

"You still have your lease, don't you?" he growled. Then said to me. "Stand up a minute, baby doll."

When I did, he sat on my chair, then pulled me onto his lap. Across the table, Megan did the same with Teague, and as soon as Harley-Jane unwrapped herself from Cowboy's frame, they shared her chair as well.

"All this stress can't be good for the kid," Marty said glancing around.

"What stress," I asked, gazing over my shoulder at him. "Geez, you weren't kidding. Half your eyebrows are gone."

"Makes me look distinguished," he assured me. "Don't change the subject. "Did you go back to see the doctor for the follow up exam?"

"Do not start with the medical stuff." I didn't hide my impatience at the idea of spending my night out discussing my blood pressure.

"Well, is everything all, right?"

"Maxine says a possible pervert wants to date me, but everything else is fantastic."

The lights dimmed around us and I squirmed on his lap, making myself comfortable. I couldn't believe how relieved I was to see him. And if the growing erection under my bottom was evidence, Marty was happy to see me as well.

Marty

"IF SOME GUY'S chasing after you, sweet cheeks, as your tenant and co-parent, we're going to have to talk about it." I slid my arms around her waist and enjoyed the way her bottom fit snug against my groin. *Perfect fit.*

"Being my tenant entitles you to a room. The guy at Maxine's is nothing, and the parenting together, we'll figure that out. But, Regina's about to begin. Hush now."

Regina who? Never mind. Who cared. With Holly's body hugging mine, I figured I'd let her have the last word for now. The show was obviously about to begin.

On stage, a good-looking woman dressed in a blue filmy get-up, glided into the spotlight and stood center stage. As if looking for something specific, she gazed out at the audience.

"Good evening everyone." Her husky tones were almost familiar to me, but I couldn't say why. "Special welcome to the Smoke, Inc. crew this evening."

My mind had been wandering, as in wondering how soon I could pry Holly out of here and persuade her into Grandpa's bed at home.

But the performer had my attention when she singled out our table.

"Do I have a volunteer, this evening," she asked.

"What the hell are they volunteering for," I asked when chairs screeched against the floor. A quick glance around the room confirmed that at least a dozen men stood at their tables, looking hopefully at the woman on stage.

Instead of waiting quietly like the rest of the volunteers, Garret bounded out of his seat so fast he knocked it over. Elaine caught it before it clattered to the floor while he made a bee-line for the night's entertainment.

I settled back in my chair, curious to see what came next. The entertainer motioned for Garret to join her on stage. He trotted to the corner of the room, disappeared through a door, and ten seconds later reappeared by her side.

Music began, he raised his arms, she stepped into his embrace and they waltzed.

Okay, a dance routine. Since the kid had previously shown no inclination to participate in public entertainment, I didn't know what he was up to.

After an intricate clockwise turn, Garret settled his arm around his partner's waist and walked with her for a short promenade, then he moved forward in a smooth, fluid turn that accommodated the change in tempo when the music morphed into jazz. From there they moved into a rhumba, then a foxtrot, finishing with a steamy tango.

"Did you know the kid could dance like that?" Cowboy asked loud enough for most of the room to hear.

"Who do you think taught, him?" I answered, laughing proudly.

When the music ended, Garret and his partner, held hands, bowing toward our table. Then he left the stage and rejoined the crew. He was winded, but smiling big, happier than I'd seen him in a while.

When a stand-up comedian came on next, Elaine announced she was done for the night. "Garret, you were wonderful. It's been fun. Later." Taking that as her cue to leave, Maxine pushed back from the table as well.

"Watch your back, honey," Maxine said to Holly. "There's a squirrely one out there trolling for you."

"What the hell? Holly you said it was nothing. Who's squirrely, what do you mean he's *trolling*, and where can I find him?"

"Holly can fill you in," Maxine answered.

My questions had to wait when Holly's friend, Roger, arrived at the table. But there was no way I wouldn't be investigating further.

"You missed a good show," Cowboy told him.

"Glad you enjoyed Regina. Ready Garret?"

As soon as Garret's date spoke, I froze. Holly must have felt my surprise because she turned and gave me a smug grin.

Cowboy got it about the same time I did. "You're the dancing woman?" he asked incredulously.

"Regina," Holly supplied the star's name. "Regina packs the crowd every Friday night, choosing a partner from the audience. Garret got lucky tonight."

"Marty, you don't mind taking Holly home, do you?" The kid's eagerness to leave with his date made me smile.

"Not a problem. I'm going that way."

"Have fun you two." Holly hopped off my lap ready to leave the club. "You look tired," she said, frowning at me.

"I'm beat," I admitted, handing her the keys. "You drive. If I fall asleep, just leave me in the Hummer when we get home."

Home. God that sounds good. Fatigue hit me with such force, I staggered when I stood. After we made it to my ride without me falling on my face, I relaxed on the seat next to her, enjoying the ride to her house.

"You have a driver's license?" I thought to ask, half way there.

"You just rest up on the way home and don't worry your head about a thing," she chided me, giving me a quick glance and a toothy grin.

I laid the seat back as far as it would go and closed my eyes. If the cops pulled us over, I'd deal with it and pay the fine. Tired as I was, I didn't want to waste one moment of time with her in sleep—unless it was us wrapped around each other in Grandpa's big bed.

"We're home," she announced when she drove into her driveway.

Home. I knew with a sinking feeling, I'd invested more than lease money here. Every day, this old house and its owner claimed a bigger and bigger piece of my heart.

Chapter Sixteen
Holly

I DIDN'T KNOW what to expect when we stumbled into the house together. Part of me, a big part of me, was ready to go horizontal against the refrigerator again. A more decorous side of me, preferred the idea of going up to my bedroom and snuggling in comfort with Marty.

As soon as he entered the front door, he sniffed the air. "Whoa, something smells good."

"Hungry?" I asked.

He looked hopefully in the direction of the kitchen. "I could eat about anything you can find out there."

"As a matter of fact, I have a chuck roast and vegetables simmering in a crockpot."

Acknowledging the fine aroma coming from the other room, I put aside thoughts of seducing Marty, opting for food instead.

"You put this on for a late supper?" He unhooked the crockpot and inspected the contents.

"I can't seem to get full these days. I put the roast on just for the sake of feeding me after I came home tonight. I'll share."

Of course, the pecan pie I'd baked yesterday had a couple of pieces left. And there were three or four dinner rolls from the dozen I'd been working on.

While Marty hovered behind me, I dished up cooked carrots, red potatoes, and a couple of thick slices of beef before ladling broth over it all and handing the plate to him.

I put butter, salt, and pepper on the table, along with the pecan pie and rolls after I nuked then enough to knock the chill off. Then I filled my own plate and started to sit down.

"Coffee?" I asked before I got comfortable. "Or beer?"

"Nah. Water's fine. It's been dry as a bone where I've been. I need to rehydrate."

I served up ice cubes in water for both of us and sat down across from him.

My voracious appetite disappeared, replaced by queasy awareness as I studied his missing eyebrow.

"My grandfather was a fireman," I said, watching him attack his plate of food with gusto. "Your father-in-law knew him."

"Yeah?"

My revelation didn't slow him down a bit.

"Jack and I had a whole conversation about him."

Marty reached for another roll, and said, "Doesn't surprise me. Jack's been around so long, he knows everyone connected to the business."

"He didn't tell you?"

"Nope. Is it a big secret?"

Is it a big secret? "Not anymore." Years of tension I'd carried, began to uncoil. Marty raised the one eyebrow he had left, waiting expectantly.

"I was born Holly Anna Carpenter. I came to live in this house when my parents were killed in a car accident. I was nine years old." I paused to look around the kitchen where

I'd spent so much time. "William Carpenter, better known as Cap, was my one remaining relative. He was already retired when he took me in."

I'd been in this house for holidays before it became my permanent residence. My grandmother had passed the year before, so Grandpa and I had been on our own.

Memories I'd repressed for years flooded my mind. "He was seventy-nine, and seemed older than dirt when he brought me here. No doubt, having a kid to look after, aged him even more. But, he was good to me and we got along fine."

"What happened?"

"He died." I could hardly keep myself from sobbing. My eyes watered as if it had happened a moment before.

"How old were you then?" Marty prompted me.

"Fourteen."

"And you assumed the name Smith, because…?"

"Well, as to that," I said, my grief abating as I replaced that memory with another. "My mother was a Smith, so it's not like I just yanked some name from limbo. As to why I dropped the Carpenter part of my name… Roger and Megan lived in the group home where I was placed. I needed friends and we jelled from the beginning.

"You know, Maxine is Megan's aunt. She couldn't get custody because of her work habits but, she visited every week, supplied Megan with money to spend, and checked up on the house parents to make certain she was being treated right. When Megan claimed me as her friend, I kind of fell into Maxine's protective zone as well. I'd been there six months, when Roger was old enough to leave, Megan said she was ditching the place as well, and so…"

Marty frowned. "You were how old?"

"Fourteen. I didn't stay there, long. And I started calling myself Smith on the off-chance someone in the system was looking for Holly Carpenter."

"How does a fourteen-year-old survive on the streets of Pittsburgh?"

"I was never homeless. Maxine got me a job washing dishes for Buddy's BBQ and helped Roger find an apartment we could all three afford." Maxine was a canny business woman. She'd set us down at a table and made us do our math, figuring how much we had to make to pay the utilities, the rent, and buy food.

"'You've got to be able to take care of yourselves, she told us.' But she had our backs every step of the way." It had been our first place and finding work, balancing our budget, and setting our goals had been a better vocational instruction than any school could teach.

"She made us fit time in for real school, though," I said and laughed. Maxine was big on education. One of her baby doll employees was and still is a teacher by day. Claudia signed me up to be *home schooled,* got me the course work, and made sure I turned it in on time. Without her, I wouldn't have even known how to apply for the scholarships that got me into college."

Marty said, "I left home early as well."

His grimace let me know there was more to the story. "Share," I ordered him.

"Hopefully, our kid will get your brains. Unlike you, I was never good at school. I was too big for the desks and scared the teachers. I missed too many days in the sixth grade and the teacher said she was holding me back and I wouldn't be moving to the seventh the next year. They'd already done this to me twice, so…"

"You quit?"

"Yep. I was fourteen. When I told my grandmother, she threw me out of the house. Good thing I was big. I never had trouble getting a job."

We contemplated each other across the table. Then I reached for the pie and broke the mood.

"You're not eating both pieces, are you?" he growled.

I took pity on him and slid the last slice onto his plate. "Ice cream?" I asked as I topped mine with a scoop of vanilla.

"Oh yeah." It was good. Kind of fun sharing a late-night meal in the kitchen with him.

I wasn't sure what was happening next—upstairs together or upstairs separately—and I didn't want to ask so I ran a sink full of dish water and began meal clean-up. He carried his plate to the counter and picked up the dishtowel I'd laid there.

"When did Roger begin performing?"

I thought about Roger's Regina. "He was bussing tables at a gay bar when the main act didn't show. He came home that night, still dressed like a woman and I didn't recognize him."

Roger had been eighteen and we were all struggling to pay the rent. He'd developed the character he'd devised that night, and Regina's performances put him through college.

"He's pretty amazing," Marty agreed. "Think he likes Garret?"

I laughed. "Well, baby doc does a mean tango. I'd say he's already made a positive impression."

"Just so you understand," he said gruffly, only half teasing. "I don't want your friend to go breaking my boy's heart."

"Not my department." I shook my head, rinsed the last plate, and handed it to him. "They are both educated, intelligent, adults. I'm not about to get mixed up in their relationship."

"How about ours?"

The question caught me off guard, though it shouldn't have.

"I think I'm pretty well mixed up in, *and* about, our relationship," I answered. "It's not like either of us actually chose to have one."

"Not true," he answered me quickly. "I wanted to know you better from the start." He grinned. "I think you wanted to know me better, too. Why else make a trip to my office to return your taxi loan, when you could have simply mailed it to me?"

I'd been too invested in having the last word to consider mailing him his hundred.

Marty

THANKS TO ELAINE, I'd known exactly where to find Holly. I'd not been concerned that she might party too hard and hurt the baby. My angst was more focused on her meeting some new guy who'd sweep her off her feet. As soon as I'd arrived, seated her on my lap, and wrapped my arms around her waist, I'd calmed down. When I'd seen who'd she'd gone clubbing with—Maxine, Elaine, Megan, Garret, Harley-Jane—I felt like a complete dunderhead for worrying and settled down to have fun.

I'd never been jealous or possessive with Kit. Which is why my current emotional state had me flummoxed. I could live with not being Holly's lover. But, I didn't like the idea of her finding a different bed partner she preferred over me. Maybe it was my ego talking, possibly it was something else.

I yawned uncontrollably, exhausted. I'd been hungry, but the late meal and her relaxing company, left me swaying on my feet. "Sorry, Holly. I'm going to have to say goodnight. I'm beat."

"Me too," she agreed. "I'll walk up with you."

Holly

IT WAS A wide staircase and we mounted the steps together. When we reached the top, without hesitation, Marty turned toward the door of the room I'd rented him.

Darn it. My hormones were screaming to drag him into my big bed. I craved him as much as I'd craved that pecan pie earlier. I was tired of denying it, too.

I caught his hand and stopped him. When he gazed at me, his thoughts hidden behind his exhaustion, I stood on my tiptoes and pulled his face close enough to brush my lips across his.

It was as if I'd thrown gasoline on hot coals. He enveloped me in a hug, and I leaned in, molding myself to every part of him. His tongue penetrated my mouth, his hands roamed then settled on stroking up and down my back, rousing my lust to a fevered pitch. I groaned, rubbing my suddenly too heavy breasts, against his chest.

My nails dug into his shoulder as he cupped my ass, lifting me higher against his erection. He was cocked and ready as was I as we ground against each other.

"Time for bed," I gasped and grabbed his hand, pulling him into my room.

Without releasing each other, we somehow managed to get our clothes off, shirts and socks flying into the air until we were both naked. I groaned as warm lips found my nipple, and moaned as he first suckled, then rolled it against the roof of his mouth.

"I want you in me now," I ordered, trying to pull him down on the bed.

An evil chuckle met my demand. "But first..." He claimed my mouth again, as his fingers parted the lips of my sex and rubbed the sensitive bundle of nerves there.

His other hand rested at the small of my back, supporting my backward arch as I parted my thighs to give him better access. When one of his thick fingers slid in and out of me, he crooned, "Come for me baby doll."

With a keening cry, I obeyed, losing any semblance of control in this mating dance. He kept working me as I plummeted to earth from the orgasm, wringing every ounce of pleasure from me before lowering me to the bed.

When I lay on the sheets like a limp noodle, he moved between my legs and began to push inside. Even with my slick readiness, I couldn't help squirming in discomfort as his thick shaft made a place for himself.

Before I caught my breath, he drew my legs up to either side of him and slowly began to withdraw until only the tip of him rested inside me. And then of course, with a powerful thrust, he seated himself again. Unbelievably, I began the climb toward another orgasm.

"Hurry," I whimpered, trying to readjust the pace to fit my needs.

"I'm boss, remember," he growled, "I set the rhythm."

Oh yeah? Planting one foot firmly on the sheets, I twisted my hips and heaved, rolling him until I ended up on top seating him deep inside of me. "Yes," I muttered triumphantly as I lifted, twisting and grinding down on his cock, loving the delicious pleasure that tingled in every nerve ending.

I teetered on the precipice, ready to leap into heaven again, when he flipped me onto my back, caught my hands above my head, and began thrusting faster and faster. He reached between us and rubbed that lovely spot of nerves he'd found before.

My orgasm exploded through me, tingling every nerve and tightening my channel where it gripped him, convulsively milking him with rhythmic pulses. His cock swelled inside me, announcing his own climax as I neared completion. I wrapped my arms around his back and held on. He held my gaze, thrusting harder and moving faster as our bodies slapped together, dancing in counterpoints to the same song.

Dear God, I could love this man... I teetered on the edge, gasping for breath as he thrust harder and moved faster until I could wait no longer. My nails bit deep into his shoulders, and my gasp became a scream. As he found release, we shuddered to the finish-line together.

Marty collapsed and we lay sprawled together who knows how long. Eventually he shifted to his side, spooning around me. My body ached to surrender to sleep, but I fought it to prolong this moment. Maybe he felt the same way, because he kissed my neck and then nibbled affectionately at my ear.

It all felt so good, so right. I relaxed deeper and deeper into the security of his arms and have no idea what prompted the words that escaped my lips.

"What did you call your wife?" Of course, I'd ruined the moment.

He stopped chewing on my ear and barked, "Kit, why?"

"I mean when you were being affectionate, you know, playful."

"Kitten. Again, why?"

"You've called me Little Bit, Baby Doll, Sweet Cheeks…" I paused in my recitation trying to remember all the names.

"Don't forget Wild Child," Marty supplied another of his nicknames. His arms tightened around me again, and I could feel the laughter rumbling in his chest.

"In my defense, I didn't know your *real* name for a *long* time, and it's taken me until tonight to actually discover your *full* name. It's Holly Anna Smith Carpenter, right?"

I nodded *yes* and then confessed tiredly, "I keep forgetting that I was Marilyn when we met, because frankly, it feels like I've known you forever."

"Forever's good," he murmured, kissing my neck again. That's all I remember until I woke the next morning with leg thrown over his hip and my head on Marty's chest, as he thumbed my nipple, teasing me awake.

"I have to shower," I warned him. And other things. Morning mouth is not something I wanted to share. I scrambled from the bed and into the bathroom. No sense in false modesty, he'd seen all of me and I didn't know where my clothes were anyway.

I shut the door and took care of business, then stepped into the shower. I heard the outer door open and close, and my hot shower blasted ice cold for a moment when Marty flushed the commode.

"Okay if I use your tooth brush?" he asked with garbled words, demonstrating he'd already begun. Objecting would have been too late and ridiculous as well, given our recent mouth exchanges.

"Use cold water," I yelled. My water heater left a lot to be desired and was on a list of needed replacements. But, what's a little cold water between friends.

The temperature in the shower warmed up nicely, when he joined me, demonstrating his sexual prowess standing upright with us both slippery with soap.

Chapter Seventeen
Marty

MAN, I FELT fine. Reborn. Jesus, who knew a night of sex could make sleep so deep and renewing. I woke up more than hard and horny. Someplace during the night, a page in my story had turned from bleak to bliss and I wanted more.

I couldn't quite get a fix on where Holly stood in this whole thing, but I wanted to move into her life as well as her house. In bed, there was no denying we fit. Whether she'd think the same thing over the breakfast table was another matter.

She dressed and escaped the bedroom while I fetched my shaving kit, returning from my rented room to the intimacy of her *en suite*. I wanted her to invite me to share this room with her, not glide back and forth from her bed to my bed after we'd fucked.

"Careful, boyo," I muttered to my face in the mirror. "You're getting in deep."

The aroma of bacon frying ended my mirror musing and I hustled downstairs and into the kitchen. She'd switched on some music and it played a soft background as she danced in front of the stove, turning the bacon in one skillet, then flipping a pancake in the other.

"Looks like serious cooking going on in here. Need any help?" I asked ambling up to pat her ass and peer over her shoulder.

She turned her head and said, "Nope, I've got this."

I caught her lips in a kiss, then disengaged and said, "Call me when it's ready," and headed out the backdoor. I wanted to sit in the three-seater and spend a mellow morning contemplating everything good that was happening.

My plans changed rapidly. The swing had been trashed, the wooden slats broken as if someone had taken an axe to it. It sagged in the middle, held together by one skeletal back section.

I swept my gaze over the terrain, looking for the asshole responsible. Long gone. My gaze fell on Holly's flowers once growing at the other end of the yard. Red spray-painted letters spelled foul words and stained the fence that separated her yard from the neighbor's.

"What's wrong," she called from the back step.

"Don't come out here, yet, sweet cheeks. Let me do a little clean…" Too late. She jogged across the yard to stand beside me. I don't think she'd even noticed the swing.

"My flowers," she shrieked, falling on her knees in front of the dying plants. They'd been pulled from the ground, shredded, then stomped to bits under someone's foot.

She sat on her heels, gazing at the crude words on the fence, before her glance moved to the swing.

"Who would do such a thing?" she asked, staring up at me in shock.

"When was the last time you looked out here and knew the backyard was normal?" I asked.

She frowned then answered. "It was fine yesterday when

I got ready to go out with the girls. Garret sat out here in the swing while Megan and I piddled inside waiting for Harley-Jane."

I pulled out my phone and called Garret. It took him a while to answer and when he did, he didn't sound happy to hear from me. Nor did he sound alone.

"Quick question," I said, before he could start bitching. "When you were in Holly's backyard yesterday, did you see anything wrong?"

"No. What kind of wrong?"

"Swing was all in one piece? Flowers were still in the ground? No paint splashed in ugly words all over her fence?"

"Shit no," he answered, coming fully alert. "Someone vandalized her backyard?"

"Yep. Just trying to figure out when."

Holly must have been doing some thinking while she eavesdropped on my conversation with Garret. When I hung up, she was ready to talk.

"The window over the sink gives me a view of the whole yard. The swing was all in one piece when we were doing the dishes last night, and there were no disgusting words on my fence."

I was pleased to see Holly was more angry than shocked.

"Should I report it to the police?" she wondered out loud.

"Probably should," I agreed. "I'll walk over to the neighbor that shares that fence line and see if he heard or saw anything last night."

Holly gave me an odd look and shook her head. "Unless it sold yesterday, that house over there is empty."

I thought about the old geezer leaning over the fence,

asking questions. I hadn't really paid attention to his appearance. He'd dressed like an old man, and I remember a floppy hat that shaded his features so much, I couldn't really picture anything but the hat itself.

I called the local PPD and reported the vandalism. Two officers in a cruiser arrived shortly and took pictures. I'd already taken my own for insurance purposes.

Holly

I WAS STUNNED more than anything else. I guess if I'd been alone, I might have reacted differently, as in I might have been scared spitless. But shortly after Marty's call to Garret and then the Pittsburgh Police Dept., members of the Smoke, Inc. crew began to arrive. The police came and left. They said I could come to the station to sign the report when they got it ready. That worked for me.

Before I'd really figured out what to do with the mess, the crew were already rebuilding the place. Roger and Garret showed up and immediately made the swing their personal project. I was distracted from my drama by the interesting dynamics between the two. I tried to catch Roger's eye several times, so I could get the inside scoop on his Garret adventure. But he laughed at me and ignored my non-subtle hints.

Jack fussed over the existing flower bed, took measurements, then came to stand beside me.

"Those were some pretty flowers growing there. Most of them will come back. But I'm thinking I could add a fountain inside the bed itself, give you a light feature and the sound of running water." He scratched his jaw and studied the broken flower bed before drawling, "While I'm doing it, I might as well add some low lighting back there along the fence."

Marty, who'd taken a wire brush to said fence and had most of the red filth scrubbed off as soon as the police left, was currently repainting it. Megan arrived with Teague followed by Harley-Jane and Cowboy. When Elaine carried boxes of donuts to the backyard my stomach growled, and I remembered the pancake breakfast I'd abandoned in progress.

Teague and Cowboy huddled with Marty a moment then left my yard to walk to the house next door.

I retreated to the porch steps where I sat watching.

"Hate what happened to your place, but hey," Harley-Jane observed, "it's amazing what a crew can do in one day."

"You've got that right." I felt as if I'd tuned into a TV segment of *Fixer-Upper* or *This-Old-House*.

Part of me wanted to retreat to my closet where I could think about what had happened. But a bigger part of me wanted to participate in the backyard party that evolved. Church arrived, boxes of food in hand and set up Marty's new grill.

Marty finished the fence and brought the H/K outside to add music to the event.

"It seems more like fun than a disaster," I told him when he slung his arm around my shoulders and ask me how I felt.

"That's exactly what we want it to be," he said. "And if the fucker who did this is watching, we're thumbing our noses at him while we find out his name."

"Are we doing that?" I asked, impressed.

"Already on it babe. Nobody is doing this to your back-yard and getting away with it."

Looking at the smoldering anger beneath his pleasant expression, I believed him. I wasn't certain if he'd factored in the police inquiry, but from the way the two officers had listened to Marty, I felt comfortable that he'd coordinated the search on all fronts.

It didn't escape me, that instead of the basket case hiding in my closet for unknown days, I was sitting on the back step, basking in the sun, and admiring my new swing. Marty was good for me.

"Holly, come over here and test this for us," Garret yelled.

I hustled that way, ready to change my position in the sun, as well as maybe get chat time with Roger.

Marty blocked my access to the swing which had turned out to be far superior to the original aging version. With my permission, they'd constructed a canopy over it with open walls on each end.

"Hell no, you're not risking yourself on a job that has no safety and security clearance. Church, get over here."

I devolved into a fit of giggles as the two giants plopped down none too gently, bounced up and down testing the chain strength, ease of use, and comfort potential.

"Needs a set of cushions," Church announced as he shoved off, stretching his big frame, getting comfortable, before slinging his arm around Marty's shoulders to slap him in the head. "Lift your feet, dummy. Have you forgotten how to swing?"

"You've served your purpose, here. Move your ass back to your grill and let Holly sit down," Marty growled.

"I've got a surprise coming for you," Church said and grinned, lumbering up from the swing. He didn't elaborate on what the *surprise* was.

I took his seat next to Marty and he wasted no time throwing his arm around me. Then he kissed me on the top of my head. "Feeling okay?" he asked, nudging the swing into a rocking motion.

How did I feel? Truthfully, I wanted to crawl into his lap and escape into sleep. I don't do drama well.

"Good job you two," Marty said to Garret and Roger. Garret gave him a thumb's up, Roger winked at me, and they ambled off together, toward the food.

I'm not good at describing things, but to my mind it seemed like I'd just had a huge upgrade without losing the flavor of what once was. I felt certain that Grandma would have liked Jack's fountain which turned into a cascading waterfall.

"I don't know how I feel," I answered him. "Confused? Unnerved? Vulnerable?"

"Yep. That fucker fouled the yard while we were asleep. And I didn't hear a thing. That will not happen again."

Oh yeah, Marty was more than mad. The yard itself was still a hub of activity. Marty's crew had used the existing trees to install motion sensor lights. The back fence had been strengthened, Jack's low lights were enhanced by staggered lantern lights on poles.

"When Eazy gets here, there won't be any house security issues, either," he announced.

"How many rent checks is this costing me?" I wasn't about to protest the offer of built in home protection. But I didn't want him to lose sight of the fact I was boss of what happened to my house. And I would pay for any upgrades. Maybe over a long period.

"Is E.Z. part of your crew?"

"Nah, he's a farmer."

"What's E.Z. stand for and why's he coming?"

"Ezekiel. Eazy's a hell of a lot easier to remember. He's a licensed electrician. So, he's going to supervise the wiring of your new home security system."

"I thought you said he's a farmer. And stop pushing this stuff at me. I can't afford…"

His mouth flattened into a grim line and he silently dared me to continue. *Okay, maybe there's a low interest plan.*

I forgot all about the interior home upgrades taking place after Eazy arrived, wearing work boots, tool belt, flannel shirt and jeans. I don't believe I've ever seen anyone dress the part of country, better.

"Howdy, Church," he drew the words, slowly, looking around as if to size the place up before he continued into the yard. When he spoke, I could hear him, though he didn't seem to be projecting to anyone but Church.

Church escorted Eazy to the swing, grinning ear to ear as he talked. "Want you to meet Marty's woman. I'm hoping Gertie will—" Eazy interrupted Church with what sounded like, a reminder.

"Ain't no influencing her, you know. Gertie decides what's what. I'm just here to wire the place."

Gertie, Church's promised surprise, was a hundred pound (at least) white coated, Great Pyrenees guardian dog.

"She's beautiful," I breathed, leaning out of the swing for a closer view. Before the end of Eazy's visit, he'd installed the security system and apparently, I would be hosting a guardian dog for an unspecified length of time.

I'd never owned a dog, or had a pet. When I expressed my concern to Gertie's owner, he shook his head.

"She's here on a job. She knows that. Feed her the mix I'm leaving, give her a scratch on the head for praise when you think of it. She's taken to you. You'll get along fine."

"Is she supposed to sleep in the house with me?" What the fuck did I know about hosting a canine?

"No, ma'am. If you want to let her in during the day, especially if it turns hot, that's fine. But at night, she'll be outback on guard duty. Any problem comes visiting here again, Gertie will bite its head off."

I better understood the rushed security upgrades later in the afternoon, when Marty explained he and the crew were only here for a short break, and would be flying back to the west coast fires early the next morning.

I wanted to cry, but I sucked it up. He was a firefighter. Among other things, that's what he did. I thought about their discreet, advertising tagline. *If it's dangerous, let us do it for you...*

Whether I learned to live with Smoke, Incorporated's hazardous assignments or not, Marty wouldn't be abandoning his company or line of work to hold my hand.

Marty

DAMMIT, I DID not want to leave Holly so soon. Or at all. My feelings for her seemed to be growing faster than I could get a handle on them. Shit. I was so caught up in worrying about everything at home, it was torture blocking it all out once we hit the fire zone.

Before I'd taken off, we'd discussed the incident and I'd asked her if she'd had anything else happen recently.

"You know," she'd admitted. "I think it's been going on a while. Maybe since I met you."

She'd looked at me with dawning awareness. "I left my purse, holding my phone and money in the taxi the night of the dance. That's why I borrowed cab fare from you. They returned the purse and phone to me the next day. The money was still there, and everything looked fine."

"Who dropped it off?"

"I don't know. It was just waiting there on my porch when I went out to get my paper that morning."

"But then, I got some weird calls asking to speak to Marilyn. After the second or third *wrong number,* I got a new number. I thought that had taken care of the problem."

"Don't forget the van that almost clipped you," I reminded her. "And the shelving that collapsed the morning you were supposed to be in that area of Humble Homes."

"And I quit walking to the store in the evening when I got a creepy feeling someone was following me."

Christ, by the time I got done lining up all the probably incidents that we'd ignored, it appeared Holly might have acquired a stalker the night of the dance.

I'd asked for specifics, but she had no idea who. Nor could she describe the van that had almost run over her, and she had only a vague notion of how her phone had been returned.

"I think it was a courier service. They left it on my front porch, next to the door, in a gift bag. At the time I had you and the dance on my mind, and I didn't think about the method of returning the phone. Now it's seems kind of hinky."

I called Mel's Cab Company and inquired about their delivery system for lost items.

"What the hell?" Mel himself answered. "You expect us to underwrite the cost of returning packages to people too stupid to hang onto their valuables? Fuck that."

I'd assured him that as I was also a business man, I understood completely. Then, as a peace offering, and after guaranteeing we'd refer all customers to their cab line when we had out of towners visiting, I managed to coax the owner into giving me gold.

"I had night duty, answering the phones that date," he confessed. "Crappy roads, icy conditions and not much going on. So yeah, I remember. I watched you and Marilyn on television raising money in that dance-a-thon. That's why I remember her call."

"Who organized her phone delivery the next day?"

"Nobody from here. According to our records, we turned it over to her brother who came in to pick it up."

I wasted no time calling Jack and gave him pertinent dates. "Hack still owes that favor. Holly changed her number a while ago. See if he can trace the old number and see who called her on those dates after the dance-a-thon. Then have him track it back to the caller's address." I planned to visit the sonofabitch and put the fear of *me* in him.

But, I couldn't linger in Pittsburgh to help the investigation along. The west coast situation had worsened. With no rain in the forecast and an already dry spring, local areas were trying to control outbreaks as they occurred, and we'd been offered a healthy contract to return.

Besides the money, Harley-Jane's brother was a member of a west coast Hotshot crew. Cowboy was all about giving them back-up too, if they needed it. We were leaving, and we'd be gone a spell. I hated it. But, there was no point in pretending it wasn't so. If Holly and I were going to have any kind of a life together, she'd have to get use to the risk factor in my business.

It made it damned hard for me to convince her to stay home from her waitress job. When I said it was too risky, she said, "Right, carrying a tray from the bar to the table is scary shit. But you, chopping wood in a burning forest, is a piece of cake."

I ignored her logic and explained my concern. "You have to go out, and once you're there, you have to come home. Both points of vulnerability."

"Jack will be with me, you know it as well as I do. I couldn't shake him off if I tried."

I didn't so much give in as much as get run over. There was no way in hell she would call off work. I didn't like it. But I admitted I might be overacting a bit. Still, I called Hack and ask him to hurry up and locate the guy. I didn't like knowing there was a predator stalking Holly and I wasn't home to protect her.

Chapter Eighteen
Holly

A̲FTER MARTY LEFT, I felt a giant hollow emptiness inside. Elaine had work piled up, she wasn't interested in my help, and so I played with Gertie in my recently refurbished backyard. I tried to coax her into the swing with me, but she refused the offer, plopping down in the grass to watch me instead.

With her presence, as well as the motion sensors that flooded the yard with light at night, I felt safe. For the most part, Gertie trotted inside with me during the day when I retreated from the weather.

At night, she stretched out on the elevated back porch, hidden in the shadows, but alert to any intruders.

The first night, nothing much happened, not even a flicker of the new lights.

The second night, though, Gertie roared from her back-porch perch, bounding into the yard when the lights streamed on. I didn't see anything from the view of my upstairs' window. Jack appeared in the backyard, rubbing sleep from his eyes, and I wondered if he'd been asleep in his SUV.

I fixed him a late-night slice of pie, had one as well, invited him to sleep on the couch, and went back to bed. I still felt safe.

Eazy stopped by once that week to check on Gertie. I gave them privacy and was wounded when I saw the big dog climb into the swing and lean on him.

Did it mean she didn't trust me? Like me? When he stood, ruffled her coat, and gave her a hug, I sidled out to the backyard for a moment.

"Is she upset? Did I do something wrong?"

"You think Gertie's got her tail in a twist? Might be personal." Eazy frowned at his dog, concern written on his face. "You worried, muffin? I'm working on it."

"She won't sit in the swing with me like she did you," I explained quickly, pretty sure we weren't talking on the same subject. "I thought she and I were friends."

"Nope. She's on guard duty with you. With me, we're just discussing family business."

"I'm sorry you're having problems," I offered.

"Custody battle," he told me, gruffly. "That's why I stashed her here with you. Not that Gertie would have stayed if she'd taken a dislike to being here."

When I went back into the kitchen, Elaine eyed me. "Saw you talking to Eazy out there," she said, her nosy-gene in an uproar. "He's an odd one. What did he say?"

"His wife wants her dog back. Gertie wants to stay with him. She was hiding out here."

"Like I said, he's an odd one."

That was the most excitement unfolding in my world, and given the recent vandalism I should have been grateful. However, I had cabin-fever out the wazoo. When Marty had tried to talk me into calling off work during the Championship Playoffs that weekend, I snarled at him. No way.

Friday night, Balls & Bones was rocking. Nobody wanted to go home, the customers replayed, reenacted, and rejoiced together over beer. I loved it. I'd been so cooped up at home, I wanted to dance on the bar all night long.

As predicted, despite my protests, I had a bodyguard. Jack had planted his ass on a stool and waited for me to get off work. It was clearly no pain for him. His team won, and he was having fun arguing with half the customers and celebrating with the rest.

On a foray into the kitchen, somebody handed me a trash bag and pointed me at the back door where more bags were piled. I didn't mind, everyone had dumpster duty eventually, and I was on deck this time.

I hauled six bags out, two at a time, and stacked them by the huge green container. Once I had them all lined up, I tossed two up and in, bent over to pick up the next bag, and whammy, someone grabbed me from behind and wrapped a skinny, shirt-covered arm around my throat.

When I'd bent over to lift the bag, apparently, he didn't allow for me being taller than him. Before he could step backward, I hunched in on myself as much as possible and powered up, breaking his strangle hold and hauling him up with me.

He twisted my right arm behind my back and I felt something pop as he went back to choking me with his other arm. But again, he didn't allow for the angle because of our height differential. I couldn't get loose, so I slammed my head backward and hit him.

I almost blacked out when my skull crashed against solid bone. He grunted and loosened his grip enough for me to draw breath and shove backward again. I tried to scream. My throat wouldn't work.

Jack finally remembered he was babysitting. Thank God.

I knew this because I heard him let out a yell and in two seconds I sat on the ground watching Jack kick the guy's ass.

Ted came to the back door, saw me bloody and propped against the dumpster. He grabbed his cell and dialed 911 before he rushed down to me.

"Stalker," I croaked, nodding weakly at the guy, now laying prone on the ground, his cheek smashed against the dirty alley way.

"Jesus, Mary and Joseph, girl. I look away for ten minutes and you're in trouble." So much for my bodyguard's tender loving care. I didn't go to Garret's clinic. Ted had called the police, and I went to a real hospital, this time in an ambulance.

"Company insurance?" And saying that hurt like hell. But damn, I sure hoped Elaine had filed those papers.

"What the hell? Would you stop worrying about that shit. You're covered. If you weren't, I'd pay it out of my own pocket. I should have been watching you." Jack stayed with me the whole time, helped clear the alley after the attack, and helped the medics load the gurney with me on it.

"I'll take care of this and be at the hospital when you arrive," Jack promised.

I could hear him sharing information and names with the two new officers so that they could coordinate their evidence with the two cops who'd investigated my backyard vandalism.

I still had no idea why he'd targeted me. It wasn't for money. He'd seemed a lot more interested in choking me than getting my tips, which were still safe in my apron. I was glad to have the money, but that left the question of why he'd been trying to kill me. He'd failed, but not for want of trying.

"Baby," I told the EMT guys. "Pregnant."

"Already know," one of them answered. "You got a friend called the dispatcher who called us."

I wanted to sleep during the ride, but they both kept talking to me which I found irritating. I wanted to tell them to be quiet, but my throat hurt too much.

After they wheeled me into the emergency room, they passed me into the next set of waiting hands, Garret, wearing his stethoscope. Elaine stood next to him.

"Baby okay?" I made a feeble attempt to touch my belly, but my arm wouldn't work.

"We've got you, Holly," Garret said. "Dr. Spencer's on her way. But I'm not going to wait to fix your shoulder so…" He helped me into a sitting position with my legs over the side of the bed.

I hadn't been able to move my fingers for a while. Garret examined my arm, murmured, "This will hurt for a minute…"

Before I could brace myself he simultaneously pressed, pulled, and twisted, blasting excruciating pain from my shoulder, down my arm, and into my fingers.

"I'm going to puke," I warned as a wave of nausea hit me.

"Have the lab check for blood," I heard him tell the nurse.

I tried to give the vomit a look when I quit barfing, but the nurse whisked it away. When she came back, Garret had moved onto other issues.

"We need to look at your head now. The medic said he couldn't find an open wound but the back of your head is covered in blood."

It turned out the blood wasn't from the big lump on my head. It belonged to the guy who'd jumped me.

"I won," I muttered, my voice barely a whisper.

"No, you got beat up and nearly killed," Elaine snapped. So much for support from the peanut gallery.

"She's family," Garret intervened when one of the nurses suggested Elaine wait outside.

"Not," I managed to croak a denial, but Elaine defended her territory.

"I'm her grandmother and I'm going nowhere." She took my hand, and I suddenly didn't want to let go. She'd never appeared to be a touchy-feely person, nor was I, but she let me hang onto her just the same.

"We're moving you to a private room." Garret supervised my transfer instead of handing me over to a nurse and leaving.

"Patch me up, I want to go home," I told him.

"The baby doctor says no, and Garret says no. You're staying here until they agree you can leave," Elaine announced.

"Dr. Spencer will be in soon," the nurse volunteered, looking sympathetic. "She wants you to remain here where we can monitor your baby's condition for the next twenty-four hours."

"I want to go home and sit in my closet." I didn't mean to say it aloud, but it had been a sublevel thought for a while. As I remembered the attack, panic caught me in its grip. "Ohmygod, ohmygod, ohmygod…"

Elaine squeezed my hand. "I'm here. Aw, sweetie." Until she handed me a tissue I hadn't realized there were tears streaming down my cheeks.

"Delayed reaction," the nurse said sympathetically. "It should make you feel better to know you probably broke the guy's nose. Maybe the police will match the sample we sent to DNA in their data base and they'll use it to put the asshole away for a while."

I really didn't want to think about him. Jack had turned him over to the cops when they arrived, and he was currently in a holding cell in the downtown jail. I hoped I had broken his frigging nose. It gave me a horrible kind of satisfaction, remembering the feel of my skull crunching against his face.

While I entertained myself with blood-thirsty thoughts, the nurse wheeled me to a l room rivaling a five-star hotel suite for luxury. Once she'd transferred me to the bed, and hooked me up to the monitors discreetly stored behind an oriental screen, she left.

Elaine remained. I was embarrassed she'd seen me blubbering like a kid.

"What really pisses me off," I wheezed, mopping my face. "I got caught flatfooted—again." You'd think with Jack grabbing me recently, I'd have been on my toes.

I'd been thinking about Marty, how I was going to spend the tip money, as in cradle or crib, and having fun along with everyone else who'd cheered the Cavaliers to victory. I hadn't even scouted the alley before I waltzed into the corner where the dumpster stood.

I groaned in frustration.

"Are you in pain? Should I call the nurse back?" Elaine asked.

"No. Tell me Marty stories. Secret stuff nobody knows."

"You're the one pregnant. You tell me." Elaine rolled her eyes at my attempt at humor. She didn't volunteer much Marty information, but she pulled a table and chair closer to the bed and produced a deck of cards from her bag.

She won more than I did, but I didn't embarrass myself too greatly. The cops came and left. Megan and Roger both came to check on me and offered to stay.

Elaine remained fixed in place and both eventually left.

Dr. Spencer arrived early in the morning and Elaine evidently judged me to be safe with her, because she left the room for a bit and gave us privacy. After the doctor examined my external injuries and touched different spots on my belly, she patted my hand.

"Your blood pressure is elevated, but not dangerously so. The baby's been bothered enough. I'm not going to poke around inside you if it's not necessary."

"Then let me go home. I can rest better there." My throat still hurt but at least I could say more than a word now.

I desperately wanted out of here. The fact it was a very nice private room didn't keep hospital employees from roaming through whenever they felt like it. I didn't know one from another and even with Elaine sitting in the chair next to the bed, I felt vulnerable here.

Dr. Spencer touched the bruises on my neck. "You had a close call."

"Yes." Instead of relaxing in safety, I sat in bed watching the door for another attack. "I'm eventually going to crash, and I need to be somewhere safe when I do."

"Do you have someone to stay with you at home?"

"Yes. Gertie." I was knee-deep in volunteers, but I would take the calming effect of the visiting guardian dog over the rest. Both Megan and Roger had offered to stay with me, plus Elaine, who seemed to have put herself in charge of my convalescence, probably wouldn't shake loose when I went home.

"I'd like the nurses to monitor your condition today. If you have no cramping or bleeding, no unexplained internal pains, and your vitals remain steady, we'll see what we can do this evening."

My shoulder hurt, my head ached, and my throat felt as if I'd swallowed broken glass. But those were things time, not the hospital would heal. As soon as the doctor gave me the heads-up on the baby being okay, I intended to go home.

Meanwhile, I remained on guard, sitting upright in the bed. The nurses tried to get me to relax, I didn't. After a while, when apparently, the danger zone for mild a concussion had passed, they encouraged me to close my eyes and rest. I didn't.

When Marty followed my lunch into the room, Elaine smiled for the first time all day. "She's had a bad time. I'm so glad you're back."

Marty

As soon as I had heard from Jack, I'd had him call Garret. The kid called me back via my SAT-phone and his headset and kept me with him on the trip to the emergency room. Once there, though, he cut me out of the loop as soon as he found Holly. For fifteen minutes I was left gnashing my teeth, waiting for answers.

"Update me," I ordered him as soon as he reconnected. Garret had been with me during Kit's illness and he knew I wanted information with no sugar.

"Dislocated shoulder, bruised throat, and a lump on the back of her head, maybe a mild concussion." Garret hesitated, then added, "Dr. Spencer's already examined her and she's keeping Holly in the hospital for observation. I don't want to upset you but sometimes babies don't hold tight after a mother experiences significant trauma."

"I figure he's got a strong grip on his mama, him being my kid; but Holly's health comes first. And check Jack's blood pressure, he's a basket case."

Jack blamed himself for taking his eyes off Holly during the championship match. I told him, if he'd tried to help Holly do her job she would have clubbed him upside the head. Besides which, if I'd been there, my ass would have been parked on a stool in front of the game and the same thing would have happened.

The police were connecting the dots on the stalking incidents. I talked to Elaine and she said Holly was pretty shaken up. Well hell yeah.

"Can I talk to her?"

"Honestly, not long."

"Hey, baby, heard you were in a brawl. Who won?" I thought I'd insert some humor and maybe make Holly smile when Elaine gave her the phone.

"Kicked. His. Ass." Her rough whisper shocked me. Despite Garret's information, or maybe because of his clinical delivery, I'd mentally minimized her injuries.

"I'm on my way, baby doll. Rest and heal." I wanted to

talk to Holly, but shit, I could feel the pain it cost her in every word she spoke. I had a driver waiting, and when I deplaned, I went straight to the hospital. I figured it was more important to be there than prettying-up.

When I walked into her room, I'd be lying if I didn't say I expected tears, or maybe even a little hysteria. Thank the fuck I didn't get either.

"Bout time," she muttered, giving me her version of the stink-eye when I gazed down at her. "Glad you're here."

"Aw, shit, baby. What can I do to make you feel better?"

Christ. She could barely whisper, bruises marked her throat and jaw, her eyes were puffy, the left side of her face swollen, and her right arm was in a sling; and those were just the things I could see. I wanted to kill someone—slowly.

"Hungry," she said, looking pointedly at the lunch tray.

"Me too. How about sharing?" Evidently the menu didn't change for patients in the fancy rooms. I investigated a milk-carton-like box, warm but not too hot to pick up.

"Soup, I think." After I opened the top, and confirmed the content, I handed her the spoon, crackers, and the carton of noodle soup.

"Well, it's not Church's chili but it will have to do." When she fumbled to hold the spoon in her left hand, I fed her soup and ate the hamburger and limp French fries.

After the soup, we split the applesauce in the plastic cup and the strawberry gelatin. After she finished off the chocolate milk, I moved the tray to the hallway and then came back inside.

"We'll wait to see what the doc has to say later today. Meanwhile, you look like you could use a nap." I figured I'd sit in the chair next to her and doze while she slept. She had a better idea.

"Hold me." She took my hand and pulled me onto the bed next to her.

Hey, it worked for me. I curled around her back, snuggled my groin against her bottom, threw my arm over her waist, and laid my head on her pillow.

"You smell like burned matches," she told me.

Shit. I'd cleaned-up but it had been in a two-by-two shower on the plane here.

"Want me to move?" I hoped not. My body had already molded itself to hers.

Her answer was to rub her behind against my package and tug on my arm until my hand lay on her belly.

"Are you saying you want me to light your fire?"

Her laughter piddled off as she snuggled closer and fell into sleep.

Her hair smelled more like disinfectant than green apples today, but she felt good in my arms, and I closed my eyes and rested beside her. I held her until her breathing deepened into true sleep. I would have preferred staying there until she woke, but a nurse entered, eyeballed me and frowned, before she left quickly. Garret returned.

I eased from the bed, and he took my arm, urging me toward the door.

"I'm not leaving," I told him. I knew that for certain. Nothing and nobody was getting between Holly and me. "The sooner I get her out of the hospital, the better." I studied the room, looking for vulnerabilities.

"Dr. Spencer's outside. I want you to talk to her." When my blank expression telegraphed my confusion, Garret clarified. "Holly's baby doctor."

"Okay." Jesus, I'd forgotten all about the kid while I'd been in bed with Holly. I scanned the room for threats one last time, followed Garret to meet the baby doctor, and stopped outside the door, facing the woman in the hallway.

Dr. Spencer's expression changed to disapproval as she gazed at me. "Miss Smith will have to give approval for your team interaction. Please don't call and harangue my nurse again."

"I've never spoken to anyone in your office." I wasn't impressed with the doctor's communication or organizational skills. "Cut to the chase. How is she?"

When she looked confused, I verbally nudged her. "Is there a problem?"

"It's good to meet the other half of our baby's parent team in person. Our previous conversations have been unproductive." Her eyes were icy chips as she glared at me.

Our baby? And what phone calls? I could feel red creeping up my neck. I didn't need attitude, I needed answers.

"Sorry. I was out of town on work. I'm Marty Jones. Holly's significant other, *and* the baby's father. I'd like to know how they're *both* doing." I held onto my temper as I considered replacing the wonder doctor.

"Her external injuries are not life threatening. We're monitoring the baby for the time being."

For the time being was the best I could get out of her. We didn't bond. I wondered if Holly could be pried away from the hot chocolate and swank robes. Then, remembering the doctor's credentials, I sucked up my irritation.

"Let me know what you need me to do to secure Holly and our kid. If she needs to stay here, fine. But I'm staying too."

"If you're not the man who called, and speaking to you I am assured you're not, who did call my office? Someone certainly did."

"I'll pass that onto the police detective when he shows. He'll want to talk to you. Sounds like her stalker tried to talk his way into her medical information. Thanks for being so alert."

I did my best to make myself look like a respectable business man. If need be, I'd promise to donate a machine or something they needed at her office. Having helped Garret set up the clinic, I knew that shit didn't come cheap. And part of me wanted her to know I could afford the best for Holly and my kid.

I retreated into Holly's room, closed the door behind me, and stood gazing at her soft and vulnerable form. Fear tangled with an emotion I thought I'd left behind.

I'm in love with her. I admitted it to myself as I carefully slid back into the bed. I didn't know how things were going to play out for us, but damned if I wasn't looking forward to the ride. Meanwhile, Holly's situation seemed clear to me.

"I think we should get married, Sweet Cheeks," I murmured, cuddling her closer. "Without Garret running interference, I couldn't even get close to your room. Fuck that shit."

Holly

BEFORE I COULD decide whether that had been a real proposal or just Marty bitching about hospital rules, someone knocked on the door.

Marty stopped the detective who entered at the doorway, and checked his credentials before he'd let him in.

"I know you're not going to want to come down to the station for a while. But I need to get the ball rolling. Wondered if you'd take a look at this picture and see if you recognize the perp."

I shivered at the idea of having someone stalking me, spying on me.

Marty took the picture and held it in front of my face. My dithering ended when I really focused on the guy they'd arrested.

"You really did a job on his nose," Marty noted with pride. The white tape holding it in place contrasted nicely with the black rings surrounding his eyes. His face was so swollen, had he been a well-known friend, I might not have recognized him. I started to hand the picture back when I paused.

Those ears. Huge ears. Sticking out on each side of his skinny head. I'd seen those ears before.

"Dance-a-thon," I whispered, my throat screaming.

Marty handed me a pen and paper and I wrote, *The guy minding the business phone in the back. I had to borrow his cell to call the cab company and leave a message for Megan.*

"We've got this guy now," the detective assured me and took back the pic. "Got him on cyber stalking based on his early calls. He escalated after you blocked his access to you.

"A couple of your crew checked out that house next door and called us when they found an open window. We've got prints and DNA. He was squatting in one of the rooms, had it filled with Marilyn Monroe pictures mixed in with assorted pieces of women's clothing in all sizes. We found a brown glove and a B&B Tee that have been identified as belonging to you."

Shit. I remember those things going missing. The guy was so close...

"You mind not scaring the shit out of her now that we caught this guy for you," Marty muttered.

"Sorry," the detective apologized. "It looks like you were just one of his targets. We're sorting through his collection of fifties memorabilia mixed with weird shit right now. If it's any consolation, it's Marilyn he's fixed on, not you."

"Maybe so," Marty snarled. "But, it sure wasn't Marilyn he'd tried to strangle. If the day comes when he's not locked up, I want to know."

After he left, Marty returned to the bed and slid his arm under my shoulders. I know I should have been scared or feeling vulnerable. But, I'd never felt so safe.

"You understand we're going to talk about this sooner or later," he murmured against my hair.

"What?" I croaked, trying to look puzzled. *Like I'd forget he'd broached the subject.* I'd thought maybe I'd have to casually find a way to slide it back into the conversation.

"Nod your head if you'll marry me."

When I nodded yes, waiting for him to say something romantic, he went all drill-sergeant on me. "Sooner is better. I already have Elaine working on it."

I should have known that. I rolled my eyes at him and he leaned close enough to plant a kiss on my forehead, my nose, and then my lips.

"You probably think I'm doing this to get Grandpa's bed. You'd be partly right. But, the truth is, I don't want to spend a moment anywhere, including the bed, without you.

You understand? I love *you* for *you*, baby doll, not just for the *kid*."

I never doubted it. I nodded, mouthing the message, *I love you too.*

Epilogue
Holly

I CLIMBED OUT of bed at five this morning, not because I had to, but because all the online bloggers described their turkey feast preparation as long and arduous and I wanted to honor the tradition. I had to make our first big deal, memorable. So far, I'd gotten my wish. I'd pretty much watched, but Marty's efforts would go in our scrapbook.

I stared at the carcass of the roasted turkey, waiting to be bagged and trashed. The thing had weighed twenty-six pounds before I'd stuffed it, and even picked clean, it was an impressive sight.

"Maybe you should preserve the skeleton to commemorate this experience," Roger suggested after the turkey's carnage was complete. While he and Garret engaged in a conversation about skeletal processing, I shuffled to the counter and picked up a garbage bag.

"Boss man," I murmured, looking across the table at Marty to get his attention. Silly me. I always had his attention. Last night, I'd woken during the night and found him watching me sleep.

I'd pulled him back under the covers and told him to knock it off. We cuddled a long time until I knew his snores were real. Then I did the thing I love doing the most these days. I slept.

Marty's kind of cherishing has pretty much eliminated my forays in the closet. Except when I'm just plain hiding out from the continual traffic pattern of males tromping through the house. I hate it when he's gone, and he has been a lot. But when he's home, the house and yard become Grand Central Station on steroids.

The company worked most of the last three months on the West Coast. The situation there has reached monster fire proportions and I'd be lying if I didn't admit, that just like Megan and Harley-Jane, I spend a lot of my time worrying. But, it's what Marty does and I suck-it-up.

My gaze settled on the turkey whisperer across the table. He winked, nodded toward the denuded bird, and mouthed the words, *I told you so.*

I'd Googled recipes online to find out about the stuffing and almost opted for a separate casserole. I'd found some of those stories about poisoning guests with undercooked dressing intimidating.

Once Marty assigned himself my cooking assistant, he'd urged me to *do the right thing,* and *fill that baby.* He spends a lot of time grinning and talking to himself these days. I'm not sure he hasn't regressed into childhood. If he has, I'm right there beside him, doing my share of head talking as well.

Last night, while we were trying to make each other go to sleep, we'd talked.

"Do you think about Kit a lot?" I'd asked him. Probably none of my business but I knew he did, and shallow me, wanted some part of him in that too.

"All the time," he'd answered promptly. "I talk out loud

to her. Shit, she seems more real to me now, than she has for the last six years."

"Yeah?" I thought about that, understanding. Sometimes I have discussions with various members of my family, just to get feedback in a strange kind of way. Like we're having a powwow in my head. After we'd zoned out and gotten quiet on that for a while, I switched topics.

"I feel like I'm supposed to be humble at the good fortune we've received," I'd confessed, not feeling particularly humble.

"Fuck that shit, babe," Marty had barked immediately. "Between the two of us, we've had enough bad luck for forty people. This is our time now and I'll beat the shit out of anyone who tries to piss on our parade."

I agreed. But I sure didn't see it coming when I managed to finally buy back Grandpa's house. Sometimes I stare at the old hardware in the sink and shiver. If I'd never coveted the new Kohler faucets that are currently waiting to be installed, I might not have gone to the dance-a-thon, I wouldn't have met Marty, and … Yeah. I shiver.

My earliest vision of Thanksgiving dinner had been me, Roger, Maxine, and Megan clustered around the kitchen table having mashed potatoes and turkey together. Once the Smoke, Inc. crew got involved, the dinner became an event and grew… and grew.

I stared at the dirty plates and cutlery soiled by thirty plus people. When I'd suggested that having a meal in the basement would add extra clean-up work, since everything would have to be hauled back upstairs, Marty had offered a brilliant suggestion.

With my permission, he'd expanded the plumbing

downstairs and added a kitchenette in the utility room. It was a sweet set-up I wouldn't have thought of. I'm still waiting on my kitchen remodel upstairs, but I'm not complaining.

I looked around. My girlfriends were busy. Elaine, using the rolling cart she'd brought for the occasion, stacked dirty dishes and cutlery to be wheeled to the new dishwasher.

Janie and Megan were parceling out leftovers in take-home bags for anyone who'd accept. I'd just finished cleaning out the refrigerator upstairs, and no way did I want it glutted with aging food.

It was good to see Elaine and Jack speaking again. As soon as they'd discovered the house next door for sale, they'd gotten into a bidding war and if Marty hadn't intervened, they would have jacked the price up sky high.

They'd bought it together and were turning the old house into a duplex, with Elaine taking the main floor and Jack remodeling and living in the basement.

Both names were on the deed, since Jack claimed Elaine couldn't be trusted to not gamble it away, and she swore he didn't have enough sense to manage his own affairs.

Cowboy and Teague folded up the long tables, clearing the floor for dancers, Church pushed a broom, removing the detritus from our first Thanksgiving together, and the H/K pumped out a heavy bass sound, making my shoulders sway and my hips skitter sideways on the stool where I sat.

Marty's cell pinged, and I felt my stomach muscles tense in dread. *No, not yet. This is our first...* He caught my eye and shook his head in a *nothing to worry about here* move, and I relaxed.

But as soon as he quit talking, I willed him to me, to

share. "Who was that?" I asked, as soon as he reached my side.

"Eazy. Said Gertie sends her love."

"Ohhh, she is so sweet. What did Eazy want?" I had no doubt that more than holiday good wishes had transpired.

"Gertie's got trouble," Marty said.

"Wife making claims again?" I asked sympathetically. I hadn't met Eazy's other half, but from Marty's description, she was a force to be reckoned with. Mackenzie Sierra, FBI. Hey, I was intimidated just by her title.

"Nope. Not Mac. It's Gertie. Eazy blames you by the way. Remember the last time they visited?"

"Of course, I remember." Gertie had snuffled her muzzle over my tummy, then stood in front of me, her eyes closed and her body still, as if listening to the baby inside me. Then she'd climbed into the swing and we'd leaned, communing with each other and nature.

"Apparently she favors your condition."

He lost me. I tilted my head, puzzling over his words. "My condition? You mean pregnant?"

He nodded, his smirk beginning to show. "Eazy says she took off for a week after their visit with us. Says she spent her time away, carousing. He doesn't know what canine or other she might have been familiar with, but the vet checked her out and Gertie's…"

"Pregnant," I whispered, thinking about her impeccable pedigree. "Has Eazy shared the news with his wife?"

"He's still alive so I'd guess that would be a negative. He called to make sure we know we're getting a pup. I said I'd ask around and help him find homes, but he says nope. He'll interview and select his own prospective pup parents."

"A puppy will be nice." I pictured a baby and puppy rolling on the floor together and yawned, suddenly exhausted. I needed a nap. "There's still too much work to do down here. I'm going up. Maybe I'll sit in your recliner and look at my feet."

Upstairs, I didn't make it to the front room. Instead, I stood in front of the kitchen window, listening to the happy sound of Alesso & Anitta drifting up from the basement. Marty wandered into the room and stood behind me as I gazed outside and bounced to the music. "Full circle," I muttered, having a flash-back to Thanksgivings here as a kid.

"What are you muttering about now?" he growled.

"Pinch me. I need to make sure this isn't a dream," I answered.

"How about this?" He moved, hugging me against his big frame as he wrapped his arms around me and squeezed my pregnancy enhanced boob.

"Are you awake," he teased, nibbling on my earlobe.

His other hand rested on my no longer flat belly, stroking the baby bump I carried before me. "You okay?" His breezy question masked his underlying worry.

"Define, okay," I answered. "I did a job for Maxine, connected with a dancing mob-boss, survived a stalker, got knocked-up..." I turned around, my belly jutting between us. "Look at what you did to me," I playfully snarled. "My ankles are swollen, my back aches continuously, the kid in my stomach never stops kicking, and..."

Before I'd even gotten a good start on my list of complaints, Marty caught my hand and carefully spooled me out, then pulled me back into his embrace.

"Wanna dance?" A familiar, wolfish, gleam twinkled in

his eyes, promising decadent fun.

I held tight to his hand and grinned up at him. "Of course."

The End

Taboo Frequency, Smoke, Inc. Book 1

When ultimate impulse collides with maximum control...

It's all about taking charge. Luke Danvers has his future planned to the nth degree—until he steps on an IED in Afghanistan. Bitter, angry, and emotionally adrift, he returns to the States, ready to spend the rest of his life pissed off at the world.

Kiley Endicott has never been a poster child for moderation. Married and widowed young, she's raising twins on her own. Since impulse has always ruled her life, it's not easy being a sedate parent under the critically watchful eye of her family.

A Friday night moment of insanity, leads Kiley to a hook up with Luke Danvers. Even in the cab of a truck, he's an awesome lover. She wants more. But she's got to be circumspect, nobody can know.

Luke hasn't had fun in—forever. But he can't stop grinning after he meets Kiley Endicott. It's more than her being a totally uninhibited lover, but God knows he can't get enough of that either. She makes him laugh.

She says nobody can know. Okay, he's trained in stealth. He sets up a call system, a taboo frequency, guaranteeing her twenty-four-hour access in every way. But he's not just waiting for their secret meets. He's planning a take-over.

An Excerpt:

O N THE TRIP back to Doug's place, Luke's uninhibited partner sat on the seat, her hands folded primly in her lap. Even though he'd aired out the cab, he still inhaled the erotic mix of sweat and sex.

Other than that, it was hard to believe that they'd both gorged on lust moments before. He couldn't tell if she was regretting what they'd done or was too sated to talk.

He didn't have a clue what to say, so he didn't say anything until they'd almost reached her car.

"I'd like to see you again." As soon as he said it, he wanted to retract the words. "But, I don't really have time for a relationship." The man who had nothing but time on his hands tried to make his life seem busy. "When I'm not working I'm thinking about working."

That sounded pompous as hell and he floundered, knowing he was blowing the moment and dammit, he didn't want to. He looked at her sideways, before pulling her closer, sliding his arm around her shoulders so her body rested against his.

Risking a quick glance from the road to look at Kiley, he took in her swollen lips and flushed cheeks. She laid her hand on his thigh, and he liked the feel of her palm there.

"I'm busy, but that doesn't mean I'm a eunuch," he amended.

"Noted," she agreed, patting his leg as she gave him a speculative look. "I'd also like to do this again." She squeezed his thigh and it didn't surprise him when his cock stirred, already half aroused and ready for more of her.

"Maybe we can help each other," she said looking up at him. He didn't know what she had in mind, but he listened to find out.

"I'm a single mom. I don't have a steady man because I don't want one hanging around my two kids who are right now with my mom. She doesn't babysit often and aside from Marcie, I don't leave them with anyone else. I have a full-time life that includes a job and no time for a relationship."

"And?" He squeezed her shoulders, urging her to make an offer he wasn't going to refuse regardless of what it was.

"And—I have certain biological needs I'd like to satisfy with something other than plastic." She closed her eyes, her blush denying the intimacies they'd just enjoyed at the same time her hand stroked his thigh, promising more.

"Well as to those biological needs—seems like we can find a way to get them satisfied. When you've got the time, I'll find the place." He pulled up next to her car and put the truck in park, idling in front of her sister's house, waiting for Kiley's answer.

When she remained mute, he decided coaxing was in order. "You do the calling," he said, switching on his truck's overhead light to search in the glove compartment for paper.

"I'd just as soon the whole town not know we're carrying on," Kiley murmured, her blush turning her pink cheeks to ruby.

"Carrying on?" After the uninhibited fucking they'd just engaged in, her old-fashioned description made him smile.

His quick rummaging turned up no paper, so before shutting off the overhead light, he held her hand and wrote his number on her palm. "If you change your mind and don't call, it's okay. I'll not bother you. If you do call, I've marked your number a TF."

"TF?"

"That's military speak for *taboo frequency*—an open line strictly for emergencies. You call when you're able to get free and I'll make sure we get together."

He let her get half out the door before he added his last addendum to their deal. "As to the plastic, you might want to bring it along for a ride or two. No sense in letting it feel neglected." He liked a little variety in the sheets and he figured he'd let her know up front, he wasn't all vanilla. He had a feeling neither was she.

End of excerpt

Cowboy Burn, Smoke, Inc. Book 2

Pittsburgh artist, Harley-Jane Arthur plans to sketch herself out of debt. With that in mind, she's thrilled when she gets a commission for a kid's party in an upscale part of the city. If all goes well, she should earn enough to pay her January utilities, put a down payment on a new roof, and buy a bottle of Red to toast New Year's Eve—alone.

Gable Matthews, a.k.a. Cowboy, has waited patiently for years, hoping Janie will notice him. When she's stranded during a snowstorm, rescuing her provides an opportunity to finally get her attention.

Snowbound in Gable's apartment, they wait out the storm. But while they countdown to New Year's Eve, more danger than a raging blizzard lurks outside.

An Excerpt:

I EASED MY eyelids open. *Ouch. Oh God. My head.* I must have moaned.

This is awkward. Stealthily I eased my hand lower, investigating my state of dress. My fingers touched silk camisole, found no bra, but squirming assured me I still wore panties.

"Something wrong?" From next to me, Gable reared up on his elbow.

"Uh. I don't remember too much," I admitted, staring at his chest.

"Is that right? Might have been those Moscow Mules you were throwin' down." He ran his finger from my arm to my chin, lifting my gaze to meet his.

"You want to ask me something?"

"What did I forget?" I closed my eyes guiltily.

"You don't remember kickin' Cheryl's ass?"

My eyes flew back open. "I don't know a Cheryl."

"You called her *Yeehaw Girl.*" Gable was clearly enjoying my misery way too much.

"I fought her?" I didn't remember that. I might have poked her shoulder. But…

"You don't remember downin' three more Moscow Mules after that, dancin' until everyone left, then draggin' me back here to bed?"

"I… I…" I gnawed on my lip, trying to remember.

"You don't remember strippin' down and bumpin' uglies with me until we both passed out?"

Bumpin' uglies? No. I most certainly did not remember that. Gable didn't have an ugly spot on his body.

I managed to wrinkle my forehead in a frown and glare at him although the gesture hurt like hell. "None of that happened, did it?"

"Nope." Wearing knit boxers stretched by a prodigious morning erection, he rolled out of bed and strolled to the bathroom.

I admired his backside and assured myself there was nothing significant about Gable climbing from bed wearing a hard-on.

As soon as he closed the door, I scrambled up and pulled his gray flannel shirt over my New Year's Eve sexy underwear. I needed coffee. By the time he emerged from the bathroom, I was sipping from a mug and had regained my wits.

He tossed a bottle of aspirin my way, filled his own mug, and said, "Gotta check the furnace."

I nodded and stared into my cup, avoiding his gaze until he did the chin thing again, lifting my head until I had no choice but to look into his eyes.

"Trust me, Harley-Jane?" he asked.

I took a moment to admire the way my full name sounded when he got serious, then nodded.

"Of course, I trust you."

Taking the cup from my fingers, he set it on the counter and moved into my space, sucking most of the oxygen from my brain as he covered my lips with his. When the kiss ended, I blinked, trying to reorient myself and find reality.

He brushed his thumb over my mouth as he growled, "Trust me on this, sweetheart. When we do, *do it*, and that will commence happenin' soon, there won't be anything ugly between us, and you sure as hell won't be forgettin' what we do."

End of excerpt

A Note from the Author

Hi. I'm Gem Sivad. Nice to meet you. I live in the southern part of an enchanted kingdom where I enjoy the slow pace of life, study the world, and tell stories about incredible things. Whether my characters live in present day Pittsburgh, nineteenth century Texas, or a paranormal world of witches and shifters, my heroines are always resilient, resourceful, and smart, and my heroes are wickedly dangerous and seriously hot.

Although I have hermit tendencies, occasionally I come out of the writer's den to meet readers at book signing events. Hope to see you there. But in case we miss each other, you can find me at the cyber locations below.

Happy reading,

Gem Sivad

FACEBOOK AUTHOR PAGE
Facebook.com/GemSivadAuthor

GEM'S WEBSITE
GemSivad.com

NEWSLETTER
GemSivad.com/Dreamcatcher

TWITTER
Twitter.com/GemSivad

More Books by Gem

Historical Westerns
Eclipse Heat series:
Quincy's Woman
Intimate Strangers
Wolf's Tender
Tupelo Gold
Five Card Stud
Breed True
Trouble in Disguise
Whispering Grace

Unlikely Gentlemen series:
River's Edge
Outrageous Pride
Cerise Amour

Stand Alone Titles:
Staged Affair
Pinch of Naughty

Historical Paranormal
Jinx series:
Cat Nip
Blood Stoned

Contemporary Paranormal
Bitter Creek Holler series:
Call Me Miz
Miz Spelled
Ursus Horribilis

Contemporary Romantic Suspense
Smoke, Inc. series
Taboo Frequency – Hell Yeah
Cowboy Burn – Champagne and Cowboys 2017
Rhythm – 2017
Phatt Farm – Coming in 2018

www.ingramcontent.com/pod-product-compliance
Lightning Source LLC
Chambersburg PA
CBHW031702170626
46808CB00005B/1578